Those eyes.

They were blue, maybe—hard to determine in this subtle light. He held her stare for a few seconds longer than a stranger should. And in those seconds, his eyes glinted. And that glint sneaked into Mersey's being and glittered darkly about her wanting heart.

Yes, wanting.

Mersey Bane believed in love at first sight. A girl had to believe in something. Because that portent her mother had made years ago about there being but *one* man for her? Not so much belief in that.

She stepped forward and, stretching up on ~~er~~ tiptoes, kissed him. A bold move, but it felt ~~a~~dently dangerous and right. Exhilaration ~~~~her veins. There had to be more, so much ~~~~fill her fathomless want.

~~~~s body stiffened within her greedy, ~~ex~~ploring grasp. "—can't do this right now."

The hard steel of the huge rifle he held banged her elbow as he drew the rifle high and stretched his arm out over her head.

And then he pulled the trigger.

MICHELE HAUF

When polled, Michele Hauf's friends will generally report that she is the weird one. But then, weird doesn't quite define her, either. More like different. Her musical interests range from flamenco to heavy metal to soundtracks (most especially *Chitty Chitty Bang Bang*). Her spare time is spent collecting and shellacking rocks, decorating dragonflies and thinking about France and when, exactly, she was a musketeer (and was that the Black or Gray regiment?). Toss in a fascination for the art nouveau time period and season it with chocolate, dumplings and gallons of Orangina. Faeries and cats are also always welcome, as well as vampires, crosses, glass doorknobs and any kind of high-tech gadget. Yeah, different is good.

Michele has been writing for over a decade and has published historical, fantasy and paranormal romances. She lives with her family in Minnesota, loves the four seasons, even if one of them last months and can be colder than a deep freeze. find out more about her at www.michelehauf

FAMILIAR STRANGER

MICHELE HAUF

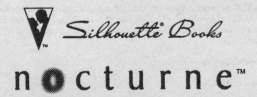

Silhouette® Books

n🌙cturne™

SILHOUETTE BOOKS

ISBN-13: 978-0-373-61768-5
ISBN-10:   0-373-61768-2

FAMILIAR STRANGER

Dear Reader,

A dozen years ago, four unpublished writers found each other on the Internet. We were assigned as critique partners, and were eager to learn and grow as writers. We are Nina Bruhns, Cynthia Cooke, Michele Hauf and Pat White. We've become true friends, each of us now published in genres such as adventure, suspense, fantasy and inspirational romance. We've celebrated each other's triumphs and offered much cyber-support, when needed, to overcome the lows life sometimes tosses our way.

We wanted to do something together, hoping to introduce our fans to each other's work. So we give to you the DARK ENCHANTMENTS series. Together we've created a world of glittering enchantments, populated with demons and faeries and vampires—and always, a sexy hero who will not stop until he holds the woman he loves in his arms.

I'm proud to kick off the series with an adventurous pair of demon hunters. Yet it is the hunt for true love that remains elusive to them. Isn't the hero's name in the movies always Jack? Well, I have a Jack of my own, and he's no less stubborn, motivated or haunted than all the rest. He'd never stand for my telling the world how brave, dedicated and forthright he is, so I'll leave you to read his story and decide for yourself if this Jack can hold a place in your heart, as he does in mine.

Michele

To: Marty Enerson and Vicki Cortese

Special thanks to Helen Taylor, across the ocean in England, who made suggestions for proper usage of some British terms. Any mistakes, of course, are my own.

I am so pleased to have been able to work on the DARK ENCHANTMENTS series with my friends Nina Bruhns, Cynthia Cooke and Pat White. Cheers to you, ladies! Here's to many more wonderful years of friendship.

Four hundred years ago a secret, hermetic order was created by the first Earl of St. Yve and a handful of initiates who pledged their lives to keep the world safe from evil paranormal beings. Ever since, the Cadre has been dedicated to maintaining the delicate balance between the mortal and Dark realms through research and observation of otherworldly entities. Seldom does the Cadre interfere.

But not all mortals seek peaceful understanding between the realms. In recent decades, an opposing force has been created by the British Security Service. This covert group, called P-Cell, has but one directive: destroy paranormal creatures of all kinds.

As the two organizations fight faithfully for their separate causes, unbeknownst to either of them the dark forces of evil gather, preparing to overtake the mortal realm....

Prologue

Shrewsbury, England

Jack Harris didn't like his life right now.

This morning he'd overheard his folks whispering about Dad's lung cancer. Treatment could prove more deadly than waiting out an inevitable death, the doctor had informed Dad. Mum had started to weep.

She'd put on a smile as Jack entered the room. He'd faked a yawn and rubbed his eyes, mostly to hide that he'd been crying, too. Mum had placed a parcel into his hands and patted him on the head. From Aunt Sophie in Scotland—that *particular* aunt that his mother always whispered about, but never spoke her name aloud.

Yesterday had been Jack's eighth birthday.

Now, loping across the hay meadow toward the forest, Jack thrust up the glass gazing ball Aunt Sophie had sent him. The glass, though marred with a few murky flaws, captured the sky and fit the whole world into the ball.

Plunging into a soft thicket of grass, Jack rolled onto his back and held the globe high, zooming it to the left, then to the right, as if it was an airplane cutting through the clouds.

"Wager I could make a wish on this," he said, to no one but the crickets chirping near his head.

Was his aunt a witch? Had this been one of her magic balls? He didn't believe in magic, or all that faery rot his mum often whispered about.

But maybe. Could it make his dad better?

Holding it high stretched out the captured sunlight in brilliant white beams. What if these powerful beams were inside his father's lungs? Surely something so strong and important as the sun could cure his dad.

"Whoa!"

Startled at the press of paws across his chest, Jack dropped the ball. He pushed up onto his elbows just as a cat leaped from his ribs and pounced off into the wilds.

"Blimey! A black cat stepped right on me."

And while his mum would have Jack pay heed to a black cat crossing his path, Jack scrambled to his knees and parted the grass to observe the critter's scampering trail across the clearing.

Brilliant. To have a cat traipse right across you! And a black one, at that.

Jack groped for the glass ball and clutched it to his chest. But the real spectacle had just begun. The cat transformed—within twenty human strides of where Jack sat—into a woman.

Jack huffed out a gasp. "No bloody way."

His jaw fell wide open, and his eyes grew even wider. His eight-year-old heart pounded faster than after a good bogeyman scare that found him huddled at the head of his bed, his feet tucked under the blankets so nothing could nibble on them.

He rubbed his eye with a fist. He couldn't be seeing right.

And yet, he'd seen it with his own eyes. The cat had changed to a woman. Fur had melted away to reveal human limbs that had stretched and grown to support an upright-standing woman. Long, shiny black hair fell like a mourning veil to her waist. Skinny legs tromped across the clearing. And…she didn't wear clothes!

Jack averted his gaze to the ball in his hand. Aunt Sophie had written on his birthday card that the gift would "spark his imagination." No mention of magic. Had it made the cat change to a woman?

When Jack again cast his gaze across the clearing, the woman paused and turned toward him—she had a huge belly—and then she winked at him. A winking, fat, naked woman!

Too astonished to be frightened, Jack swallowed. Suddenly, something dark appeared in the sky above the woman's head.

"Watch out!" Jack yelled. His fingers clenched about the ball. "Lady! Look!"

Jack's world suddenly tilted into deep dread. Yes, even more dreadful than knowing his dad was not in a good way. Every piece of him shook, from his freckled ears down to his knobby knees.

Big as a bull, the monster hovered. It was red. It had horns.

It was going to hurt the woman, Jack felt it deep inside, like when he knew he was going to get a switching for staying up in the lookout tree past suppertime.

He'd never run from the switch. Nor had he feared it all that much.

"No!" Standing up and stretching back his arm, Jack threw the glass ball through the sky.

The woman noticed the monster, let out a cry and bent at the waist. The growling, horned thing lunged. The glass ball landed on its target, right between the monster's eyes.

And Jack, overwhelmed with shock, horror and the excited elation of making his target, collapsed backward onto the summer grass. He hadn't fainted. Only girls faint. But he did close his eyes for a moment.

And when he opened them, the red monster hovered above him.

Something smelled like the rotten eggs his mum had found in the henhouse last week. Yellow eyes took his measure. A foul string of spittle dangled from its sharp teeth.

Feeling his bones stiffen, Jack opened his mouth, but no sound came out. He wanted to cry blue murder. Or better yet, lift his arm, so he could punch the creepy in the snout.

A long black tongue snaked out from the monster. The touch of it burned Jack's chest. He barely had a moment to realize it made contact with him before the monster vanished.

The next thing Jack was aware of was something soft touching his cheek. He opened his eyes. *She* knelt over him. The naked woman.

"Jack the Demon Frightener," she declared with a smile.

He felt the cool weight of the glass ball press onto his spread palm.

"You preserved my freedom. Thank you, Jack. I will not forget your bold act of valor."

And away she skipped, her giggle like sunshine sparkling on a pond.

Jack slapped a hand over his chest. His finger went to the small hole burned through his Sunday shirt. Mum would bring out the switch, him ruining a good shirt and all.

But it didn't matter. He'd frightened off a real demon.

Wicked!

Twenty-four years later...

Jack Harris stormed through his front door, tugging the ill-fitted black suit jacket from his shoulders. He tossed it onto the couch and searched the afternoon shadows of the stark living room.

Inside him, a storm raged.

Jack had spent four years with MI5, and before that, six years in the British Security Service. While in MI5, he and Monica Price had partnered for two memorable years. And now she was dead.

The funeral had affected him in unexpected ways. It had torn through the numb that had crept into his bones. Every tear he'd tried to hold back since her death had escaped as he'd sat in the car park below his building. Unspoken emotion clawed for release, yet, alone in his car, he hadn't had anyone to talk to. So instead, he'd pounded the steering wheel with his fists.

He should have told her how he felt about her.

You didn't have time to love her, mate. Or is it you lacked the courage to love her?

Either was a poor excuse. He did love her. *Had* loved her.

Love, he did not deserve.

Had he been the one to bring bad luck into Monica's world? Bad luck? Hell, the incident resulting in her death had involved no luck whatsoever.

Life had been swimming along fine until Jack had received that package two weeks earlier. Where was it?

He sighted the parcel his mum had sent him. After cleaning out the old house in Shrewsbury—she'd purchased a home in Las Vegas, of all places—she'd sent along a box of things from Jack's childhood she suspected he might want. He'd sorted through the contents, tossing the dirty print-smeared football cards, handing the collectible Marvel comic books to the kids down the hall and leaving the insignificant detritus from his past still nestled in the packing material.

He'd ignored the most obvious evidence of his childhood. Until now.

Lunging to the side of the couch, Jack reached into the box. His palm fit about the cool glass ball, as round and hefty as a grapefruit.

This…this *thing*. It had come back to haunt him.

"Bloody bit of bad luck."

He threw hard, backing the force with anger and guilt and, most prevalent, the hunger for revenge.

The ball hit the wall with a thud and busted through the plaster board. White dust spumed out and settled onto the hardwood floor. Suspended there, it had fit itself halfway into the wall, a colorless eye that had shown Jack remarkable horrors.

"Sodding...bloody—ah!" Jack released the last bits of anger in a throat-aching cry.

He'd thought he'd left the eerie bad luck behind with his childhood nightmares. Now, it had begun again.

Two hours later, Jack received a call from Dirk Marcolf. The man identified himself as deputy director for a black ops division of MI5.

"Harris," Marcolf said over the phone. "I'll need you to come in for a thorough debriefing."

"Already been debriefed, Mr. Marcolf." Jack had given it all up during debriefing. Shell-shocked, he hadn't had control over the words as they'd spilled from his mouth. He'd said all he could say about the horrific event.

"Sorry, Harris, but you've seen things."

"Things I'd like to erase from my brain."

"And you'll probably have questions."

"You can't begin to imagine."

"Oh, I think I can. Ever hear of P-Cell, Harris?"

"No."

"Good. That's us. And tomorrow morning, you're joining the team."

"But what if—"

"We chase monsters, Harris. And if my guess is right, I know you're going to want in on that action."

For the longest moment Jack breathed into the receiver. He didn't need to roll over the words Marcolf had just said. He understood them perfectly. And he didn't need to think on his reaction.

"See you in the morning."

Chapter 1

London—three months later

Jack Harris had committed to this mission of destruction. The road, not up from his indiscretions, but one that threatened to parallel it all the way to hell.

He had been given a license to kill. Not mortals, but instead, the dark denizens from another world. A world called the dark realm. A world he'd never imagined to exist months before now. Yet, for all purposes, it had once touched him.

Since joining—make that being *recruited*—into P-Cell, the covert paranormal section of MI5, life had not been the same. Normal people did not dream about demons, or stalk the hallway in the middle of the night and reconnoiter the loo before taking a leak on the off chance a demon might be clinging up on the ceiling.

Yet, in all his years with the British Security Service, and then working as a spook for MI5, he'd never before felt quite like this. Confident *and* hungry for the kill.

Sure, confidence was second nature to Jack, but to hunger for destruction? Such an appetite was new, yet not unwelcome.

Jack hefted the M4 carbine, positioning the butt of the rifle upon the crook of his elbow. A salt grenade was locked into position. He'd only get the one shot.

The electromagnetic-field gauge he held in his left hand registered a faint blip. Something occupied the cavernous walls of this building. And he knew it wouldn't be all ducks and bunnies.

Slowly, he took the iron stairs in the abandoned warehouse, twisting at the waist to ensure the hand-size EMF gauge could pick up readings to cover his periphery.

A flick of his finger switched to GPS function. This model had been designed specifically to pick up the electromagnetic resonance of ley lines and map them on screen. A network of ley lines stretched across the earth, meeting and aligning at key mystical sights and resonated with a magnetic energy that attracted the otherworldly.

Demons always came through to the mortal realm via a ley line.

Combat boots tread stealthily. His stripped-down gear shifted silently upon his sturdy frame—flame-resistant black shirt and trousers, Dragon Skin vest, and at his belt a night-vision scope, combat knife and salt spray (pepper proved ineffective against the creatures he stalked). And he carried a silver dagger tipped with a UV cartridge, if by chance he stumbled on to a thirsty vampire.

In the past two weeks, Jack had gone out nightly on patrol. Direct orders from the deputy director of P-Cell. The paranormal activity in this area had increased measurably, of late. And the kicker? The hot spot was just up the road from his flat in Bermondsey. Much too close for comfort.

He had embraced the job at P-Cell with an angry heart and a keen eye.

He was still fighting terrorists—though now they were otherworldly. Demons were terrorists with uglier faces and supernatural methods. The challenge was that all bad guys had faces a man could read and react to—but not all demons did.

As a demon hunter, his objective was to shoot first, ask questions never.

P-Cell's array of weapons kicked arse. He used the M4 more often than he utilized his martial skills. Didn't get to physically kick a lot of demon arse because he still hadn't figured out where, exactly, that portion of the demon was on their strange anatomy.

Well, some, he could. In his short stint, Jack had learned the variety of demons was vast and varied. No two were alike, though they were classified into two genuses. *Daemon sapiens,* the modern demons were more refined, wise and always appeared in human form. The *daemon incultus* were the ancient, nastier breed that Jack preferred to hunt.

The latter usually appeared in demonic form, which worked for him. Jack could spar with them until they tired of the daft mortal's antics, and then the demon would attempt to take him out with a lash of burning tongue or some nasty exhalation of fumes or slash of talons. Confrontations kept Jack on his toes. He'd been hospitalized briefly last month for a deep slash through his kidney. Good thing he had two of those.

According to the GPS, he stood on top of a ley line. The electromagnetic field meter had a six milliguass range and picked up virtually all demon activity within shouting distance.

Some*thing* was in this building.

Of course, the somethings never showed themselves until Jack was close enough to be slashed, spit on, knocked down or all of the above. Which is why he wore Dragon Skin, a new scaled form of Kevlar that provided ease of movement as well as protection. Had to protect that last precious kidney.

Hell, he had to protect himself, because he wasn't going down until the dread demon that had murdered the woman he loved met the same bloody end.

The encounter with that particular demon had not been his first. No, Jack had recognized Monica's slayer. Last time he had seen that nasty thing, he'd been eight years old.

These days he wasn't tossing about silly glass balls. Now he relied on semiautomatic firepower.

Reaching the top of the third-floor stairs, Jack placed the palm of his left hand over his chest—there, where the subtle ache beneath the small scar never stopped.

Tonight, it was him or the demon. Take no prisoners.

The air was charged with the inexplicable, and it sent prickles up Mersey Bane's spine. She intended to get lucky tonight. She needed a fix.

Long sinuous strides moved her down a quiet pavement that paralleled the Thames. The moon waxed gibbous as the night crept up on morning.

Arms bent and hands held before her waist, she gripped the witching rods lightly, thumbs pointing skyward. The handles were ash columns, a hardwood resistant to influence. The copper rods, bent in an L-shape—the short length inside the handles—moved slightly with the rocking motion of her steps.

Two hours earlier, back at base, Mersey had received instructions to track down the leak in *paras* traced to this Bermondsey neighborhood. *Paras* were entities that were not human or mortal and usually apported here from the dark realm. Demons, faeries, elves, weres, the whole shebang.

The common man would be surprised to know how many nonhuman entities walked this earth. It was Mersey's job to keep that influx to a minimum, utilizing as little violence as possible. She loved tracking and capturing. Demons were her specialty, for reasons beyond her control—she'd never been given a choice in the matter.

Eyelids falling shut, she concentrated, walking slowly forward. She could scent things humans could not. The ever-changing odor of the Thames drifted up her nostrils, the river but a jog away. Tonight it smelled of cut grass and rotting hardwood.

A slight movement in the rods diverted her senses. She smiled. Getting closer. Beneath her steel-toe boots she could feel the vibrations rising up from the earth. Must be a ley line close by—an obvious place for a tear in the mortal fabric to transpire.

Something had to be torn. Four *paras* of the demonic persuasion had been reported within the last forty-eight hours. That was positively an invasion. Mersey hoped they were *daemon incultus;* a genus of demon that didn't use mortal disguise, but rather showed itself in all its natural, creepy glory. They were much easier to capture than a tricky human-form *daemon sapiens.*

Her mother had taught her to witch for ley lines when she was six. It hadn't really been an education, more like unearthing a talent already there. Mersey could witch a ley line, an underground trickle or stream, or wend her path toward an infestation of demons merely by concentrating and allowing the innate energies within her to connect to the otherworldly forces. Those forces were everywhere; most, invisible remnants from an unwarranted visitor, but some were definite trails.

Her connection to the otherworld was like breathing. Natural. In fact, it was mortals who gave her the most pause, if not, on occasion, out and out terror.

Trailing her wake by fifty paces, Mersey knew a white cat padded along. Ever curious about her, felines. If a cat prowled within shouting distance, it would eventually find her and cozy about her ankles to give a discerning sniff. Good thing she liked cats.

Suddenly the copper rods crossed. Mersey stopped straight away. The vibrations flowing up from the ground and through her body were unmistakable.

Cocking her head to the right, she assessed the dark warehouse beyond a chain-link fence. Three stories. Windows smashed out. Possibly abandoned.

"Brilliant."

She folded the customized rods and tucked them inside the pocket of her ankle-length suede coat. It was late September; though an early autumn chill warranted a cap and she had gloves stuffed in her pockets.

"Stay out here, puss," she directed. "This could get ugly."

The cat obediently sat, curling a moon-white tail about its forepaws.

Ducking through a tear in the stiff chain mesh, Mersey then crossed the dirt courtyard and quickly located an entrance through a broken ground-floor window.

The building was cold, but her coat, rimmed about the collar and wrists with sheep's wool, kept her warm. A snug black leather aviator cap dangled over her ears and static-charged wisps of her shoulder-length hair clung to her neck and cheeks.

Scents of industrial grease and dust permeated her nostrils. Must have been a factory once outfitted with machinery that had dripped the huge black oil stains on the wood floor. The moon served as a pale white lamp.

Stretching out her arms, she walked through the empty warehouse. Her right hand, each finger stacked with protective hematite rings, divined for otherworldly vibrations, while her left, unadorned (for her past needed no protection), swept along in parallel. Her paces were steady, same as witching a line. Now was no time to introduce fear. Awareness became paramount.

She could feel something hum through the veins of her right hand, though the signal was blurred. Whatever it was, it wasn't on this ground floor.

Locating stairs at the end of the murky room, she flew up the debris-littered steps two at a time. No worry for making noise. If there was a *para* in the building, it already knew she was here.

Fine with her. She didn't need to see the thing; she just had to capture it.

"Heck of a way to spend a Saturday night," she murmured, topping the third-floor stairs. "On the other hand—" three strides took her into the vast empty room "—no one's been knocking down my door to go dancing, of late."

"You want to dance?"

Frozen in a beam of red light, Mersey instinctively put up her hands to shield her eyes. This wasn't quite the sort of luck she'd hoped to find tonight.

Chapter 2

"Who are you?" a male voice demanded.

Squinting against the beam of red light, Mersey looked down the long steel barrel of a huge gun.

"Hullo, what is that?" she asked. "Did you raid the *Star Wars* prop room, then?"

Dropping her hands, she stepped forward into a slash of moonlight. The man stood in the shadows and the light from his gun prevented her from seeing anything more than the outer edges of him. And those edges were impressive. Broad shoulders always did it for her. That meant the man was strong and capable of carrying things— like a woman—off to the pub or, better yet, his bed.

From where had that thought come? A girl ought to be cautious around strangers wielding big-arse weapons.

"Hands where I can see them!" He prodded the weapon toward her. A retractable bayonet engaged with a click.

Mersey flinched. "Watch it, will you? You could poke an eye out with that thing."

"Ma'am! Name, rank and ID number, if you please."

She smirked and crossed her arms.

"I'm on a mission, ma'am. Let's be having it. I need to verify you are a civilian."

A civilian? What else would she be to the average man on the street? Of course, there appeared to be nothing whatsoever average about this muscle-bound bloke with a macho rating that tipped the scales.

"Mersey Bane," she offered. "Sounds like the disposition, but spelled like the river. As for rank, I think I'm on about the third floor. And you're not getting my ID number, mate."

"Ma'am!"

"I am hardly a *ma'am*." She thought to stroke a hand through her hair, but the aviator cap kept it out of sight, so instead she shoved her hands to hips. "And no numbers. How do I know you're not going to steal my identity and spend thousands on eBay to support your convoluted weapon habit?"

"Convoluted?" The tip of the gun tilted downward, along with the red laser.

Towering over her by more than a head, Mersey fancied he must be six and a half feet high, at the very least. She had to look up to meet his eyes. Nice.

"Who do you think you are?" he barked at her.

She sidled closer, the flaps of her full-length coat winging out beside her. She wanted to get a better look at him, to answer the tempting curiosity that burned hot within her breast.

"I've told you who I *think* I am. Mersey Bane."

She contemplated reaching out to offer a handshake, but the weapon kept her at bay.

Moonlight stole across the side of his face. The man's square jaw pulsed. Hair cropped military short hardened his stern features even further. His expression screamed menace.

Yet those eyes. They were blue, maybe, hard to determine in this subtle light. He held her stare, for a few seconds longer than a stranger should. And in those seconds, his eyes glinted. And that glint sneaked into Mersey's being and glittered darkly about her wanting heart.

Yes, wanting. A girl shouldn't go so long between dates when she was young, eager, and oh, so—

She smiled a teasing grin, hoping to soften his sharp edges. "And you are?"

"None of your concern, Miss Bane."

"But how to get to know you better without a name?" she said, pouting. And why she had suddenly pulled on the temptress act startled her.

"Tongue!" he barked.

"Tongue?" She delivered him a catty tilt of the head. Yet her casual stance hid a sudden twinge of anxiety.

So the man knew the situation? She knew exactly what he was asking for. Unfortunately, it did not refer to anything sexual. And if he did have a clue, then she wasn't dealing with an average civilian.

Taking the location and his weapon into consideration, to judge from his attire—combat boots, dark clothing and a flak jacket— he must be a rogue demon hunter stalking prey. What luck. Tall, dark, handsome *and* in the know.

So long as he did no harm with his big bad toy, she decided to like him. But if he should use the weapon, all bets were off.

Tongue? What she wouldn't mind doing with her tongue to his broad shoulders.

He offered a smile then pulled it smooth. "Please, miss, I know it sounds strange—"

"I understand what you're asking for."

"Then you'll oblige me."

Obliging him drew the inner temptress farther from her hideout. Eyebrows briefly flashing up and down, she smiled inwardly when he gave her a quick lift of brow to counter.

Poking out her tongue, Mersey waggled the tip—a non-forked tip.

The man lowered the gun to rest at his side. Yet, his finger remained close to the trigger.

"All right then." He exhaled and gestured toward the stairs. "Best you get on your way and leave the dirty work for the big boys."

Big boys? Before a protest could get past her lips, the sheer size of the man's moonlit frame forced Mersey to reconsider. Blimey. Difficult *not* to give him that one.

"Obviously you're stalking paranormals to ask me such a thing," she tried. "At least, I hope you are. I haven't walked into a police operation, have I?"

"I…"

Couldn't say. Probably had to remain covert. As if that big gun didn't give him away.

"Fine, I know the drill. So give it up," she prompted. "I deserve the same consideration. Tongue."

"Miss, I—"

"How do I know you're not a demon?" she said, flashing him a wink.

He obliged her request by sticking out a flat, pale pink tongue. Perfectly human.

Demons, though they could mimic the human form completely, could never get the tongue right. Red, blue and forked were the most common indications.

"Right," she said. And that dark glitter squeezing her heart overtook all remnants of reluctance. *Go for it, Mersey.* "But I've a better method for the tongue check."

Stepping forward, she spread her hands up the man's arms, gliding across the rough protective vest. Her reach wouldn't go all the way; she couldn't touch her fingers together behind his back. Oh, bountiful bit of brawn.

The man didn't immediately react as she stepped up onto his boot toes. She pressed her hands against the back of his skull. The short hairs on his scalp shifted stiffly under her palms as she fit her fingers along the muscles tensing his neck.

He breathed a gasp into her, but didn't break the kiss. It had been a while since she snogged a handsome lug like this one. And after only knowing him for a moment? What was the lug's name?

Now was no time to question principles. It was as if she were acting outside herself. Sexy, wanting Loose Lucy had stepped up to take what Mersey needed, while the logical, practical Mersey protested—albeit weakly—from too deep inside her psyche to cause more than a nuisance.

She believed in love at first sight. A girl had to believe in something. Because that portent her mother had made years ago about there being but *one* man for her? Not so much belief in that.

Her lug smelled faintly of spicy aftershave and warm flexing muscles. The scaled vest exuded a slight chemical smell. The shadow of a mustache tickled her upper lip. A deep groan signaled his willingness.

Mersey sucked in his lower lip. A bold move, but it felt dangerous and right. She couldn't get enough of his rugged sensuality. Danger exuded from him. Exhilaration filled her veins. There had to be more, so much more to match her fathomless want.

"Mph," he muttered against her mouth. He pushed gently, his wide hands spanning the girth of her rib cage. He might completely enclose her torso with his forceful grip. She liked the vulnerable position. "Miss?"

"Mersey," she said on a sigh. Clinging to his shoulders, she had to hold herself up to meet his mouth for another quick kiss. "Didn't catch your name, stranger."

"I—" His body stiffened within her greedy, exploring grasp. "Can't do this right now."

Mersey felt his arm slide along her torso. The hard steel of the huge weapon banged her elbow as he drew it high and stretched out his arm over her head.

And then, he pulled the trigger.

Chapter 3

The trigger gave under Jack's touch. A burst of brilliant red light momentarily illuminated the entire third floor of the warehouse. The carbine grenade launcher kicked hard, but Jack caught it with an unmoving shoulder that bore more than a few scars from rifle kickback.

Meanwhile, he held the woman tight to his left side, his arm wrapped about her narrow frame, while he lowered the gun in his right hand. Her warmth and that she melded into him without protest did not go unnoticed. Clinging to unexpected salvation while he dug himself deeper into a disparaging hell.

Bad form, Jack.

An unholy yowl clawed the rafters. The demon had taken the salt grenade in the maw. Heavy, cold wodges splat Jack's face, shoulders and arms as a rain of demon fallout settled about him. Sometimes they did that—splatter before dissolving to dust.

The gorgeous bird in his arms squiggled free and stumbled

backward. A full rifle barrel shorter than he, she had been literally standing on his toes to kiss him.

"Dash it all! What did you do?"

She shook her arms of the globulous demon particles and bobbed her capped head forward to do the same.

"Target annihilated," Jack confirmed. He tilted the rifle barrel back against his shoulder.

Now, to convince her to forget this night ever happened. The last thing P-Cell needed was a civilian in the know. And yet, she'd known about the tongue thing.

"You were a bit preoccupied with coming on to me to notice the danger. Never been kissed while hunting."

"Danger? Target dead!" she shouted. "You—you scruff! You can't do that."

"Take no prisoners. Not wise to leave them kicking."

The woman slapped away more demon bits and shook her fingers to fling the offending substance in all directions. A few angry stomps placed her in the line of moonlight beaming through the window.

"You must preserve the subject for interrogation and deportation back to its own realm. Bloody imbecile!"

That was two names she'd called him in less than three breaths. This saucy bird was not going to rail on him for doing his job.

Jack strode over to Mersey. "You're going to forget what you've witnessed, little girl."

"Little? Of all the— Who put you in charge?"

"That is priority information."

"Oh, really? And that big bad toy of yours? A salt grenade? You're nothing but a freelance demon hunter, blasting indiscriminately. It is absolutely inhumane. You, you…death merchant!"

She was calling it as she saw it, and she saw quite plainly. Jack couldn't argue her surprise, or the fact that he should have done his best to keep her from witnessing this incident.

But if she suspected he was a hunter, then that verified her knowledge of demons. Which made her no less a civilian than he was.

She stomped an obstinate beat upon the floor. Her coat cut narrowly down her petite frame, dusting the tops of well-worn combat boots. Jack caught her by the upper arm.

Moonshine spotlighted their encounter. Underneath the skull-fitting aviator cap (with goggles) he noticed bits of dark hair had been tied back behind her head. Huge, green eyes belonged on a puppy dog begging for favors, not this spunky woman with an attitude. A pert, slender nose led to lips that begged to be snogged. Again.

She smelled like a niffy demon. But still…

"I suppose you're not up for snogging now?" he tried. But his heart wasn't in the proposition. The hunter needed to resume the hunt.

"I can't believe I actually kissed you. You're a…"

"Just doing my job, miss."

"You—" she stabbed the air between them with a finger "—are a violence-loving, gun-toting cretin!"

Yet another name! Jack straightened his shoulders and cast a glowering sneer on the frantic bit. "The cretin thanks you for your accurate assessment of his nature, Miss Bane. And, he'll have you know that violence just saved our arses."

"It's Mersey," she said with a sniff, "not Miss Bane. And you are?"

"Not eager for small talk." He sighed, but then blurted, "Jack Harris. Now look, the situation is dangerous. I can't be responsible—"

"I can take care of myself, Mr. Harris."

There was plenty brass about this woman. She cocked out a hip. Skin-hugging black leather wrapped her long slender legs. Sexy. Jack could go a round or two with her. *If* he weren't concerned for the fate of the world. Which, he was. Or, at the very least, a small portion of London.

"Are you even aware of the chain of fallout that occurs each time you kill a demon?" she countered.

He guessed the only possible explanation for Miss Bane's knowledge—beyond her being a conspiracy theory wacko—was that she must be professional. They were out there, demon hunters and witchy sorts; freelancers of the nature she imagined him to be. Which he was not. All orders came directly from P-Cell. Jack avoided the freelancers like the bloody plague, their hocus-pocus rot was generally nonsense.

Though, for all purposes, he did call himself a demon hunter. P-Cell boasted werewolf and vampire hunters as well, with the gray seekers covering all OEs—otherworldly entities—not considered a constant and irrevocable threat.

"The fallout is pretty obvious," he said and flicked another fragment of demon from his shoulder. "Demon approaches. Demon endangers innocent civilians. Demon dies. Simple as that."

"It is not so simple!"

He wasn't in the mood to argue. And unless this bird got real serious about snogging, he wasn't prepared to waste any more time here.

"Who do you work for?"

"Me?" She shrugged up the lapel of her coat and adjusted her stance to stretch up her petite frame. The commanding look *almost* worked on her. "You tell me who you work for first."

"Don't know what you're talking about, miss. I'm just a private citizen who thought he heard something suspicious. I work independently. Call it pest control."

"Pest control?"

"That's what it says on my business card."

"Fine. I know the drill, Mr. Harris. Whoever you are, you probably don't exist, right?"

"I'm dead serious, Miss Bane, you need to vacate the premises." He glanced toward the ceiling. Where there was one, there was always another.

A combination of a sneer and a tongue-lashing mocked him from those sassy plump lips. *Now* she had tapped his last nerve.

Jack stalked up to the obnoxious bit of cheek. Brimstone pervaded the air, growing stronger as he gained her—standard demon scent. It was from the fallout. He fitted his stance right up to her boots and pressed his face close to hers. Beyond the layer of demon gunk, he smelled lemons. Yet her kiss had been the furthest thing from tart.

Bad form, Jack. You're not here to make out with a strange woman. But you could get her number for later.

Right. Now he was thinking like a stupid civilian who would get himself killed. Must be the weird fresh smell of her. Just so…intriguing.

"If you don't leave now," Jack growled, "you'll be in serious danger."

"And if I refuse?"

She was pushing it. Flirtatiously sliding her eyes up and down him from head to waist.

When had obstinacy become so alluring? Jack had been so wrapped up in the quest for demons, he had seriously fallen away from real life, which included socializing and, oh, yes, women.

But were they making them this way nowadays? So…attractively impudent?

"If I can ask," he said, calmer, checking his anger. Yeah, it was in there. The anger never completely left him. But he could pull on the charm if need be. "What's with the goggles?"

She reached up and tapped the plastic lens of the goggles. "Demon spit is toxic. They would have come in handy *if* I'd known the splatter was coming."

Jack smoothed a hand over his scalp. Hair short as razor stubble was slicked with demon residue. He'd left his own night-vision specs at home.

"As for being a freelance hunter," she added, "you guys aren't as covert as you like to believe. We've been bemoaning your trigger-happy actions for decades. And now I completely understand why."

Stalking away from him, she started toward the stairway.

"We?" he called.

"Yep. We."

"Wait!" Shoving the gun over his shoulder and taking off after the elusive bit of demon guts and defiance, Jack took the iron stairs two at a time.

We? If someone was going to compromise his mission, he needed facts.

The woman stopped on the second floor and walked swiftly to the center of the vast room.

"What is that thing?" she muttered. "It's not standard issue."

"Kitchen sink," he said with a proud grin. "Night-vision scope, trigger-controlled camera, rocket-propelled grenade and much, much more. She's my baby."

"Uh-huh. Point it away from me, will you, hotshot?"

"Sure." But not before he pressed the photo button.

The digital camera fitted in the scope snapped a flashless shot of his partner in crime. He'd send it on to headquarters later and get to the bottom of Miss Mersey Bane.

This floor was similar to the previous. Stripped to the bare walls and in preparation for remodeling. Plastic had been stapled over the glassless windows and construction dust littered the stained hardwood floors. Oil and dirt scented the air.

Pausing, Mersey motioned to Jack. "Shh." She pressed a finger to her lips and looked upward.

Jack followed her gaze. Dread tightened his scalp and drained the warmth from his extremities. A feeling he'd been tapping into a lot of late.

"Human or demon?" he whispered, reaching for the EMF clipped at his belt.

"Demon."

Mersey dug into her pocket and produced a pyramid-shaped stone, the point of it fitted between two fingers that were stacked with black rings. The size of a tangerine, she displayed it on her palm before him. Quartz?

"It's my turn now," she said. "Pay attention, hotshot. This is how the professionals do it."

Jack smirked. He was humoring her in hopes of gaining information about the mysterious *we,* so he cautioned his anger.

"It's here," she whispered. Holding up the crystal, she closed her eyes, seeming to read the atmosphere. "Not an overly threatening force, maybe…more curious. Like the one you took out."

"And how do you know—"

She put up a palm for silence. "Please, Mr. Harris, could you and that big-arse gun just hold quiet?"

"You get a lot of boyfriends wielding that charm?"

"Don't need boyfriends."

"Lesbian, eh?"

"What?"

He chuckled at her affront. "Didn't seem that way when you were studying my tonsils."

"Of all the—" Her attention averted quickly.

Jack slapped a hand to the rifle stock. The hairs on his neck prickled. Something was about.

The nonsense verse she began to whisper flowed as easily as a child's nursery rhyme. Jack didn't recognize the words, but figured it for Latin.

Intrigued, even against his better judgment, he decided to play along, watch her show. Should something actually come at her, he'd have her back. And she *would* need him.

Through the murky darkness Jack spied the shadow rippling across the ceiling. The demon did not try to disguise its presence. The faint odor of brimstone drifted closer.

Still chanting, Mersey moved forward into the room, her focus increasing and intent aimed for the demon.

"This is not going to be good." Jack aimed for the moving demon.

"Hold off, hunter!"

"Oh, no you don't." Flicking off the safety emitted a high-pitched tone from the rifle's computer. Jack tracked the laser across the high ceiling beams. The demon would materialize first as mist. They always did.

Yet there, at the back of his concentration, sang her chant. Knowing, intent and bold. Inexplicably intrigued by the rhythm of her voice and the evocative tone of the musical words, Jack tilted his head to the side.

Who was this odd woman? And why did he allow her antics? Never had he exposed a civilian to the dangers of his work. Not that he expected she would have left if he'd given her the boot.

Dark mist apported above them. No time to struggle with inaction.

Mersey lifted the quartz pyramid high and commanded, *"Te vincio!"*

The air in the room changed, swiftly brushing over Jack's face and shoving at his shoulders. But while he maintained position, he lost aim. It happened so quickly, he only knew it was finished when he saw Mersey's hand drop to her side, the pyramid clutched securely.

The demon shadow had disappeared.

"Where the hell—?"

Chapter 4

Dark lashes dusted her eyes, and she sent a triumphant grin toward him. "Told you I was a professional."

"That was *it?*" Where was the bang, the fallout, a payoff from the kill?

Hefting the quartz, Mersey strode to a nearby window where the plastic had torn away and whipped outside like a flag. She studied the crystal in the streetlight that shone through.

Jack joined her. The clear quartz was now completely black, and when Jack squinted he could see minute movement, like swirling mist, inside the stone.

"It's in there?" he asked. "The whole demon?"

"Safe and sound." Dropping the pyramid into an inner coat pocket, she then pressed a palm against the window frame, leaning there. "A lot less messy than your method, wouldn't you say?"

Straightening his shoulders, Jack said, "I use technology, not...hocus-pocus."

"Get over it, hotshot. I'm not a witch. No hocus-pocus up my sleeves. But now, I have a viable entity to bring back to base for interrogation. If luck is with me, I'll have the source of this demon's entry before the sun rises."

"And where is base?"

"Ah, ah. We're not sharing that much."

"Forgot. First date, right?"

"Sure." Her gaze dropped down his torso and when she looked back up, a tickle lit in her eyes. Cocky bit of sass, wasn't she?

Jack knew exactly what to do with women who tossed out silent propositions.

He leaned in, briefly eyeing the bulge in her pocket that contained the crystal, yet ultimately aiming his focus on the woman's brilliant eyes. She smelled like spoiled demon, for the bits still clinging to her hair and shoulders, yet with a tinge of fruity freshness.

"I'll have you know I'm not put off by demon-coated women."

"Really?" She tugged the white T-shirt away from her ribs, displaying the rusty residue that coated it. "I've demon guts crusted all over me, and I'm really not turned on by men who carry big weapons. But if you're up for it, give it your best shot."

This bird was easy. Or not. One minute she was kissing him, the next she stood there aloof and challenging.

"You're not much of a romantic, are you?" Jack asked.

And he was?

"Romance—" she looked aside and sighed "—is for faery tales."

"I agree." He pressed a palm to the window frame above her head. "But let's see if this will change our minds."

He touched her jaw and smoothed the back of his hand along it to stroke the powdery residue from her cheek.

Are you doing this, Jack? Making out with a complete stranger in the middle of a demon-infested warehouse?

Why the bloody hell not? Jack always opened the door to opportunity when it knocked. Sometimes he even got lucky.

First contact with her mouth tasted slightly metallic; must have been the residue. She didn't protest their contact, yet she did not answer his kiss by pressing back. Just…accepting.

Stepping into her space, Jack tilted his head down to keep the kiss. She didn't attempt to make it any easier by moving into him. He couldn't get close enough to press their bodies together because he was so much taller.

But for the moment her mouth was reward enough. Thick lips, soft beneath his own, opened to release a wintergreen sigh. Her breaths came faster, and he liked that. Not impervious, then. Her Jekyll and Hyde approach to seduction was confusing, and yet, it had got him to forget about demons for a few moments, hadn't it?

Right. Demons. The mission. *You ruddy idiot.*

When Jack drew back from the powerful contact, he couldn't help notice she inhaled as if drawing in the scent of a flower. Couldn't resist taking one last piece of him?

"Nice," he said. But he hadn't remembered to slip the pyramid from her coat. *Not smart, Jack.*

Mersey didn't say a thing. And yet, her next move released her inner Hyde. She reached for Jack's shoulder and pulled him back for another kiss. No sweet, tentative touching this time around. This woman liked her kisses hard and deep, if a little unpolished. He reacted to her tongue tracing his mouth and let in her wintergreen cool.

Yep, it had been far too long, and Jack had become a dull boy. No longer.

Lifting her by the thighs, he walked forward a few paces, pressing the sassy bird up against the wall. Her shoulders fit between two vertical framing boards and she wrapped her legs about his hips.

Jack moaned as all the right parts snugged against all the right places. Instantly hard, he ground his erection against her. Sex with a stranger. He could go there. Hell, he was already there.

Shoving back the coat from her shoulders, he heard the hard clank of what must have been the demon crystal in her pocket. A deadly creature contained in that bit of murky rock, capable of swift murder, and without remorse.

An unwelcome image flickered in Jack's mind. *She hadn't even seen it coming. One moment Monica stood there, looking to Jack for reassurance—rescue—the next, she was dead.*

"What are we doing?" Jack pushed from the kiss and paced away toward the stairs, and then as quickly, reversed and returned toward the object of his lustful curiosity. "I don't know you. You don't know me."

He turned and again strode away. Petite, feisty and attractive, yet unlike the usual eyelash-batting pretties, Mersey Bane was one of those women who wanted to hold their own, without a man to back them up.

There was nothing wrong with women like that—unless he couldn't get there fast enough to protect them when they needed it. And they always needed it.

"What's bugging you, hotshot?" The tip of her tongue glanced out to trace her lower lip. "Did I do something wrong?"

"Wrong? We're kissing when we should be saving the world from demons," he said.

"You kissed me first," she accused. "Do I scare you, Jack?"

"Scare me?" Nothing scared him.

Almost nothing.

When memory reared its demonic head *that* put a fright to his calm pulse.

He averted his gaze to the sharp-pointed lump in her coat pocket. "You bloody terrify me to know you're toting a dangerous demon in your pocket."

Fingers gripping the air, then splaying out, she punctuated her silent frustration with a curt. "Right. I think that's my cue to leave."

"What do you intend to do with that thing?" Jack demanded.

"Take it back to base and interrogate it."

He thrust out the stock of the M4, catching her across the chest with it. "You don't know what trouble you're getting into, little girl. You can't release that thing. It'll tear you apart."

"Listen." She shoved away his gun. "I'm not telling you how to do your job, so don't tell me how to do mine. Deal?"

Jack clenched his jaw so tightly, his molars scraped.

When she started down the stairs, he decided one more try at Mr. Nice Guy, and then the gloves were off.

Jogging toward the stairs, he fished a card from his inner vest pocket. He still carried them, having done so when working upstairs at MI5 as a spook. He handed Mersey the business card, which listed his last name and his cell-phone number.

"Pest control." With a smirk she flicked the card with a forefinger. "Two kisses weren't enough—" her eyes averted to his crotch, where the pain of his restraint tormented "—big boy?"

Jack lunged and gripped her by the coat collar. Fighting the aggressive need to lash out, he growled. Infuriation had never before challenged him with such intriguing green eyes.

"Call me if you need help," he said through a tight jaw. Releasing her, he did not step back, yet maintained eye contact, which forced her to crane her neck to see him. The struggle not to sink back into her luscious scent threatened. "You will need help—you just don't know it yet."

"Sure." Smiling a wicked grin, the woman tucked his card into a pocket and then started down the stairs.

"Sure you don't want that help right now?" he called. The urge to follow her could not be ignored. "I can give you a ride home, or to your base."

Without replying she waved back as she exited the building.

You going to let her go, Jack?

By rights, he should let go of Miss Cocky I've Got a Demon In My Pocket. She was a dabbler, like those stupid numskulls had been the night of his encounter with the dread demon. And that had ended horribly.

He couldn't allow Mersey Bane to end up as Monica had. He had to follow her and blast that demon in her pocket to bits.

And if he could gain one more wintergreen kiss while at it, then this night would turn out all right.

Chapter 5

Mersey Bane got on a city bus down the roadway from the warehouse. An easy follow. Jack tailed the red double-decker through London as it headed northwest. The streetlights and businesses were lit for after hours and pub crawls. Bands of drunken compatriots wobbled from one pub to the next. Jack was always up for a crawl, but not when he was working.

He kept an eye to the capped head seated toward the back of the bus. The demon in her pocket must not be released, most especially, on a bus. She wasn't capable of handling it—in proof, her sexy come-on showed Jack where her mind was. Not on protecting innocents, but instead, focused on sexual endeavors.

It was a little odd because he didn't get the I'm-a-loose-girl vibe from Miss Bane. But he could be wrong. Jack Harris had never won any awards for knowing a woman's mind.

One hand on the steering wheel, he leaned across to the passenger seat and popped out the compact flash disk from his weapon. Inserting it into the drive in the car's dashboard, he uploaded the photo he'd taken earlier. The screen was stashed in the glove box, but he didn't need to view it.

Sliding his mobile phone from a pocket of his vest, he dialed up headquarters. The phone was answered on the first ring.

"Good evening, Jack, how may I help you?"

"Belladonna, do you ever sleep?"

The female voice purred, which made Jack smile, despite the situation.

Jack had come to rely upon the sweet lady's voice behind the frequent calls he made to check in with P-Cell or gather information for an assignment. Her title was communications contact, and she was definitely high in P-Cell ranks. Belladonna had yet to steer him wrong. And P-Cell's secrecy was guarded by her anonymity.

He figured her to be older, probably in her sixties, but had never met her, nor had any others with P-Cell. The creepy thing? She always answered a call on the first ring. No matter the time of day.

"After all these years, I require little beauty sleep, Jack. So what's the situation?"

"One confirmed kill to report."

"Excellent. Did you ID the culprit first?"

"Standard nuisance demon." Or so he guessed. His attention had been diverted toward the woman in his arms. Diversion entailing ensuring her safety—and snogging. "Got something else for you. I've uploaded a photo to the mainframe."

"I'm accessing it right now. Oh, she's an interesting take."

"Name's Mersey Bane. Pronounced like the disposition, spelled like the river."

And why he repeated that bit of trivia, he just didn't know. Had the woman got to him? Slid her sensuous yet awkward allure beneath his skin and imprinted herself on his psyche? Ah! He was tired. Head full of muck and all that.

Or was it that wintergreen kiss that still tickled his mouth?

And the feel of her body crushed against his like a sparrow clinging to a hawk.

A glance to the bus spotted his prey.

"Is that something on her face, or is she that pitiful?"

"Demon residue, Belladonna. And she's not pitiful, just in trouble."

"If she's with you, then yes, I'd call that trouble."

She teased. The woman couldn't begin to guess at he and Mersey's earlier interaction.

"She was in the area when I destroyed a demon."

"You've never exposed yourself to civilians before, Jack. Bad form."

Belladonna always called things exactly as they were. Jack hated the sense of failure, but he always made a point of learning from it. And what had he learned tonight? *Don't mix business with pleasure.*

"She's not exactly a civilian. She… Well, there was another demon, and she captured it in some sort of crystal, then hightailed it out of there like she was all it. Her last words were that she had plans to take it out of the thing when she returned to base."

"Base? What base?"

"Don't know." Belladonna's sudden urgency put him on alert. "She called me a lot of names, too, but—what was that one…? Ah yes, a death merchant."

"Oh, dear. Who is this woman?"

"Well that, Belladonna, is why I gave you a bell. I need all the information you can provide on her. I'm tracking her at the moment."

He glanced up. The bus pulled to a stop. The capped head remained seated.

"Heading east toward Westminster on a double-decker. I don't know what the deal was with the crystal, but if she tries to set it loose—"

"She must be in the know." Jack heard a keyboard clattering in the background. "It is possible to imprison a demon within crystal for storage and later release. But you've got to know what you're doing. Most importantly, you must have some talent. You didn't compromise yourself, did you, Jack?"

He swiped a palm over his face, shaking his head. He hadn't purposefully compromised himself, and yet, the woman had managed to fix her own ideas of his cover to him.

"Jack?"

"I didn't say a thing. She thought I was a freelance demon hunter. No worries. She'd never pin me for P-Cell, because no one knows about us."

The silence on the line was incredible. Jack glanced up and around the rearview mirror. The bus took off. The capped head was no longer in position.

He scanned the pavement where the riders had dispersed. No sign of a petite woman in an aviator cap and long coat. Shifting into gear, he took off after the double-decker.

"No one knows about P-Cell," Belladonna agreed over the radio speaker. "Unless... She specifically named you a death merchant? There's only one group— Could be one of them."

"Them?"

"You're still new, Jack. There's plenty P-Cell history you don't know about. I'm going to search the database for your Mersey Bane. I'll give you a bell if I find what I'm looking for. I believe in you, Jack."

He didn't know what to say to that.

"You've got it in you to do great things," Belladonna added. "Whatever you do, don't lose the subject, or that demon."

"No intention, Belladonna." He hung up, and gunned the Range Rover to parallel the bus. No sign of the woman on this side. "Sod it, if she slipped off..."

Angry at his lack of control over the situation, Jack sped up to park behind the bus as it performed another stop. He ran out and sorted through the riders as they spilled from the bus. Pushing through to step up inside, he scanned the seats. It was empty!

"If you want to ride, find a seat," the driver prompted. "Haven't got all night, mate."

Slamming his fist against the steel handrail, Jack jumped out to the pavement, right before a stairway that led down to the tube train.

Intuition screamed that she'd taken the evasive maneuver. "She went underground. Sneaky. I will find you, Miss Bane. You're not going to slip from my life like a demon misting in from the dark realm. This hunter never loses his prey."

The depths of London's underground system were brightly lit and smelled stale, and tainted with the metallic rub of wheels along the electric track. Hurdling the turnstile, he dashed out onto the platform and slipped into the same carriage he saw Mersey's coat disappear onto just as the doors closed.

The carriage was packed, all seats taken and floor space crushed with standers. Must have been near a concert hall for the late crowd.

Jack pushed through, but no one was cooperative. He didn't want to force his way past the pregnant woman, so he gripped a teenager bopping to an iPod by the collar and hauled him out of his seat. Offering the seat to the pregnant woman, he slid by her as he slapped the teenager's hand to a standing pole.

By the time he made the end of the carriage, there was no sign of Mersey Bane. He scanned back over the seats. The teenager flipped him off. How could he have missed her?

"Meowr." A black cat curled beneath the seat of an old woman who worked her crochet with blinding speed.

"Someone brought a cat onboard?" What they didn't think of. "Did you see a woman?" he asked those about him. "She wore a cap with goggles and had a long coat."

No one paid him mind.

The carriage came to a stop and half the passengers pushed out. With one last scan around, Jack stepped out onto the platform. Scratching his head, he watched the train pull away. The black cat pawed at the closed door.

"Not good," he muttered. "Not bloody good."

Now who would protect Little Miss Attitude from the demon?

The connection between the familiar and the demon hunter could prove most conducive to his reentry into the Cadre.

The dread demon lingered in the otherwhere above London, following the sensory trail left behind by both of them. The girl trailed a stream of giddy urgency behind her. And the male couldn't decide whether to be angry or release his lust.

Interesting.

Now, to send in a minion for a closer look.

The Cadre headquarters sat nestled in the lush St. Yve forest fifty miles southwest from London proper. It mastered half the Maybank manor, home to Lord Lawrence Maybank, Earl of St. Yve. A secret organization fronted by the Department of Anachronistic Research of London University, the order boasted a virtual who's who of paranormal research academics.

As current head of the Cadre, the earl's castle served as its headquarters, as it had for centuries. Set upon a man-made double-terraced hill that had once harbored an ancient fortress, access to the manor was privileged. No outsiders could ever find a way in, thanks to the many magical shields set around the area. And if an innocent did wander onto Cadre ground—most likely, the surrounding forest—they would chance upon the threshold guardians, and thus, would forget ever trying to seek the Cadre in the first place.

Thanks to Mersey's initiate level, access to the main grounds was cleared with but a flash of her smile at the sentinels who arched over the drive. Their wingtips stretched ten feet across and, though carved of stone, appeared amazingly lifelike. Which was the point. The stone gargoyles didn't move, but they were alive and observant, ever watchful.

Mersey left her little white Volkswagen to the footman and

stepped across the pebbled walk beneath the porte cochere. Nearby, hornbeam hedgerows were thick and bursting with growth, yet always trimmed perfectly. Too perfect, Mersey often thought, and, out of habit, she plucked a few leaves from the wall of hedge, allowing them to flutter in her wake to the manicured grounds. She smiled to know she could institute a bit of much-needed disorder.

Before her, the ancient limestone facade of the castle gleamed and beckoned all to enter. But the St. Yve manor rarely received visitors. Least not if those visitors knew what was good for them.

While the earl was the head of the Cadre, his daughter, Lady Aurora, was in line to inherit the position, and it was she who dealt most frequently with the initiates and handled the day-to-day running of the order. Though meetings and field assignments kept her quite busy, and Mersey rarely bumped in to her for more than a moment once or twice a week.

The mansion was quiet, the grand draperies pulled over the windows, and but a few dim lights that were always on in the corner of the foyer.

Detouring on the way to her room, Mersey dropped off the demon-filled quartz in the dungeon with Squire Callahan, the storage manager—but she referred to him as *demon storage dude extraordinaire.* He was always over the moon to get a new specimen, and figured Interrogations would be able to work her magic before noon.

It was 4:00 a.m. by the time Mersey shuffled into her private rooms. Her favorite scent, a mixture of lemon and thyme, tinted the air. After she'd had to shift shapes in the subway, she was knackered. Shifting always drained her. She was surprised the hunter hadn't figured her out. Maybe he wasn't as in-the-know as she'd assumed.

The manor offered private suites for initiates. Mersey's room had belonged to her and her mother, and following her mother's death, Mersey had remained. Only on her twenty-second birthday had she finally got up the courage to rent her own flat in London. She spent little time there, though. London didn't feel right. This was where her memories remained. But she still wasn't sure what home should feel like. Her flat didn't offer homey vibes but neither did the manor. It was missing a certain presence.

A male presence.

You will know the one when he comes to you. Mysterious, and not terribly helpful, her mother's pre-death portent.

Mirabelle Bane had been certain of Mersey's future mate. Too bad Mersey hadn't got the same memo. If there was a man out there—looking for her—then roll out the red carpet, and show him the way, because she was ready. For love.

Perhaps a distraction like love would move her focus from her dissatisfaction with the Cadre. To remain here and continue to work for the Cadre, or to permanently leave for London and cast out on her own? It was the question that bothered her a lot lately. She loved her work, but felt more and more like an outsider here. There was never anyone around interested in chatting about simple things like the latest fashion fad or where the best nightclubs were. Mersey had but one real friend, Squire, yet she suspected he had a crush on her, while she thought of him as a brother. Everyone at the Cadre was focused on their jobs. *Social life* did not exist.

Mersey believed people were drawn to that which they most needed. And what was she drawn to? Of late, nothing in particular. Which didn't bode well for her supposed needs. But she sensed it was no longer this manor or the people within it.

You were drawn quite close to Jack Harris.

Mersey sighed.

Her goggles were splattered with demon residue. Thick, oozy stuff that had dried and crackled. It would dissolve to dust and leave behind a reddish powder. Peeling off her residue-coated clothing, she then donned one of the thick terry monogrammed robes the house brownie always laid out on her bed, and wandered out toward the washer.

She'd easily given Mr. Jack Harris the slip. *And* a slide up against his ankle. Bet he was feeling pretty ticked off right now.

Smirking, she padded back to the bedroom and plopped onto the bed.

Drawn to him? Yes, she had been.

The man wasn't classic handsome. *Alluring* came to mind. That and *strong.* Attractive, in a macho, blast-'em-all-to-bits way. He'd smelled wonderful, like every dream she had ever had of masculine heroes saving the day. A bold, bent nose had mastered his face, and more razor stubble on cheeks and chin than hair on his head. The fierce blue eyes staring her down had done things to her insides. Made her forget things—like the mission.

She never got distracted. Yet when Jack Harris had gazed into her eyes, he'd stirred up a sensuous, uninhibited side of Mersey she'd not known she possessed.

And why upon all whys had she *kissed* him?

Mersey caught her forehead in her palm with a smack. "You were such a Loose Lucy!"

This was not her modus operandi. Walking up to a proper stranger and planting a smacker on him? She wasn't uncomfortable around men, but generally Mersey waited for a first— official—date to snog.

It had been that sensation in her heart. That dark glitter of invitation. Well, she'd read it as invitation, a cry for her to step inside and become a part of his world.

"It wasn't awful," she muttered. In fact, it had been very good. *Let's do it again soon* good.

"Think of the mission," she chided.

It wasn't every day she ran into a demon hunter while out reconnoitering. In fact, it had never happened before. She needed to identify his alliances and ensure his objectives did not interfere with the Cadre's mission.

Was he a freelance hunter as he'd claimed? There was one other organization in the area that would send out a man on such a dangerous mission, but they were stealth and covert. Much like the Cadre. They were rivals with her people, for the very reason she had witnessed—the idiots simply blasted. Death merchants, the lot of them.

There was so much to be learned by safely capturing the *para* and later interrogating it. All demons were not harmful to humans. In fact, most humans required demons for their existence. How else to know the deep, dark wanting of desire or the exhilarating fear of terror? Mortals called their darkest demons to them, without knowing, and experienced a wondrous realm of emotion and human experience.

And if any man thought to indiscriminately remove those experiences from this world, then Mersey had in mind to change his perception.

Jack stomped into his flat and set his weapon on the floor. *Always keep it handy,* and by the door was the most necessary place. He had weapons in every room and near all the windows. Survival skills learned during his stint for the British Security Service. MI5 had further bolstered his covert skills.

Now, if only he could remove the demons from his dreams. Real guns didn't work in dreams. Even the imagined ones fired—and struck—without results. Like the evening he'd fired his pistol at the dread demon stalking closer to Monica. It hadn't felt the impact of the bullets at all. Jack's efforts had been most ineffective.

And tailing one petite bird had further proven his ineffectiveness.

"Bloody. Incapable," Jack muttered as he stalked down the hallway. He tugged out the UV-tipped dagger from his belt and tucked it away in the storage cubby in the hall, followed by the belt.

Tearing his shirt over his head and unzipping his trousers, he strode into the bedroom and shucked off his clothes so he stood in only his black boxer briefs.

Stretching his arms and twisting at the waist, he worked at the tension that clutched his spine. The tightness taxed his flexibility and he had to strain to reach behind his opposite shoulder. But he knew how to take care of job stress.

Jack grabbed the gravity boots on the floor at the end of the iron-framed bed.

"Sodding…" he muttered as he stomped toward the inversion bar installed near the ceiling at the midpoint of the hallway. "Idiot…stupid…gorgeous!"

She had been a pretty bird, no doubt about that. Even beneath the comic-book attire and demon residue. Those eyes. When had he ever seen eyes so big and bright and—that kiss!

Made it difficult for a man to remain morose, which he'd mastered, thank you very bloody much. What else could he be after all he'd seen in his lifetime?

But he knew deep inside, there was a soft part of him he wasn't so familiar with. Had Mersey seen that soft side? To think it was okay to step up and kiss a man who towered over her by a foot and who had wielded a semiautomatic weapon? That irritating softness must scream out to the world like some kind of welcome mat. How not to crawl into a hole and tuck away his heart from inspection with a microscope and teasing, roaming female hands?

"Girl's carrying a load of trouble in her pocket. Should have never let her get away. Bugger it!"

Slapping on the boots, he then gripped the bar suspended high in the narrow hallway and, swinging up his feet, locked in. He let go and hung upside down.

For a few moments he hung there, allowing the blood to rush to his head, reveling in the gush of skull-squeezing fluid that pushed out all other thoughts. His back lengthened and he twisted his shoulders to stretch out his spine.

This always felt first-rate after a long day. Good old military exercise to get the blood pumping and force out the toxins that he'd taken on during the course of the day. And man, did he take on the bad stuff.

Morose was an excuse. Jack strived to shift beyond the horror and make his experience worth something. To others. All his adult life, he had refused to allow others to be hurt through terroristic methods. And demons were the ultimate terrorists.

Pressing his bent arms close to his body, he curled up at the waist and went for that first muscle-stretching crunch. *One. Two.*

He wouldn't stop until he reached one hundred.

Seven.

He'd let the girl get away. She still lived in his senses. He should have been able to track that lemon scent like a bloodhound.

Thirteen. Fourteen.

Already the sweat began to build. That meant the toxins were purging. His gut tightened, working his abs, and his quads strained.

To stuff a demon in her pocket like that? What if the thing had got loose on the underground? Or later, when she was all alone, heading back toward base.

Base? What a nutty piece of demon-chasing fluff.

And yet, Belladonna had got him to wondering. Rarely did Belladonna not immediately have the answer to any question. Further research in the database must mean something important. Them? Who were the mysterious *them* Belladonna had mentioned?

Twenty-eight.

Sweat dripped up the bridge of his nose and ran down his forehead. Yeah, he liked the world upside down and sweaty, and all alone.

Alone was good. Alone meant he wasn't responsible for anybody or anything. Just himself. The way it should be.

Thirty-three. Jack increased the pace of his pull-ups. *Thirty-four. We protect the world from the otherside.* P-Cell's motto.

He'd adopted their motto and their ask-no-questions policy. It worked for him. Demon hunting had become routine—yet always a challenge—but Jack remained vigilant to find the demon that had killed his partner.

Forty-two. Forty-three.

Mersey Bane needed someone to keep her safe. For Christ's

sake, she even had a comic-book name. Must have delusions of fighting demons and saving the world.

Jack could get behind saving the world.

Sixty-three, sixty-four.

And yet, destruction never felt right. Violence begat violence. How to make it end?

Seventy...

And now there was a woman standing in the path between him and the big bads. She thought to fight the demons? Well, she needed a kick-arse weapon to do that. And muscle—*seventy-five*—and a death wish.

Which he had.

Out in the kitchen, the phone rang. Curled up and gripping the bar for a pause—his abs straining—Jack huffed and decided it must be Belladonna. The answering machine was turned on high, so he could hear her from here.

He swung back down. "Eighty—oh, sod me."

An upside-down demon face grinned at him.

Chapter 6

There were horns. Everywhere. Jack head-butted the grinning demon. One of the horns cut through his temple, embedding a deep, stinging pain above his eye.

"I hate horns!"

He didn't take the time to assess for damage. Swinging backward, which was really forward, he couldn't gain enough momentum to swing all the way up to grip the inversion rack and release his ankles.

"Jack, I've some information on your Mersey Bane," Belladonna's voice announced over the answering machine.

"Brilliant." Jack swung back—this time it was backward—and fisted the same spot where the demon had been squatting, but his knuckles punched through air.

In the brief flash of his surroundings, he didn't sight the demon. But it wasn't gone; he could smell the brimstone and hear the sepulchral chuckles that seemed to echo out from the very walls.

"So it's that way, is it?"

Another swing toward the doorway spied what he didn't want

to see. Demon in the nine o'clock position—wielding a bronze floor lamp like a cricket bat.

Jack curled his arms up over his face as he swung into the demon's attack zone. The lamp shade prevented the hit from being too painful, but he did take the stiffly corrugated linen shade beside the eye.

His attacker yowled in disappointment and sent the lamp flying toward the plasma television. Jack winced as he swung away. He did favor his high-tech toys.

"You've found yourself an interesting woman," Belladonna said. "Good job, Jack. A dynamic find."

Not nearly so dynamic as his houseguest.

He swung once more to gain momentum. The demon slashed a razored appendage. A snarl splattered toxic spit across the floor. Heavy droplets steamed and sizzled through the varnished surface of the hardwood.

"You piqued my interest when you mentioned she called you a death merchant," Belladonna said. "There's but one organization known to label hunters that way—the Cadre."

What the hell was the Cadre? Sounded vaguely familiar.

Jack swung up to the target. He wrapped his arms around the pumpkin-sized head, peppered with horns. In that split second, his body hung horizontally in the air. A jerk of each leg unhooked the gravity boots from the inversion bar. He used inertia to fall backward, flipping the demon over his rolling body as he did so and kicking at the swishing black mist that hung at the base of the creature instead of demonic feet. Though fitted with deadly claws that could halve a good-sized sofa with one swipe, it was a small demon in body, so the toss proved an easy one.

"P-Cell has been trying to nail the Cadre for decades," the answering machine continued. "We can never get close enough to their guarded establishment. We suspect they are somehow linked to the Department of Anachronistic Research at London University, since all roads lead directly to Lord Lawrence, Earl of St. Yve—er, one of his twin daughters currently heads the department.

I did a background check on your Mersey Bane and she's a former student, and a suspected Cadre member."

Jumping upright and landing in a defensive crouch, Jack surveyed the room. He positioned his arms, ready for fisticuffs. "Come on, you ugly scruff. Show your face!"

"This is quite a coup, Jack. You've made contact with the Cadre. You've orders from Dirk Marcolf to track Mersey Bane."

The demon untangled its limbs with a wicked clack of talon. Its roar hummed in Jack's sinuses. It wasn't the volume so much as the wretched smell of sulfur that lifted the bile up Jack's throat.

"You likely know little about the Cadre," Belladonna continued. "Haven't been with us long enough, I'm sure. We believe they may have existed for centuries. P-Cell, and those we've suspected to be with the Cadre, have been at odds since P-Cell's inception in the forties. They're a bunch of parapsychologists and demonologists. And get this, they like to study and preserve the demons and then return them to the dark realm. Isn't that a hoot?"

"Completely," Jack uttered. He eyed the M4 still propped by the front door. Twenty paces away. The next closest weapon was the .45 down the hall inside the bedroom.

The gravity boots slid down and over his ankles, making flexing his feet—and thus running—difficult.

"P-Cell has never had access to the Cadre. Their base is protected by some sort of magical shield. Most frustrating, for a few agents have almost succeeded. Or so we can guess. Lost their memories, they did, when they got too close. Marcolf wants you to verify the location of the Cadre," Belladonna said. "Destroy all demon activity, if necessary, to obtain admission. It'll be a real feather in your cap, Jack."

Click.

Feathers, he didn't mind. It was the snarly, horned, niffy things that put up his hackles.

"And what did I do to deserve you?" Jack muttered to the swaying demon whose glowing red eyes were to be avoided.

Staring into its eyes could enchant the *daemon incultus*—at the expense of a man's sanity. "Now you filthy lot are showing up in my own home?"

"Ave magister, Ba'al Beryth!"

"I don't speak demon, but I'll take that as an unflattering comment on my living quarters. It was tidy until you crashed the party. Stinking bit of—"

The demon lunged, claws slashing the wall near Jack's ear. Deep trenches cut through the plaster. Jack dove backward, catching his right shoulder on the floor and rolling his body up into a run.

It was at moments like this that the little boy inside Jack stood up and thrust back his shoulders. Jack the Demon Frightener? *Don't let the big hunk of glass hit you on the way out.*

Or rather, do.

It was an awkward race with the gravity boots clunking about his ankles, but he made the bedroom door, gripped the frame and swung himself inside just as the demon soared by, growling and gnashing its teeth.

The .45 under the bed was loaded and ready. Salt rounds always did the trick. Jack sat up, aimed and blasted the face that appeared in the doorway—if you could call drooling black lips, red eyes and horns a face.

"Spot on."

A perfect hole opened between the glowing eyes. Jack could see through it to the slashes in the wall on the opposite side of the hallway. No splatter. Sometimes they didn't do that. Instead—

Jack slammed his body flat, facedown on the carpet. Behind him the demon hardened and cracked, as if sprayed with liquid nitrogen, and then exploded. Hard bits flew about the room. Something conked the back of his head. An eyeball rolled under the bed.

The chunks began to sizzle and *pouf,* they fizzled and broke apart to a simmering red ash.

"And I just had this ugly carpet shampooed," he muttered.

Sitting upright against the door frame, the pistol clutched and ready, Jack peered down the hallway. He didn't smell any others, but wasn't about to let down his guard. If one had entered, then others must surely know the way.

P-Cell's job description hadn't included entertaining weird snarling, horned creatures in his home. He'd been living in a surreal horror flick ever since that bust had gone bad months earlier.

Something had happened that night. The demon in the warehouse, it had...touched his heart. Literally.

Jack placed a hand over his chest. A thin line of scar tissue above his nipple proved that he hadn't imagined the strange happening. Each time he traced it, a weird vibration gripped his heart.

Engaging a salt round into the chamber, he muttered, "What did I do to piss off the demon realm?"

He knew the answer, and it hadn't been anything recent, he felt sure. This war had begun over twenty years ago when a little boy had thrust a wishing ball at a monster to save a beautiful woman's life.

Swiping a finger across his eyebrow, Jack felt a cut. Blood curled into the whorls on his fingertip. Another scar to add to his collection.

From his doorway position, he eyed the red light blinking on the answering machine. Mersey Bane was involved in a covert demon-hunting group? The Cadre?

Now that he had a moment for clear thought, he had heard of the organization. Dirk Marcolf, P-Cell's deputy director, had mentioned them once during training. Marcolf made routine visits to the Department of Anachronistic Research at the London University, to check up on them, hoping to catch anything untoward going on. They'd not sniffed out a solid lead to the Cadre headquarters yet.

I believe in you, Jack.

Belladonna's support felt strange to him. He couldn't muster belief in himself, so how could any other manage it?

Brushing off a scatter of demon ash from his forearm, Jack disengaged the pistol. Another female's voice shattered Belladonna's comforting statement.

Are you even aware of the chain of fallout that occurs each time you kill a demon?

He wasn't sure what Mersey had been talking about, but he wondered now. Demon annihilated. Job complete. What more was there?

Fallout? Beyond the mess settling into his carpet, he hadn't a clue. But he'd find out because he had just been given a new objective. Tracking Miss Bane.

Four hours later, Mersey tugged on cigarette-leg jeans and a soft green sweater, still warm from the dryer. Her boots were polished, along with the buff coat (cleaned and folded). Attribute that to the house brownies who did their work on the periphery of usual perception. She'd see to leaving them some rosehip wine in thanks. They preferred the French appellations, as she'd learned years earlier when she'd thought to leave cheap English ale and returned to her room to find her sheets stained with ale and the chairs nailed to the ceiling. Brownies were offended by overgenerous gifts, but true affront rose at thoughtless, cheap presents.

Stuffing the goggles and cap in her coat pocket, she then donned the coat and headed below to see if the interrogation had begun.

She had lain in bed for hours, but was pretty sure she had only gotten fifteen minutes of real sleep. The rest of the time had been a lucid dream of sexy, sweaty bodies doing the nasty. Starring herself and a particularly fine male body, with a muscled back, tall stature, gruff manner and commanding kisses. Oh, and the kitchen sink of a rifle he wielded propped by the wall three feet from their bed of passion.

She wondered about those kisses. When she'd initially kissed Jack, she hadn't been sure, and being out of practice, she'd been more than a little nervous. But nervousness had fled with the warmth of the man's commanding touch. And the overwhelming feeling of safety she had felt nestled in his powerful embrace.

What the hell was she doing?

"Mersey, you so need to get back in the game."

For years she'd truly believed in her mother's portent, and had simply waited for *the one*. Then, realizing nothing would come to her—not even romance—unless she put herself out there, she'd begun to explore the idea of a relationship. Brief, noncommittal relationships that hadn't felt right to continue beyond a few weeks of dinners and sex.

She'd never had a real, devoted boyfriend, though there had been two lovers in her past. Mersey had come to learn that mortals didn't do it for her, but neither did *paras*. So what remained?

The one faery she'd kissed had left her with a sour taste for the sidhe. Yet, she still hungered for Raskin in her dreams—an ostracized prince from the Black court. A girl couldn't dream up more of a bad boy than that.

Mersey wasn't sure where she stood on the scale of acceptable partners. It was difficult being a familiar in a realm that didn't even believe in her existence.

Her parents had been familiars, and so Mersey had been born a familiar. Even though a familiar's principal habitat was the mortal realm, she was not considered mortal, and she had never felt *right* out there in the populated sectors. Though, certainly she did function and fit in just fine.

Her paranormal skills were particular, yet few. Besides being a vessel demons tapped to bridge to this realm, shifting to cat form was her most outstanding. Shifting was a carryover from the ancient familiars who were once cats, with the ability to shift to human form. Over the centuries her kind had adapted. Her senses were heightened, especially her eyesight. She could see like a cat, which made her world a gorgeous abundance of texture. And her connection to the organic electromagnetic structure of the world made it easy to locate ley lines, and sense *paras*.

As well, she'd studied martial arts. The Cadre didn't offer the training as a means to kill opponents, but rather defense. They frowned on violence.

Here at the St. Yve manor she was accepted. But never really loved.

Would love be possible? Had her mother unknowingly sealed her destiny so many years ago?

Rubbing her right hand along her coat, Mersey toyed with the hematite rings, rolling them around her fingers. Mirabelle Bane had chosen a mate for her daughter—and had given that person a ring like the ones Mersey wore, so her daughter would know the man when she met him.

As if she would ever meet *the one* out of billions.

"Thanks a lot, Mom," Mersey muttered, as she did so many times when her thoughts drifted to her lack of mate. "A photo would have been more helpful... Oh, no."

A quick count resulted in seven rings instead of the usual eight she wore. Had one fallen off? Broken?

Her heart sinking, Mersey swallowed.

She'd always worn these rings. They were bespelled to protect and warn her of demon presence—one very dangerous demon, in particular.

"One gone," she whispered. "This doesn't bode well."

But what to do? She did keep one ring in safekeeping. "No, I'll save it. I still have eight total."

Pressing her beringed fingers over her heart, she strode the quiet manor hallways. The lab was on the lower level in the dungeon.

Mersey found Squire Callahan bent over a microscope, his long fingers enrobed in thin blue latex gloves and a pristine white lab coat cutting below his hips—he was beyond six feet high. Blond hair that might never see a comb twisted this way and that on his narrow skull.

The raucous noise of a rock band was flipped off as he noticed her entrance. "Oh, hey, Mersey. You're looking spiffy."

"Feeling it, too, Squire. So, what's up?"

He nodded toward the far end of the lab, where the interrogation was already in progress.

Segregated behind a massive Lucite wall that was bulletproof, claw-proof, fireproof and reinforced with magically enhanced nano-bars to keep whatever magic may be released inside, the interrogator paced the white marble floor below the floating demon.

Known by her distinctive moniker, Interrogations was a slim, short woman with severe straight brown hair and equally severe black plastic-rimmed glasses. Mersey often mused that if the woman would remove the glasses and add a bit of pink to her dour wardrobe she could be a real looker.

The interrogatee was plump and a blushing shade of salmon. Short orange hairs stuck out all over the thing and the glossy green eyes bugged as it took in the room. Obviously a *daemon incultus,* for the other, *daemon sapiens,* always wore a mortal form.

"A lesser *incultus* demon?" she asked Squire as they observed. "Turn the volume up."

Squire tapped the console before them. "A mischief demon, to be exact. Interrogations has almost broken it. It's peckish. And we have rats."

Mischief demons were the bawling babies of the dark realm. They were easily upset, very loud and craved rodents. Interrogations always had rats on hand. Mersey was never too interested in discovering how the woman came by the demon treats.

Mersey listened as the expressionless woman mercilessly questioned the quivering demon regarding its entrance familiar. The majority of *daemon incultus* required a familiar to passage to the mortal realm. Find the familiar, and the Cadre would have their source of the leak. But Mersey's thoughts strayed.

She wondered how Jack would handle such an interrogation. Likely he'd forgo talk and instead blast the subject to Kingdom Come. And then he'd turn on that sexy smile and kiss her.

She sighed and hugged her arms to her chest. Last night was the first time she'd met anybody in the know who wasn't a Cadre initiate, though certainly she had heard of freelance hunters.

The idea that there was someone out there—who wasn't a Cadre member—who could relate to her world, intrigued her.

He had stood over her, locking her in his sight with deep blue eyes the color of a twilight sky after the rain. And her heart experienced delicious palpitations.

Jack. Wasn't that the standard name for the hero in all the action movies?

Heroes were well and good, but…ah, blimey. She could use a tall, dark and muscular man to rescue her from indecision and answer her quest for fulfillment.

Things like a relationship, and companionship, and love sounded pretty good to her right now. She wanted passion. Dash it, she *craved* passion.

Hmm, Mersey wondered if the hero was in the mood for damsel rescuing. She was far from helpless when it came to tracking *paras*. However, when it came to flirtation, desperation made her kiss perfect strangers.

"Mersey?"

"Yes," she answered dreamily.

"What's with you?" Squire shrugged a hand through his tousle of springy curls. "Are you paying attention?"

"Huh?"

"Ah, she's got men in her eyes, she does. Or is that faeries?"

Only Squire would be so audacious to use her past to tease her. "Will I ever live that down?"

"Oh, you have. That's why someone needs to remind you."

"Raskin is not so awful. He was just…having a bad day."

"Mersey, you continue to defend him after he humiliated you."

"It's just his manner. He *is* a faery."

"Why do women do that?" Squire pounded the stainless-steel lab table with a fist. "They ignore the average bloke to swoon over the charming rogues, when we all know they are lecherous and only out for one thing. You're too good for that, Mersey."

Nice to hear it said, even if it was hard to believe sometimes.

She didn't want to be so good that all her male prospects were ruled out. "I prefer to remain on Raskin's good side, Squire. He does like his mischief."

"Point taken."

"But no more kissing faeries. So." She looked to the interrogation. "Back to work."

The mischief demon had fitted itself into a corner and its orange fur shivered. The subject eyed the steel cage that harbored a fat white rat. It began to bawl like a spoiled child.

"Name the familiar," Interrogations repeated. She stabbed a glance toward the nervous rat. "Then you can indulge."

"Jack!" the demon howled, and lunged for the cage.

The interrogator stood over the cage, eyeing the demon. The demon's jaws morphed hideously into a complaining but silent moan. "Jack Harris!"

Stepping back, and almost missing the step down to the main floor, Mersey clutched the edge of the steel lab table to steady herself. "No. Bloody. Way."

The demon had given up the familiar who had opened the passage to this realm. But, that couldn't be right.

"Jack? But he didn't…"

He hadn't given her any sign, impression, or even a feeling that he was a *para*. Not that she had the ability to recognize another familiar with their clothes on. It wasn't possible—unless she witnessed the familiar shift shapes or saw the crescent-shaped witch mark that all natural-born familiars wore somewhere on their bodies.

Or perhaps he was a mortal who had been tapped by a demon?

Jack Harris had stepped into her world with guns blazing. He'd kissed her. He'd…killed a demon. Which could have also resulted in the death of another familiar, if said demon had bridged here via a familiar.

Fallout.

Mersey jerked her gaze back to the demon. A thin twitching white rat tail streamed out from between its tight orange lips.

"Could it be lying?"

Squire stepped down and sorted through a collection of quartz pyramids and various storage and collection stones arrayed on the steel table. "Doubt it. Give a demon its favorite treat and it won't lie. Bitch when we get the war demons in here. Their favorite is human babies. Not that we have ever sacrificed—"

"Squire, I..." She didn't know how to react to this information. Besides racing back to Jack Harris and punching him in the kisser.

And yet, why should she expect him to reveal himself to her? It wasn't as though she introduced herself to others as "Mersey Bane, demon familiar. How'd you do?"

"We're sending it back." Squire tossed a perfectly round hunk of pink rhodonite in his palm. "I've got enough of those things stored in the archives. You keen with that? Mersey? You don't look so well."

She clutched her scalp and turned from Squire's imploring hazel eyes. "Jack Harris was there last night in the warehouse. I thought he was a freelance demon hunter, one of those nuts who *believe* and take on the quest by themselves."

"*The* Jack Harris the demon gave up?"

Mersey nodded. "But I didn't know. How to know when in the presence of another..."

"Familiar?"

She looked to Squire and nodded, unable to voice the many weird thoughts running through her brain. Foremost being that she had kissed a stranger without getting any of the important credentials.

"The demon is lying. It can't be right."

"Demons do lie," Squire agreed. He tapped the Lucite divider, and the mischief demon shivered. "But this one is telling the truth. It has no reason not to."

Then that meant... Mersey had been drawn to what she most needed.

"I've got to get back to London. Now."

Chapter 7

Jack stretched his arms over his head and pushed into the cushy leather office chair until it tilted against the wall. Below MI5 headquarters, deep in the basement rumored to house the tech geeks, was where P-Cell made its home. Only P-Cell agents had access. By now Jack had learned to offer a smirk to former MI5 colleagues ribbing about his being a basement geek.

He'd been destined for this job since he was a boy. Even though he had been recruited *because* of Monica's death.

As had become ritual, each Sunday morning, he'd check in the archives and pore over the textbooks and grimoires kept under lock, key and warding.

Books spread before him across the long glass conference table. An open laptop displayed an ancient scanned text. Today, he'd hit pay dirt. Finally, he'd found a picture and description to resemble the demon he'd seen months earlier. A dread demon.

A *daemon incultus,* dread demons were powerful denizens of the dark realm. Their prime directive was raising dread in their mortal victims through macabre means such as violence, shock, even murder. A mortal's dread could call a dread demon to this realm. A direct order from the Grigori, the ruling council that oversaw the dark realm, could send it here as well.

Though the varieties of demons were vast, some were concentrated to one element, and worked their powers through the earth, air, fire or water. Dreads used air, including mortal breath as a means to feed off their dreadsome nightmares.

And yet, for all that power the dreads did require a familiar to bridge to the mortal realm.

So who, or what, had allowed that nasty son of a bitch to bridge to the mortal realm on the night of Monica's death?

Jack tapped a finger on top of the drawing and read the caption below. "Ba'al Beryth, Minister of Devilish Pacts and Rituals. Quite the title."

Red horns curled back from its forehead, hugging the side of its skull, to point at the row of sharpened teeth fit into a scythe grin. Emaciated so that its ribs showed, and yet wrapped in red muscle, it bore skeletal wings at the back of its shoulders. The hands were humanlike, yet stretched and curled with black talons.

This was the demon he'd watched murder Monica. Was it the same he had seen as a child? Maybe.

Obviously, a familiar had to be attached to the dread demon to allow it to passage to this realm. More than the one demon must currently tap the same familiar, for all that had been appearing in the concentrated area in Bermondsey. Unless some of the demons didn't require a familiar, but merely an open passage.

Hmm...

Was there a familiar living in the area?

Jack scoured the texts to refresh his memory on familiars.

Virtually human—familiars were the closest OE to being mortal—yet familiars could shift shapes at will, most always feline.

Hmm. Jack gave pause. That black cat in the underground last night...? Nah. Impossible. That would mean Mersey was a—no.

He read on.

Most familiars freely allowed their demon cohorts to tap them, but some were tapped against their will. Even common mortals could be tapped by clever demons. The bridging to this realm caused the familiar brief yet excruciating pain, but otherwise, they lived a normal life, until their demon master required a recharge, so to speak.

Mine.

Jack shook his head to obliterate the nasty whisper. Better not to think about those things, and to look to the future. Like destroying Beryth. No, he would not give it the preceding *ba'al,* which pronounced it a lord.

And the easiest way to do that? Locate its familiar.

However, besides finding a demon, Jack had a new assignment to contend. P-Cell wanted him to track Mersey Bane to the Cadre.

After searching the computer database, he found a small article on the Cadre, which had been written in 1960 by the founder of P-Cell, William Hanlow.

The Cadre was believed to be a hermetic order. Hanlow also believed the order existed behind the veil of the Department of Anachronistic Research at London University—but he'd never gained substantial proof. He postulated that members of the Cadre were recruited from the department, and, according to the text, various forms of *paras*—the Cadre's term for otherworldly entities—were also commissioned to serve the deceptively benevolent group.

To Jack, a hermitic order was some sort of religious cult that believed in the woo-woo. He didn't buy that stuff. Good solid firepower was the only magic he believed in.

Hanlow suspected the Cadre researched all forms of otherworldly beings, possibly even experimented on and stored them. Lord Lawrence Maybank, Earl of St. Yve, had inherited command of the Cadre from his father, as it had been handed down to sons through the ages, and had served as head of the department for forty years before his daughter, Dawn, had taken over.

There was a notation in the updates, made in 1976, of twin daughters born to the earl the previous year, Dawn and Aurora. Tough bit of luck there. Not a son in sight to inherit.

All that background information helped Jack little. What concerned him was there had been no recorded infiltration of the Cadre by P-Cell. Seems the country manor where the Cadre resided was protected by a sort of shield that kept out intruders. If anyone were lucky enough to pinpoint the cottage inhabited by an elderly couple—alleged preternatural gatekeepers—they could get no farther, and often returned with complete confusion as to where they had been. Oftentimes memory loss was involved.

The Cadre kept P-Cell at bay, and P-Cell continued their attempts to thwart the Cadre's daft endeavors to befriend dangerous OEs. It was too dicey to allow any demon to inhabit this realm, even the ones that didn't prove a danger. For if you allowed one access, then others followed. A crystal clear fact to Jack.

Clicking out of the database and putting the computer to sleep, Jack stared at the picture of Beryth. His palms felt warm and sticky upon the paper. He realized suddenly that his breath had increased.

He slapped a hand over his chest. Beneath his shirt the scar heated, yet didn't tingle as it sometimes did when he touched it.
Mine.

No. And no! He was not connected to Beryth.
I would know.

"So, I've to find a familiar to stop the demons. And…"

P-Cell believed Mersey was a Cadre member? No problem. He had merely to follow her home, and mission accomplished. *If* he could find her again.

How to track a woman whose only known location was on his lips?

"Lure her to the ley line that's been leaking demons."

Right then.

He swung around and, tapping out the access code on the desk console, the steel wall behind him slid open to reveal an array of weapons available to the hunters and seekers. Silver and black steel glinted. Guns and knives and throw stars were displayed. Laser scopes, GPS enhancements, grapple hooks and grenade launchers. P-Cell ordered the salt for their weapons directly from Egypt; only Dead Sea salt would work against a demon.

He selected a few salt grenades and then, tucking the demon directory under his arm, headed out the back door, a secret exit that put him topside into a car park.

"Look out, Beryth, your days are numbered."

The London Eye lit up the boardwalk and twinkled in the dark waters of the Thames to Mersey's immediate right.

Witching rods in hand, she hadn't yet picked up *para* activity, though she did sense a ley line in the vicinity. She wanted to patrol the length of the river in London proper. A huge task, but the hot spot she'd located the other night could spread.

She didn't worry that people stared, remarking on her curious activity. Cadre members were particular to avoid allowing civilians to accidentally witness a crystal capture. And if they did? Memory wipe was used. Mersey prided herself on not once having to utilize the wipe—she'd always felt it morally wrong.

"Jack!"

Mersey spun abruptly, spying the couple, and the woman who had named her lover Jack. They kissed and giggled and walked opposite Mersey's direction.

Jack.

How to determine if Jack Harris was a familiar?

Her knuckles tightened and Mersey realized she was gripping the rods for life. Relaxing, she then marked her paces as she strode the boardwalk, cautious not to bump into anyone.

She supposed it wasn't something that should have come up in their previous conversation. "Oh, by the way, love, I'm the one who's been letting those demons run free. Fancy more snogging?"

Should she reveal to him that she was a familiar? Like trusting like?

Mersey tried to be as honest as possible. Lies never came easily to her. And it wasn't as though she were lying to the Cadre about her contact with the demon hunter; they hadn't asked after her liaisons, so why start a row over something even she wasn't sure about?

"I will tell him." Relieved, she let out a long exhale. "Yes. Then, he'll feel comfortable enough to confide in me."

She walked onward.

Jack propped his forearms on the Westminster bridge railing. An evening breeze sifted the Thames up into his face, and he zoned out on the spin of the 440-foot high moving observation wheel that he considered a blight on the cityscape—the London Eye.

Thinking the way to track Mersey was to return to hunting, he dug out the EMF from a pocket of his canvas jacket and checked the readings. Close to a ley line.

The mere fact she tracked demons, and captured them in crystals to stuff into her pocket, was wacky enough. And that getup with the goggles and cap? Definitely two steps to the left, that bird. Yet, Jack liked any woman who would rather snog than talk.

Mersey seemed to be both. A talker and a kisser. Toss in a few demons, and he had a right fancy mix. Conversation, action and romance. Not that sex was romantic, but he never argued against a woman's sexual demands. Or his own. It had been weeks since he'd last shagged. A man shouldn't go that long unless he was near death, and even then—

"Harris!"

The EMF registered a faint activity. Weird.

Jack turned to spy a rather normal young woman striding toward him. No cap and goggles tonight. She wore the long buff coat over slim black jeans and a green turtleneck. And was that a hint of makeup darkening her eyelids and calling attention to those bold green eyes? Like a kohl-eyed Cleopatra.

"What are you doing here, hotshot?" she called as she approached and shoved the witch rods in a pocket.

"Same thing you're doing. So, you're going to poke about with your copper rods to locate the big bads?" Jack wondered.

"It's called *witching,* and I'm marking out the ley line. Demons tend to use the ley lines for entry passages to this realm."

"Good old mortal realm. How I do enjoy my feet planted on it." Jack joined her side, putting his back to the spray from the river. "Those bent wires really work?"

"Yes. And they're copper rods, not wires."

"Just don't point them at me."

"Why not? You think I'll learn something you'd rather keep secret?"

"You think I have a secret?" He had put a wall around himself. And he liked it that way. "No secrets here."

The wind blew long strands of blackest hair across Mersey's lips. It was all Jack could do to stop himself from reaching up. Why restrain himself?

He touched the strands and she bowed her head. But the wind blew the hair right back. "I tried."

"You win or lose?" she asked.

"What? Oh." He followed her gaze to his eye and touched the slash wound above his brow. "I always win. At least against the things that play by the rules."

"I see. Ever go up on that thing?" She nodded toward the Eye.

"Can't pay me enough."

"Really? Afraid of heights?"

"I fear nothing, little girl."

"Oh, really? Well, *I* like it. Especially at night." She stretched out her arms and leaned forward over the railing. The lights from the wheel reflected off the river and glittered over Mersey's face. "Up there feels like flying in a slow-motion world of flashing lights and soundless sky." A twist of her head tilted a daring look at him. "Want to go up?"

He crossed his arms, wondering what the bird was up to this time. That teasing smile and those sensual eyes never alluded to business. She was all about the tease, this one.

Weren't you going to stop mixing business with pleasure?

Bloody conscience.

And yet Jack ignored his inner voice because no man should ever resist opportunity when it knocked. "All right, then."

"Great. We can talk."

"We can—?" Why did that not sound as pleasurable as he'd hoped?

She strode away, the tails of her coat flying out, and called back, "There's something I want you to know about me, Jack!"

Well, then. Would she reveal she was with the Cadre?

Jack sped after the gorgeous bird. Business, it would be.

Chapter 8

Jack jogged up to the observation capsule where Mersey boarded. The huge wheel never stopped—unless for the occasional handicapped person—and moved slowly enough that passengers could easily board.

"I paid for you!" Mersey called and gestured that he hurry into her capsule.

Jack stomped past the brightly lit vendor stand that sold replicas of the Eye to tourists, and joined Mersey in the air-conditioned capsule. No one followed, so they had the seating to themselves. For the next half hour.

Trailing his fingers along the curved Plexiglas wall, Jack shot his gaze above and around the illuminated cell, enclosed and attached to the outside of the wheel and hanging precariously over the Thames. Nifty. Already his staunch avoidance of the thing began to waver as he anticipated viewing the city from the top. And, since the object of his interest couldn't go anywhere, he was set.

"All right, young lady." Keeping in mind this was business, he crossed his arms and worked his best authoritative stance on her. "You got me here, alone, and unable to run away. What are your intentions?"

"You get right to the point."

"And you prefer to dodge around it. Unless you jump right in with a kiss." *Jack!*

Ignoring his conscience was getting easier and easier. He leaned into her. Lemons curled inside his senses. "Is that your plan? More snogging? Because I'll have you know, I'm game."

The grin that tickled her lips cued him the bird was feeling frisky again. Oh, he could go there. In fact—

"Jack, I'm a familiar."

"What?" Shooting upright, he reacted by slapping his hip and stepping back.

Mersey stomped her foot. "Please tell me you did not just reach for your weapon."

"Huh?" Caught, red-handed. "No. I…no! I don't have a weapon." But he had reached for something to protect himself. It was how he'd been trained.

"But you feel like you need one?"

"No. I just…" Hell. He couldn't have heard her right. Feeling the blood drain from his face, Jack swiped a palm over his jaw. "For real? You're a…?"

Mersey nodded. "I wanted you to know. I'm big on the truth."

"Ah, well, right then." Bloody hell in a handbasket. This bird was a…? He couldn't even think it!

"I didn't mean to shock you."

"You didn't." He gestured dismissively, and turned from her, pacing to the end of the capsule. Like hell she did.

Just get him out of here and—no, he would *not* react defensively. There was no danger here. The woman was—not human? No, she was human, and gorgeous, and smelled the way a woman should smell, and kissed like a— He'd kissed her. He'd kissed a…?

Why couldn't he bring himself to even think the word?

Drawing a palm over his jaw again, he brushed his fingers up over his scalp and performed a covert peek under his arm and toward her. She smiled sweetly and waved at him.

"For real?" he asked.

She nodded.

"Now that we've got my identity out of the way…" He fought not to let her see him cringe as she spoke to him. "Is there anything you want to tell me, Jack?"

"Me?" Unsure what to do with his hands—because forming them into fists wouldn't help matters—Jack stuffed them under his arms and leaned forward against the row of plastic chairs queued down the middle of the capsule to face Mersey. "Like what?"

"I think you're a familiar."

His jaw didn't drop open because instead he bit his tongue, which was still sore from the previous night and the fight with the demon in his flat.

"But, for some reason—" oblivious to his shock, Mersey paced the length of the plastic chairs "—I don't think you're aware of it."

Jack turned and gripped the steel railing that curved the oval circumference of the capsule. The Houses of Parliament sat directly below him, but he didn't give them a bother.

A familiar? Previous assessment of Mersey Bane: completely off base. This bird didn't tally. And now she was accusing him of being the same?

And he was now stuck with her for—Jack checked his watch—twenty-one more interminable minutes.

"Do you do this on all your dates?" he asked.

"Do what?"

"Come out of the closet with a bombshell like that, and then accuse the guy you're with of being a paranormal creature?"

"Out of the— Jack, there's nothing wrong with being a *para*."

"I think you're playing for the wrong side, little girl. There's plenty wrong with being a monster."

"We are not monsters."

He ignored her insistence because he knew better. If anyone knew a monster when he saw it, it was Jack Harris. And yet, he winced. She didn't look like a monster. More so, he didn't want her to be one. He couldn't let her know he was having a hard time with this.

"I'm fine with you being a…"

"Familiar, Jack. It won't kill you to say it."

"Right. You're a…familiar. But I'm human. Got that? One hundred percent mortal, through and through." He lifted his shirt and smacked his hard abs. "Want to touch and see for yourself?"

Eyeing his exposed abs, she sucked in the corner of her lip. Vacillating? And what was he doing? Jack tugged down his shirt. The woman confused his sense of mission with seduction. It wasn't right.

"*Paras* are not monsters," she said tightly.

"Some are. You were there last night when I blasted that demon to bits."

She shoved both hands to her hips. The sudden fire in her eyes threatened to bring Jack around to his struggle between business and pleasure.

"You saw that thing. Mersey—"

"Miss Bane to you, Mr. Harris."

"Back to business, eh? Right then. At least one of us is thinking straight." He leaned backward and gripped the railing behind him. "If I hadn't blasted that thing it would have got out to maim or kill, or both!"

"You don't know that. You didn't even take the time to identify it. You blasted. Blimey." She shrugged a hand through her hair, and then punctuated her next statement with a fist. "You idiot hunters think you're protecting the world from imagined dark evils—"

"The evils are hardly imagined."

"In most cases they are! You could be destroying an intelligent, emotive being that is here for a purpose beyond destruction."

"Demons are intelligent, I will grant you that. At least, some of them are. But emotive? Not here to destroy? I haven't met one yet that didn't want to rip off my head and then chew it for a snack."

Jack tapped his watch. Fifteen minutes and counting. Why did she have to be familiar? "Is that how you know so much? Because you're a…"

"Familiar," she said roughly. "And yes, I do know my demons."

"And I know mine."

"I've been involved with them since I was a kid."

Jack stood tall. "Me, too."

A dark brow lifted above one of her eyes. Mersey tapped those beringed fingers against her opposite arm. Releasing an impatient sigh, she paced to the opposite end of the capsule.

"So you're the one," he said, figuring it out, and kicking himself for what he might now have to do in order to stop the influx of demons.

"The one?"

"The familiar who allowed the demons through to the warehouse."

"I did no such thing!"

"Well, I didn't." The defensive tasted so wrong in his mouth— but it was true.

"How do you know?"

"I—I know!"

He stomped away from her. Because to argue only put him to odds. Him, a familiar? The notion was ludicrous. He would certainly know if he'd been tapped by a demon.

Jack gripped the steel railing. One hand he placed over his left pec. The scar beneath his shirt tingled.

Not tapped. *No.*

He didn't *feel* different.

Just as he should not be treating her differently. She wasn't a monster. *He knew.*

Jack shoved away from the railing and walked up behind Mersey, stopping but inches from the gorgeous scent of her. If he dipped his head forward and buried his nose in the luscious dark strands—

Jack cleared his throat and admonished his straying thoughts. She was an OE. Something to be…stalked.

"You don't know me, Mers—er, Miss Bane. We shared, what, ten minutes together? Granted, half that time was some fierce and unforgettable snogging."

"Don't remind me."

"You didn't like it?"

She kept her arms firmly crossed. "It was tolerable."

"Tolerable?"

Jack lifted a hand, prepared to grip her by the shoulder, turn her around and pull her in for a tolerably suitable kiss, when he reneged. He'd kissed an otherworldly being. What had he done?

"It was a mischief demon I captured in the crystal last night, Jack. Nonviolent. It had slipped through a passage in the warehouse, left open by a familiar who—for reasons unknown to me—decided to leave the passage wide open. I took it to base and we interrogated it. Standard procedure."

"Who is *we?* And where is *base?*"

"None of your business."

"Of course not." He snapped his head to the left, cracking out the tense muscle that tugged along his neck. Too much information to process right now. And none of it particularly comforting.

"What is important," she continued, "is that the demon gave up the name of its familiar."

He could see where she was going with this, and didn't like it. "Demons do not know my name, little girl."

"Yeah?" She turned and had to lean back against the curved wall to avoid contact because he still stood close. "It spoke your name rather clearly during interrogation. Twice."

"And what sort of interrogation tactics does your *we* employ? Torture? Duress? Insinuation? You probably mentioned my name—"

"Who are you, Jack Harris? And why would a demon give *your* name as its entrance to this realm?"

Fingers fisting at his side, Jack spoke through a tight jaw. "I never saw that thing before in my life. Hell, I barely saw it before you sucked it into your little stone. *You* fed the information to it. You had to. Demons are very suggestible."

"I wasn't doing the interrogating. And Interrogations had no clue to your name. I know you're upset, but—"

"Upset?"

He moved in on her, placing his hands to the sides of hers on the railing. Why did she have to smell so appetizing when all he wanted to do was push away and be done with her? It was as if he could already imagine them together, naked, their bodies rubbing against one another. Would she come softly or match his raging release?

Ah! Here he was again, thinking about shagging the woman when he should be getting her to lead him to her secret hideaway.

Jack followed her darting eyes for a moment, and then shoved away from the railing. To look out now, he realized they'd reached the pinnacle of the iron wheel. The world was vast and open all about him. The moonless sky was black—likely blocked by the thick gray clouds—and below, the stars had fallen onto the glittering city.

He felt disembodied from the world. Disemworlded?

Steadying himself with his fingertips to the Plexiglas, he closed his eyes. His breaths came faster.

It's that she's just announced she's the enemy.

Was he still attracted to her? Yes, sod the cat, he was. The cat?

Jack dodged a look over his shoulder. "Was that you last night on the tube?"

She gave a coy shift of stance and offered a "Meow."

Bloody hell. How to take this information? He had a mission. Track the subject and locate her base. Didn't matter *what* she was. Right?

Stroking a palm over his face, Jack turned his back to the

midnight blackness. The soft interior lighting was suddenly too bright and cheery for his failing sanity.

"I've seen an innocent murdered by a bloody demon. Until you've seen it, you'll never understand my point of view."

"Don't try to guess at the things I've experienced in my lifetime, Jack. I'm sure I've got you beat, hands down."

"Is that so?"

He approached her again. She wouldn't meet his eyes. Declaring her toughness and then shunning the challenge of his gaze? He'd been right about her. Mersey Bane, familiar—sodding hell—was a little girl lost in the big bad, playing at some comic-book adventure of saving the world.

It was a world deserving of rescue. In his heart he could never stand back and allow the travesties he knew to occur without attempting to stop them. But any of Mersey's attempts would surely be in vain.

"So...all *paras* are offensive to you?" she wondered.

"If *para* means a nasty paranormal creature from the dark realm, then you bet."

"So I offend you?"

"I—" Yes, she did. And no, she did not. "Are you from the dark realm?"

"Born and raised right here on mortal turf. Though for all purposes, I'm not considered human."

Jack didn't trust himself to be able to explain it in terms that would not put her off. He had to maintain her trust so he could track her. And to be truthful with himself, he just didn't know how he felt about her. But he did hope for one thing. "You're not a monster."

They were heading down now, bless the bloody cross. He needed to be away from this uncomfortable conversation. To be doing something productive. Like stalking the real enemy.

"Monsters are the things that live under your bed," he added. "The nighttime creepies, the shadows that haunt the hallways."

"The dark shadows of a person's soul."

She had him there. "Sort of. But tangible."

"So you consider a faery a monster?"

"You bet."

"Yet, familiars are not?"

"I…suppose not."

So much disapproval in her uttered sound. Could a man get a chance to at least think, to roll this information about for a tick?

"Why do *you* hunt demons?" he asked. "Aren't familiars supposed to be like their guides to this realm?"

"If I allow it, which I rarely do. And I don't hunt them in the sense that I would then destroy them. I capture them."

"What do you do after you've released them from the crystal?"

"They're not always released. Only the dangerous demons are kept in permanent storage. The nonviolent ones, we deport back to the dark realm. We've a list of the most dangerous."

"So you keep a hit list?" Her organization actually drew up a list of the good and the bad ones? Not that Jack believed there were good ones… Because P-Cell also kept a list, and it was a mile long. "Easy to trap and release, is it?"

"Sometimes."

"Your…partner do the releasing for you?"

Now a blushing smile lit her face, but she recovered quickly. "You're not going to get anything from me, Jack, so don't even try. I'm sorry to have sounded as if I'm accusing you. I want to help. If you need it."

"Sure." He rubbed a palm over his face. "Accusation forgotten. Help un-needed."

"I believe in you, Jack."

That statement struck him so utterly out from left field that Jack just stood there. What to say to that? Belladonna had said the same thing. Neither knew his dark thoughts. A mere glimpse of the terrors his stint in the army had soldiered, and now in P-Cell, would horrify them both.

Shoulders dropping, Jack allowed his gaze to wander away

from Mersey's and down to the floor. He didn't know what to say. An angry rebuttal didn't feel right.

"There's nothing to believe in," he muttered.

Turning, he walked to the other side of the capsule and smashed a fist against the curve of the clear wall. The hit sent subtle vibrations through the capsule.

The air inside the capsule had changed, becoming thin and clear, and that made Jack feel as though she could feel his every thought, see that soft core of him, and know his need for release. To confess. To shuck off the guilt and stomp it into the ground, once and for all.

Could he ever do that? Open himself to a woman he barely knew, and…ask her to understand?

She confessed to you.

And how to accept that confession? Didn't he have enough to deal with without knowing he might be attracted to a…

"Sorry, if my confession freaked you," Mersey offered. "Now you know my truth—oh! Dash, another ring broke."

Jack bent near her feet to pick up the pieces and felt a shocking tingle as he touched the black curves of hematite. Weird.

"You can get replacements." He offered her the bits, but her attention remained fixed on her bare finger. A quick count noticed there were six others on her fingers.

"No, I can't. You wouldn't understand. Sorry." Shaking her head and not meeting his eyes, she looked like a little girl lost. Because of a broken ring? "I'm probably wrong about you, Jack." The door opened and Mersey walked out onto the ramp.

And Jack felt a piece of himself walk out with her.

What the hell was his problem? He couldn't let her leave like this. And what about his plans to follow her?

He shoved the broken pieces of the ring into his pocket.

"Back to work, Jack."

Chapter 9

Jack revved the Range Rover and pulled away from the curb, deciding to go straight, following the Thames, instead of turning toward home. In less than five minutes he sighted her. Pulling over to the pavement, he leaned across to open the passenger door.

Jack said, "Get in."

Mersey bent and inspected the interior, tapping the door with a slender finger. What was so difficult? Did she still consider him a stranger? After all they'd just been through on the Eye?

Or was it that she considered him scary?

So he'd shown her his angry side. It was who he was. Angry and pissed and not going to take it anymore.

And confused. What to think of this bird, who was also a…cat?

"You're safe, Bane. You can trust me."

"I know I can." Something in that smirk made Jack wince.

I believe in you.

Poor woman, she didn't know him well enough.

She slid onto the passenger seat, and the car peeled away.

"Where you headed? Bus station?"

"Underground," she offered.

"Right, the subway. I know that."

"I know you know that." She flashed him a crooked grin.

"I can give you a ride home," he offered. "You carrying?"

"Carrying?"

"You know, crystals. In your pockets. Filled with the big bads."
She slanted a look his way. "Worried?"

"Never. You ever accidentally release one of those things? I
mean, how do they stay inside the thing?"

"The crystal containment method is foolproof. It's locked with
a spell. Nothing inside will ever get out, until someone lets it out."

"And you do that because...?"

"Interrogation."

"Right."

Jack downshifted and the car squealed as it turned a one-eighty,
and the Range Rover fitted itself into a parking space before the
subway entrance.

Gripping the door for life, Mersey huffed. "You can't scare me."

"Yeah?" He put the car in park and leaned across the shift.
"You're playing with the big boys now, little girl—"

"Would you bring the macho bullshit down a notch? You might
carry a big gun, but that doesn't mean you know how to get the
job done right."

He quirked a brow. "Is that supposed to be some wonky sort
of reference to sex?"

She let her eyes drift to his crotch. "It wasn't," she said. "But
if you've a deficiency— For what it's worth?" She released the
door handle and let out her breath. "I think you're telling me the
truth about not being a familiar."

He slammed his shoulders back against the seat and tapped the
steering wheel. "Damn straight."

"Which means you could be tapped unawares."

He'd heard of that. Demons can tap completely normal mortals to use as familiars to bridge to the mortal realm.

But not him.

"What are you trying to do, Bane? Falsely accuse me?"

"I want to close up the leak. If you're responsible—"

"Assuming that *you* are not."

"But—"

"First you say you believe me, and now you're right back to accusations. You're a nut. Now get out of the car before I do something—"

"Violent? Isn't that original. A hunter going Rambo on something he doesn't understand."

Jack pounded a fist on the steering wheel. If he came right out and questioned her alliance to the Cadre would that scare her away? No, he'd keep that information in his pocket for now. He had to do this right.

Why was he getting so angry?

Because she was dead-on-the-doornail right about him and his easy anger. And he still had to deal with the fact she wasn't who, or what, he'd thought her to be.

"If it's violent to protect mankind from a horrendous death by demon, then I accept the accusation. I'm trying to keep one more person from being eaten for lunch, Miss Bane. But if you've got a problem with that…"

"The problem I have with you, Mr. Harris, is that you don't discern good from bad before blasting. There are *paras* that come here with no intention to harm. If you'd take a moment to observe before pulling the trigger, you might realize that."

"I know enough to understand that sometimes a man doesn't have time to observe, Bane. I'd rather be safe than sorry."

"I should hate you. For your beliefs. For your lack of belief. For your quickness to violence. For your idiot macho posturing."

"Macho idiots need love like all the rest of the blokes."

"Yes," her tone softened. "I suppose." She shifted closer, her muscles gliding into submission. "Especially when the macho bloke kisses so bloody well."

"Ever kiss a paranormal?" Weird question, but it just occurred to him, and he needed to know.

Mouth falling slack, her voiceless expression answered the question much louder than Jack had expected. So she *had* kissed an OE? Yikes.

Jack pressed back into his seat. "Not a demon, I hope?"

She gripped the door handle. "I think it's time to leave."

He hit the automatic door lock. Things were getting too interesting to let her loose now. Besides, he was allowed a few rules of his own in this game; it was only fair.

"I want to know what sort of creepy can attract a woman like you?"

"He wasn't creepy," Mersey defended. "And remember, I'm a *para*, too."

"Yes, but you're normal." Yeah, she was, wasn't she? That was where his vote cast right now. "A bogeyman?"

"No!"

"Vampire?"

"Eww. I don't do the blood thing."

"Shape-shifter?"

"Jack."

"I'll get it, give me a minute."

"A faery, all right? A harmless, forest-variety faery. When I was eighteen years old."

"And how'd that work for you?"

She shrugged and crossed her arms over her chest. "Un-eventful."

Yeah? But he'd hit a nerve. And she looked all pouty and kissable. *Jack boy, you really could care less that she's not one hundred percent human. So don't let the idea of her familiarness offend you, eh?*

"I won't."

"You won't what?" she asked.

He leaned across the seat, and threaded his hand up and behind her head to pull her in for a kiss. She pressed against his chest, but not hard enough to make Jack believe she actually wanted him to stop.

She was sweet, but the kiss verged on wicked. Soon Mersey threaded her arms around his neck and moved closer so their positions weren't so awkward. He pushed a hand along her waist to draw her up, and felt the hard impression of what he knew were crystal pyramids clank against the back of his hand. Was there a demon in her pocket?

He traced her lips with his parted mouth, liking how her grin tickled her, as if by surprise. "Why do I get the feeling you haven't done this all too often?"

She lowered her eyes and toyed with the cuff of his sleeve.

"Unless it's with faeries?"

"It was just the one," she said softly. "And he wasn't overly impressed by the encounter. But you…Jack, you don't mind kissing me? Even now that you know?"

He didn't mind, but only because he didn't want to go there. Not right now. "Your kisses are like lemon drops, Mersey—a man can never get enough of those sweets."

"I…haven't kissed all that many men, Jack. I guess…I've been waiting for the right one."

"I see." He sat back. And tried not to pay attention to his cringing heart.

The right one? Jack Harris wasn't the right anything. And he'd hate to disappoint a girl on a quest for Mr. Right. "So, ah, this your stop? Waterloo?"

"What did I say? Jack? Did I do something wrong?"

"Nope. Just don't want to let you down."

He shifted into Drive, but kept his foot on the brake.

He had let her down anyway. Not keen, Jack. But he was no one's Mr. Right. He just wanted to kiss them, take them home for a tumble in his bed, deposit them out on the stoop, and then with a pat to their heads, send them off.

Easier not to become involved. Easier because his life was

filled with too many unknowns right now. Easier never to admit his feelings because that was like cracking open his chest and exposing his heart for the world to examine. It wasn't a pretty sight. This old heart of his had seen too much, and was likely scarred for it.

"Guess I'll be off then," she said. "Do you intend to follow me again tonight?"

He smiled at her in the rearview mirror. "Probably."

"Luck with that."

Chapter 10

Jack pulled into the alleyway, looking for a parking spot. There were broken pieces of hematite on the seat. He scooped them up, starting a collection. She was leaving a trail. And he intended to follow it.

Luck with that.

He smirked. "Tricky bird."

Make that a cat.

"A familiar," he whispered, not as freaked by it as he suspected he should be.

The gray seekers at P-Cell dealt with familiars. It wasn't his specialty. Beyond knowing they served as demon bridges, he knew they were basically human. Humans who could change to cats.

Was she like other women? Her body, all her…parts? Did he care? She kissed like any other woman.

The only way to really satisfy his curiosity was to stay on her. Right then. He'd be on her tail in two seconds—

A fierce burn ignited in Jack's chest. He jerked, the back of his skull banging none too gently against the hard rubber headrest. A chill rode his spine, picking up speed with each disk it traveled upward, until prickly barbs encompassed his shoulders and neck.

He could barely breathe. Each gasping inhale seemed to close the back of his throat even more.

"What the hell?"

A visceral chill dug deep inside him. He let out an abbreviated yelp as dark shadows scurried over his eyes—evil things of blood and muscle and exposed organs. Dreadful. They screamed, they yowled. He couldn't stop them from infiltrating his brain.

"Jaaaaack," pressed in on a dead tone. It filled his veins with icy bile. "Jaaack."

It toyed with his fear. The presence seeped inside him and filled his system, occupying his very being. Dread melted over him.

Fear was a valuable gauge that kept him aware and alert. Yet the day Jack gave over to fear was the day he lost his head to a crafty demon.

"What the hell are you? Where are you?"

"You bore me, Jack."

"Show yourself!"

"It's me, Jack. Don't you remember?" The sepulchral voice slid from baritone to a sexy female whisper. "You excel at showing me the tasty bits. Brought me right to the mortal female in the warehouse. Nummy. This new bit I won't eat. Not right away. She can serve me far better alive. Perhaps better than her mother did."

Jack slapped a hand to his burning pectoral. Smoke rose from the mark on his chest. The scent of burned cotton coiled beneath his nose.

"I knew I'd chosen correctly," the voice, now male, rasped inside of him.

It was *inside* him, occupying his brain and twanging his muscles with a vibrant need to clench. How to fight something with his limbs literally paralyzed?

"Follow her, Jack. Seduuuuce her."

The chokehold unclenched from his throat—enough so Jack could speak.

"Get out of my head!"

Jack couldn't see the demon, and didn't bother giving it the pleasure of seeing him look for it. Instead, he gripped the steering wheel. Driving would do him no good.

His rifle and the salt grenades were in the boot.

"Yes, yes, you plan your attack. Blast me to Kingdom Come? Big words for so small a man."

Gripped by a clenching red ache, Jack's limbs stiffened. Shoulders pressed backward, and his wrists swung out, stretching his arms farther back, threatening to completely wrap to either side of the car seat. An impossible move. The strain of his muscles tore in his armpits and across his chest where smoke still tendriled from the scar.

"You're letting the girl get away."

"No thanks to you!"

Jack groped for the door handle. His fingers would not bend to clasp it.

"Follow Mersey Bane to the Cadre as your commander insists. Be my eyes, Jack. It is what I need from you."

"I—" His molars bit hard on the back of his tongue. Jack yelped, and the movement of his jaw released it from the tight lock. "Who are you?"

"You know not? You wound me with your ignorance. I have thought of you, Jack. Endlessly I replay our first encounter. You were lucky, nothing more."

Was it the same one? The demon he'd hit in the field?

"Ah…so you do know."

Jack exhaled, and while doing so, he felt as if he were not expelling the breath so much as it was being sucked out of him.

"Yes, the air of you. Your life. It gives me strength." The demon sucked in, its throat rattling. "Still don't remember me? If I must. Ba'al Beryth," the entity hissed inside his head. "Know me. For I know you, Demon Frightener."

Bloody hell. It was the very same. "I don't take orders from demons."

"I thought you'd be eager to follow the girl. Doesn't P-Cell want you to infiltrate the Cadre? You shirk your duties. Bad Jack, very bad form." That last sentence came out in Belladonna's chiding tone.

Everything about Jack clenched. His fingers, his muscles, even his gut. The demon was somehow controlling him.

Dreadful. The same way he'd felt that night he'd had to watch this bastard demon from hell tear out Monica's heart.

"It is what I do," Beryth purred in a voice that was at once liquid and then stone. It shifted inside Jack and hummed in his heart. Not a gentle rhythm, more a defibrillating pace. "I conjure dread in the hearts of common mortals. A neat trick, but unsatisfying after one has known mortal love—ah! Let's try this on for size, shall we?"

A face appeared in the seat next to him. A hand dropped upon his chest. Feminine, the touch.

"Jack, I need you!" The same scream he'd heard over the walkie the night he'd sat in the car, waiting for Monica's signal.

Jack closed his eyes, not wanting to look. Knowing what he would see. Her perfume overwhelmed the brimstone. Chanel No. 5, she'd once told him, in the snappy businesslike manner that signified she was a trusted partner who had his back, but no one should ever forget she was a woman.

He had never forgotten. She had been a woman through and through. But he'd never the courage to tell her...

"Jack," Monica's voice cooed. "Tell me you love me."

If he could but placc his hands to the rifle.

You never take the time to determine if they're good or bad. There is fallout.

This one was bad to the core.

He needed to focus. To master the control exercised over him. Then, he could dash for the boot and send the demon to Kingdom Come.

"Don't you want to kiss me like you kissed that strange girl, Jack? What's so special about her?"

He'd respected Monica. The fine line between work partners and potential lovers had never been crossed.

"You're not here," he managed to say. But he could see her platinum-blond curls edging the periphery of his sight. She smelled so familiar. Sitting in the car with Monica for long hours on stakeout, until he wore her scent on him, and could still smell her in his clothes the following morning. "Get. Out!"

The figment vanished.

"Perhaps you need inspiration?" hissed a baritone whisper.

"Fuck you."

Fingers kinked into distorted hooks, and Jack's legs stiffened, pressing his back into the seat. His insides froze. The icy prickles of something cut into his kidneys. *Kidney.*

Hell, could the demon know he had but the one remaining?

"No!"

That shout broke the demon's influence. Body going limp, Jack's muscles released the tension and his body seeped against the seat.

"You stay close to her, or I eat her for a snack." The demon chuckled in a mixture of female and male tones.

Jack swung out to his left. Gone? Not a tendril of brimstone in the air. He tried the door handle. It opened to let in the chill autumn air. Swinging out his legs, he leaned forward. Breaths formed before him like so much dread spilling out. Heartbeats thudding, he exhaled and pressed his forehead to the interior frame of the car, summoning reason.

The demon had demanded he track Mersey. Would it go after the woman should he fail to lead the demon to the Cadre? It couldn't if it didn't know the way. Maybe it did know the way. Obviously it couldn't access the place if it had asked him to lead it there.

Or maybe the Cadre wasn't its ultimate goal? Did it seek to tap Mersey? Why could it not?

Clutching his shirt, he fisted his knuckles against his chest. The scar felt new, freshly open and burned into his skin. A smoldering hole smoked right through his shirt.

Are you a familiar, Jack?

Attached to Beryth?

Mortals can be tapped, even familiars can be tapped without their knowing.

Any creature could put images into his head. It was what demons did; they fed off mortal emotions, shortcomings and desires.

"Tapped?" he muttered. "I can't be."

The dungeon was always cool and quiet. While the stone walls gave it an ancient, creepy castle feel, the accoutrements were all high tech. Most of the instruments Mersey had no clue how to use, nor did she wonder.

Capturing a demon in crystal was one of her skills. Very few others who were not familiars could master the crystal capture method, unless they had studied for years and reached the level of adept. It was not easy.

The four levels were novice, apprentice, fellow and adept. Lady Aurora and the earl, along with few others, were currently the only Cadre adepts in residence.

There were a few exceptions; Lady Dawn—Aurora's twin—was still at fellow level, yet she had the ability. It all depended on the focus, level of study and determination.

Mersey had been watching Squire play World of Warcraft on the computer for a while now. That the man had to go online into an imaginary world to defeat strange minions and monsters stunned her. There were so many more interesting beings right here in the St. Yve manor!

"Squire." She stood and rubbed her chin. Leaning on her hand had put a dent in her jaw. "Is there any way to verify a familiar? Beyond watching it actually be tapped by a demon?"

"You're a familiar. There." He gave her a split-second glance up from the computer. "I just verified you."

"Squire. I mean, someone else. Someone I suspect may be one."

"Not sure."

He put the game on pause and strolled down the aisle of stainless-steel tables to the bookshelf at the end of the wall. He tugged out a slim volume and Mersey saw the spine as the gold letters flashed. *Familiars 101,* by Caractacus Bane. Her father.

A shiver of longing startled her so that she looked away. She avoided her father issues as she avoided being tapped. Both were distasteful and not worth the energy spent. And yet, both provided life. Every time a familiar was tapped, their lifespan increased due to the ley-line energies.

"Let's see…"

Mersey curled her knuckles against the cool steel lab table. This was so not good on all the various scales of measuring not good. If Jack was a familiar, then it must have been he who had called up the two demons in the warehouse. Just to blast them? Familiars didn't do that. Kill a demon, you kill its familiar.

Jack had a grudge against demons. That had been obvious. But why?

Mersey could relate to holding a grudge. The memory of being imprisoned in a wee silver cage for three days by a mischievous demon that had tapped her a few years ago, would never leave her. It was one of the reasons she rarely shifted to her animal form now. Though, the other day on the tube train had been necessary. Silver held a feline familiar like iron trapped faeries. She hadn't agreed to be tapped since her imprisonment. It wasn't even worth the increase in lifespan.

Tapping required an agreement between demon and familiar. Unapproved tapping occurred when the dark denizens of the demon world tried to come through with evil in mind. Which was why Mersey had a job as retrievals specialist.

"So how's tricks up top?" Squire asked as he paged through the book. "Don't get out much, you know. They like to keep me in the dungeon."

"Squire, you do your job well. Someone's got to hold down the fort while others walk the top."

"Need a partner?" He looked up from the book. All right, so the man could use a few steaks and doughnuts to put some meat on his bones. She wondered if the UV flashlights the Cadre used against vampires might give his skin some much needed color.

"Don't get me wrong," Squire said. "I love my work. But I need to get my fingers into the action, you know? You're out there every day, stalking and capturing *paras*. I want that glory."

"You don't get enough on the computer?"

"Warcraft is pretend, Mersey. You know that, don't you?"

"As long as *you* do, that's all that matters." She sighed and toggled the corner of the book he paged through. "Squire, your job is much more dangerous than mine. I just crystallize them and hand them over. You're the one who has to determine species, and maintain the fine balance in the storage archives."

He twirled his forefinger in a big-whoop motion. "Like that's difficult. Wish the High Council would approve my deportment training. Lady Dawn promised she'd put in a good word for me."

Deportment involved releasing demons from crystal storage and returning them to the dark realm. A highly skilled talent that was only achieved after reaching adept level.

And did she want to achieve that level? Every day her heart grew less attached to this place, and sought…something. It was a deep pining that she felt sure could be answered elsewhere, but never here.

"Sorry, Squire, I work alone."

"Right. What about the demon hunter? From the looks of it—" he splayed his hand before the crystals Mersey had set on the table; they hummed with demon energy "—the two of you work well together. He helped you nab the mischief demon. Is there something I don't know, Mersey? You know Lady Aurora would not like it if she found out you were flirting with the opposition."

"It was one kiss!" she defended, and then slapped her hand over her mouth. Oops. Had she said that out loud?

"Ah. I'm assuming that's demon hunters you're kissing, and not faeries. My, my Mersey, I wonder what you'll do to keep that information a secret?"

"Squire, you wouldn't."

"I might." He bowed his head over the text and began to read. Mersey saw his huge smile, though. He teased her often, in fact, she sensed he had a crush on her. Too bad her type had developed muscles and an attitude.

"What if I bring you out on the next surveillance? You've got to promise to keep out of the way. You have no idea what stalking requires."

"Deal." He held out a hand, waiting for her to shake it.

Mersey had hoped to be a little less "bound" by the deal. Reluctantly, she shook. "I am so going to lose my job for this."

"No, you won't. But you might if someone discovered you've been snogging—"

"Stop, Squire. No mention of demon hunters within hearing distance of Lady Aurora or the earl, all right by you?"

Lady Aurora handled most operations in the Cadre, under the discerning guidance of her father, the earl.

"What does the book say?"

"You mean, what wisdom does your father have to bestow upon his daughter?"

Squire was acquainted with her family history. Caractacus Bane had always been a folk hero to her. He'd breeze in and out of her and her mother's lives, bestowing gifts and telling tales of his ventures in the dark realm. He had traveled there often, for reasons still quite mysterious to Mersey.

He'd never been a true father, in the sense that he'd shared a home with her and her mother, yet, he had been the one to guide Mersey through her shape-shifting training. But once mastered, he'd become distant. After her mother had died, Caractacus had planted a kiss on Mersey's forehead, explained she need never fear for money or shelter, and had handed her over to the Cadre. Mersey hadn't seen him since.

She focused to find Squire, chin in palm gazing at her like a lovesick puppy.

"Blimey, just read it to me, will you?"

"Touchy. But not without cause."

Squire had been a new addition to the Cadre family that year of her mother's death. They'd instantly bonded over their shared orphanage. He knew things about Mersey, but was ever discreet.

"Very well, there are a few ways to determine if one is a familiar."

He drew his finger down the page, his lips moving as he read the words. "Ah, here! You could ask his demon master for the identity of its familiar and the demon would have to tell you."

"Uh-huh. And with thousands upon thousands of demons stalking all the realms, just how am I supposed to locate the one who—"

"It worked with the mischief demon."

"I'm still not convinced it wasn't lying."

"The text claims they cannot lie about the identity of their familiars."

Right. And deep inside, Mersey did believe. Just as she believed in Jack. She believed that he was a man torn in opposite directions, struggling with right and wrong. Yet he confused her on too many levels.

She exhaled. "Anything else?"

"Familiars attract cats. Er, normal cats. Not like, er…you know."

"Cats are old school. Give me something better, Squire."

"Ah." He raised a finger and cast her a waggling blond eyebrow. "Now here's something interesting, if a bit salacious."

Couldn't be good, whatever it was.

"It's says…"

"Spit it out, Squire!"

"You could have sex with him. Says so right here." He tapped the book and shifted on the stool. "There's a certain energy shared between familiars. Supposed to rock your world to have sex with another familiar."

Sex sounds good, got stuck on the end of Mersey's tongue. Especially with tall, brooding and handsome.

No. She was so not going to do that. Never. Absolutely not.

Although...

"Also," Squire continued, "it says when you have sex with a familiar, and look into his or her eyes during climax, you see the image of their demon master reflected in their eyes. Well, if that's not a definitive way to know, then I just don't— Mersey?"

Already heading toward the door, Mersey called back, "Thanks, Squire. I'm out of here."

"Good then. Off to shag the demon hunter?"

She would not dignify that one with an answer.

Chapter 11

"How'd you get my number?"

"You gave me your card," Mersey said into the phone receiver. "Remember?"

"Right." Jack exhaled heavily into the receiver. "In need of pest control?"

Despite the nervousness that drummed her fingers against her thigh, she smiled.

When she didn't answer straight away, Jack rattled out, "Are you in trouble? Where are you? I can be there in two minutes."

"I'm not in trouble, and even if I was I wouldn't call you. Oh, let's forget this." Prepared to hang up, Mersey paused at Jack's shout for her to wait. "What?"

"You tell me. Why'd you call?"

Twisting her toes into the satin bed comforter, Mersey caught her head in her palm and winced. She had to do this. She needed to know, whether or not Jack wanted to know. "I just thought… I—er, maybe we could get together. To…chat. Like meet over dinner?"

"Sounds like another date."

Another? Had the man been counting their every meeting as a date? "Do you need it to be a date?"

"I think I do."

She smiled and twisted the phone cord about her forefinger. "Fine, then it's date number two."

"Three. The Eye was number two, if you'll remember."

"Why are you keeping track?"

"I'm a bloke. It's what we do. I look forward to yet another evening of excitement. From where shall I pick you up?"

"Oh, you're good, Jack, but not that good. Meet you at Monkey Chews in two hours?"

"Up on Primrose Hill? I'll be there."

Jack arrived at Monkey Chews early and ordered a pint of ale and chips with bacon, his favorite. The black button-up shirt he'd pulled from the back of his closet—the only one without wrinkles— was tight. He unbuttoned the top two buttons and undid his cuffs. Looked naff, but he wasn't trying to win best dressed.

Mersey wouldn't care. Would she?

He downed a few bacon-crusted chips and swished back half the pint.

This is not a date.

Right. But he had to assume the role, make it look right.

Yet, he couldn't deny his interest in Mersey. Despite her being a cat—but it wasn't as if she were a furry feline all the time, so he could deal—he just couldn't *not* like her.

He tugged down his sleeves and toyed with the button hole.

He'd been so concerned with keeping his identity secret while spooking about for MI5 that dates were rare. He had usually fulfilled his desires by picking up a one-night stand after hours.

Before that, he'd had the usual college girlfriends who'd drop by the dorm room for some pseudo-studying that always led to sex. But no official dates in there.

He buttoned up his cuffs. Civility before comfort, right?

He put back the remainder of his ale and ordered another pint. Newcastle Brown, that was his usual. It never failed to relax him, but tonight, his heels drummed up and down beneath the bench. Mersey had already seen him at his worst—spattered with demon guts and spouting angry diatribes—so what was he so nervous about?

The woman had pinned him for a freelance demon hunter. That was a good guess. And if she was with the Cadre, then it made sense that she would go there. But her accusation about him being a familiar was ludicrous.

Did she know something he did not? Could a familiar recognize their own, even a tapped mortal?

And who was he? A hunter who had allowed his prey to escape.

Jack was still learning, and obviously hadn't yet mastered the influence-avoidance technique. But that Beryth hadn't killed him in the car was even worse. The demon needed Jack to do some foulness that Jack didn't even want to imagine.

And yet, while it had glanced its tongue across him when he was a boy, it had got much deeper months earlier. It had put its tongue right through Jack's chest....

He'd just crashed through the door of a warehouse on the Thames dock in hopes of taking down a gang of arms dealers he and Monica had been tracking for weeks. Already inside the warehouse, Monica had given the signal to Jack over her hidden microphone. A very panicked signal.

Jack raced into the warehouse. Instead of an easy bust, he walked into a weird devil-worship ceremony. And the devil himself had come for tea.

No, not *the* devil; it was nasty, red, horned and spiked. A childhood flashback had made Jack falter for but a moment before opening fire on the monster.

The thing thrust its tongue down Monica's throat—and pulled out her heart.

What kind of horror was that for anyone to witness?

And Jack, though he fired his pitiful MI5-issue pistol like a madman, wasn't able to stop it. The monster didn't flinch as each bullet bounced off its leathery hide.

With a crooked, toothy smirk and a wickedly human chortle, the thing then smacked its forked tongue across thick black lips and soared toward Jack. Taloned appendages gripped him around the throat. All around them the suspects fled, while Jack was literally lifted from the ground.

Suspended by the monster's burning red clutch, Jack felt his entire body burn, as if on fire—yet there were no flames. The creature's eyes glowed as it snarled at him, patted him on the head and then dropped him at its feet.

No, it hadn't feet; the thing ended in swirling black mist. Nasty, niffy stuff. It was the first time Jack associated sulfur with the otherworld. Brimstone.

Lying there, flat on his back, arms spread across the concrete floor and spitting up his own blood, Jack felt sure this was it. His number had been called, and instead of taking the up lift, he was headed down, down, down. He didn't like the heat, never had. Hell would not be a good place for him.

The monster flicked out a forked tongue, touching Jack right over his heart—the tongue permeated his Dragon Skin vest and literally entered his chest. And then it growled in a brimstone-laced snarl, "Mine."

Jack blinked. And the whole nightmare evaporated.

Prone, and shaking, he looked around the empty warehouse, spying the long picnic table that did indeed offer neatly arranged weapons waiting for transport. And there, not eight strides away from where he lay, he saw her face, her eyes void. The monster had stolen her heart and eaten it.

He remembered the vile smell of the demon's breath, tainted with the blood of his partner as it had growled *mine* in Jack's face.

Yes, he knew now to call it a demon. *Monster* was too vague a term.

"I've got your back" was the last thing Jack had said to Monica, after verifying she had entered the warehouse to observe the goings-on.

But he had not. He hadn't protected the one woman who meant the world to him.

Tapped? He'd not given it thought at the time. But now, Mersey's suggestion that he'd been tapped did trouble him.

If she was a familiar, wouldn't she know?

"Thanks, mate," Jack said to the waiter as he plopped down another pint. The froth of foam spilled down the chilled frosty glass, but that wasn't what caught Jack's attention. "Well."

A vision had entered the dark entryway.

Donned in flouncy black lacy stuff, and her waist cinched by a black corset laced in red, Mersey Bane crossed the pub floor, turning all male—and a few female—eyes as she went.

The rings on her right hand glinted with a splay of her fingers. Long black leather boots stopped just above her knees. Little black bows attached to the tops of the boots met the tight black leather pants. Her wicked, pointed-toe black heels clipped a smart pace over to Jack's table.

Jack sat up straighter. Candy walking toward him? He was game. Even if it was a strange flavor of sweet. Hell, it kept his mind from grimmer thoughts.

Her sleek black hair had been smoothed and tamed behind her shoulders. The severe cut of her bangs—the first time he'd seen her wear bangs—gave her a touch of the Goth. Bettie Page bangs, Jack mused. This bird had transformed herself to sex on heels.

Green eyes surrounded in smoky shadow blinked at him. A small smile grew onto her pale lips. But Jack's attention kept straying to the leather clinging to her legs. Those legs. Blimey, as petite as she was, those gams went on forever. And the bows were placed as a flirtatious tease. Did he want to see what went on farther up?

Bloody, sodding yes.

Was this the same woman he'd first met covered in demon residue and sporting a feisty mouth? Now she'd been touched by the feminine—with a wicked sexy Goth edge.

Sliding onto the bench opposite him, Mersey seemed oblivi-ous to the trail of hungry eyes that had followed her progression to the table. She ordered a cream soda and settled back, offering Jack a cat-who-caught-the-rat smile. Those green eyes played up the feline similarities.

What, exactly, was she up to? Did she think to seduce him? For what reason?

And that smile. Had he seen that exact smile before?

Realization struck Jack like a pickax to the heart. He clutched his chest. Mersey reminded him of…the woman in the field.

He'd been so young. And the woman—she'd been naked—had cast him a sly wink. And then things had gone pear-shaped.

Snagging a chip from his plate, Mersey gobbled it down and gestured toward the dance floor at the back in a dark corner near an old-fashioned jukebox. "Angel Eyes," by the Jeff Healey Band filled the pub with steel guitar and mellow jazzy bass.

"I love this song. Fancy a dance, hotshot?"

"Dance? I, er…" Coordinating his feet while matching the beat? Not his cup of tea. But those green eyes pleaded with an in-tensity that poked at Jack's heart. "Sure."

Mersey was up in a moment and tugging Jack along to the small, scuffed wood floor. Another couple did a soft-shoe, lost in the rhythm.

Following Mersey's directions, Jack slid his hands into hers and she held her arms out, as if ready for something far too complicated.

Aware they had an audience, Jack leaned in to whisper at Mersey's ear, "I, er…I don't know how to do this." He stepped back and ran a palm over his scalp.

Sweet, petite and dusted with an accidental helping of Goth, Mersey beamed up at him. "Not so good with the steps myself. But I can manage something slow." She slid her palm up his chest.

Nervous as he'd been to follow her to the place where his inadequacies would be exposed, an overwhelming relief melted over Jack as Mersey pressed her head against his shoulder and they began to sway together to the beat.

The song was slow, which was good. Too much to concentrate on if he had to figure where, when and how quickly to place his feet.

None of it mattered. The heat of Mersey's body invading his pores mastered all reluctance. There at his shoulder, the sparrow nestled to the hawk's wing. Her breasts nudged his rib cage. Every part of him wanted to get closer to every part of her. The curves of her felt too good.

"I wish I wasn't so short," she said. "Of course, you are rather high."

The bright lemon scent of her awakened his senses and kept him from the deep stir memory threatened.

There was so much about her he wanted to discover. When and why had she become someone who tracked and captured demons? Was it because she was a familiar? Did they all do that?

She should be standing behind a cosmetics counter, brandishing perfume or modeling the latest shade of cheek color to Harrods's lunchtime shoppers. Though she wore feminine a little awkwardly, Mersey was much more beneath the surface.

Her fingers clutched the front of his shirt, sending a rocket blast of heat across his flesh and informing his libido that it had been too long since he'd indulged in a woman.

Right then. *Don't cock this one up, Harris.*

Jack spread a hand up the satin ribbons lacing her back, his fingers spanning her shoulder blades. With his other hand, he smoothed away the fine line of dark hairs that had got caught in the corner of her mouth.

A kiss required that one not talk, which was a very good thing, as far as Jack was concerned. He nudged her upper lip with his own. She parted her lips and a sigh drifted across his mouth.

Bending his knees, he brought himself to her level and pressed his head aside hers. "So this is your MO, eh? You lure the guy here on the pretense you've something to discuss, then, when he least expects it, you charm him with your dance moves."

"I've no moves, Jack. And if anyone is doing the charming, it's you."

"Yeah? You wouldn't be trying to seduce me, would you? To learn my secrets?"

She gave him a shy sway of shoulders. "Is it working?"

"It's definitely beginning to do something to me." Such as loosen his inhibitions and make him consider a seduction of his own. And then he remembered. He wasn't on a date. This was a covert operation to gain access to her headquarters. "So…your place?"

"It's not going to happen, Jack, so give it up. You will never learn where base is."

"Hadn't even thought about that. But now that you mention it, don't you have to check in, or something?"

"Not for dates."

"Right. A date."

"Number three, as you reminded me."

And if that sexy wink wasn't a gauntlet thrown at his feet, Jack was a sodding familiar.

"Fancy stopping by my place for a drink?"

"There's drinks here in the pub," she countered.

Did she seriously think to play the tease? No, he sensed she wasn't aware of her own vacillations between seductress and tough-girl demon catcher.

Jack had to smile at the many faces of Mersey Bane. And toss in a black cat to the mix?

"I've got some catnip in my cupboard?" he offered. "Left over from cat-sitting a neighbor's pet last year."

"Jack…" She nuzzled against him, and he felt it a move a cat would make when rubbing against a human to show affection. "You're cruel, but I'll give you points for trying. How far away do you live?"

Score.

Chapter 12

If he couldn't get her to take him to base, then an indirect approach was required. She still didn't trust him. He'd have to work on that.

Though his flat was immaculate, there were still things Jack needed to check before inviting Mersey inside.

As they topped the fourth-floor stairs, he slipped in front of her and blocked his door. "Give me a few minutes, will you? Er, need to tidy the place. Make sure I didn't leave the private stuff lying about."

"Stuff, meaning guns and ammo?"

"Cute." He kissed her cheek quickly, regretting not planting one right on her smirking lips, then closed the door on her and dashed through his home.

He veered toward the demon directory he'd borrowed from P-Cell archives and shoved it under the couch.

He'd hauled the broken television down to the trash bin last night. Living room clear. Check.

Hallway clear and one weapon stored in the cubby. Check. Loo. A towel on the floor, but no signs of life. He glanced to the ceiling, checking all corners in the dull light. Check. Bedroom? Double check.

No demons. Anywhere.

Jack exhaled and removed his jacket, flinging it over a chair as he went, and opened the door. "Such a pleasure to find a lovely bird outside my door. Come in. Can I get you something to drink?"

"I'm good."

He watched Mersey survey the living room, poking her nose through the drawn shades to check the view of the Thames. Those black satin ribbons were dangerous. If he pulled one free would the whole boot slide down to her ankle?

"Yes, you are good," he had to agree.

No demons tonight, he thought forcefully. No demons, no demons, no demons—

"Jack?"

"What?"

"You have a crystal ball stuck in your wall."

Bloody thing. It stuck there like a fist of fury, reminding and warning. "It's just a ball of glass. Childhood present. My mum was cleaning the old house and thought I would want it. Haven't got around to tossing it."

"And yet, it appears you already have given it a good toss. Curious." Mersey crossed the room. "This is the neighborhood where we stalked the demon two nights ago."

"Yes, it's close," he said. "But no demons here, promise."

Jack strayed a few glances up to the corners of the ceiling. No uninvited OEs. And keep it that way.

"You know that wasn't really me that night," she said.

"A twin, was it?"

"No, I mean, that woman who kissed you, she was a bit of a surprise, even to me."

"So you don't normally kiss strangers?"

"Never! I'm… Should I say this?"

"You're actually pausing before jumping this time?"

"All right, hotshot, here's another truth for you."

Jack braced himself. What more was there about this bird?

A silly smirk pushed its way onto her lips, as if it had won after an inner struggle against not revealing a saucy grin. "I never go home with strange men on the first date."

"Third. And I'm not that strange, am I?"

"No, you're not. But I'm feeling like it's a one-way attraction after my confession last night."

"No, I'm cool with that."

"Honestly?"

"Cross my heart," he said. And did he mean it? It was much easier to warm to a familiar having kissed her already, than perhaps not having touched her at all. She was…human, so far as appearances went. Jack could accept that. "I'm sorry if I implied that you might be a monster. I don't feel that way."

"Thanks. I feel like you're being truthful with me."

"I am," he breathed as he bowed over her head and nestled his nose against her hair.

It had been a while since he'd held softness and lace and all the other fussy stuff Mersey wore. Smooth, shiny hair. Soft, perfect skin barely blushed. Teasing ribbons brushed across his thighs.

All of it felt great. So distant from his reality.

Her fingers tripped down the front of his shirt and began to work at the buttons.

"You jump from sweet to saucy in a matter of blinks, Mersey."

"Got a problem with that?" She spread back his shirt.

"Nope." He shrugged the tight black shirt from his arms.

Jack stopped short of flexing a muscle; instead he pushed back his shoulders, which lifted his pecs. The woman switched gears so fast he wasn't convinced she was actually in control of the ride.

Did he want to slow her down? No. *Should* he?

She glided her fingers down his chest, the touch so tender it was almost painful. A wake of goose bumps emerged behind her warmth. Her fingernail bumped down the ridges forming his abs.

Jack let out a moan. Sweet mercy.

Sweet Mersey.

No, he'd let her take the wheel for now. Business had no part in this pleasure.

"You must work out."

"Hunting the big bads keeps me on my toes, and physically fit." He drew a hand along her forearm. Though thin, her arms were taut with muscle. "You must be aware of the physical challenge, Miss Demon Chaser."

"I prefer *retrievals specialist*. After the chase there's no blast."

"So you specialize in retrieving."

"Demons specifically." She traced below his belly button. "They're my raison d'être."

"Really?" Jack sucked in a breath as the delicate touch ignited all the *go* buttons inside him. Intent on giving her freedom to do as she desired, he spoke through a tight jaw, attempting to keep back an out-and-out groan, "How'd you get into this kind of work? Gotta be a hell of a choice between fashion design or demon chasing. I can't imagine that conversation with the parents."

"I was born into it. My mother and father were both familiars."

"I see." Made sense. But he didn't want to go there right now.

"It's not important, Jack. What is, is that I can feel your heart beating faster." Her fingers spread across his chest. Green eyes glittered up at him, and she whispered wondrously, "It's such a strong heartbeat. Like you. I like standing in your shadow. Makes me feel…"

Protected?

"Safe."

He'd take that.

Conscious that she would soon touch the scar above his nipple, Jack pressed a hand over her fingers. For some reason the scar pulsed now, like if she touched it, she may pull back with a burn.

"You know," she whispered, "we're attracted to those things and people we most need."

"Is that what you believe?"

"It's what I know. My mother taught me. We call all that we need into our lives. Sometimes we know what to do with it, sometimes it must be learned. It's like a demon being called to a mortal. That mortal sends out the need for such a demon, without knowing, and be it lust, sadness or vengeance the demon brings with it, it is a lesson the mortal needs."

"I can go with that. When a man feels he has dark demons haunting his soul, it could really be true."

"Exactly. But let's talk about work another time." Her breath hushed against his scar. She couldn't realize what that crazy warmth did to Jack's self-control. Or maybe she did. "Kiss me, Jack."

Mersey slid her arms around behind his neck and her knee nudged against his hand, so he gripped her under the thighs and lifted her fey weight. She fit herself to him and he had to step backward to avoid taking a tumble. The wall caught his shoulders.

The silk ribbons and steel grommets of her corset abraded his chest, a delicious torment to his challenged morals. Kissing Mersey was no chore, and yet part of him hung back, slightly disturbed by her almost staged eagerness.

She kissed with purpose, not about to tease or take the leisurely route, but there was something…just not right.

"Wait!" He set her down, and she stepped back. And his anger instantly fired. "I know what you're doing. You're trying to seduce me, so I'll give up the goods."

"But, I—"

"I'll save you the trouble."

He picked her up by the hips and set her on the brown suede easy chair like a bad child who needed a time-out. The overstuffed chair consumed her and made her look like a small child.

"I am not," Jack enunciated clearly, "a familiar. I'm human. Got it? I hunt demons. If you choose to call me a bloody death merchant that's your prerogative. Nothing, and I mean nothing, about me is paranormal."

"But there is a way—"

"Are you listening to me?"

Jack paced before her. His brain had finally caught up to his cock, and he wasn't overly happy with that development. A man shouldn't ought to be thinking when he was better off snogging.

He passed before Mersey. She drew up her knees to her chest and looked like a frail doll on the overstuffed chair. A wicked doll who had been working her charms on him.

And why not fall to said charms? Just shag and pat her on the head then send her on her way. That was Jack Harris's MO. Why change it now?

Turning from Mersey, Jack stared right at the ball stuck in the plaster wall.

Two nights after the incident with the demon and the naked lady in the field—and that weird encounter that had followed with the black cat at his windowsill—Jack had decided the glass ball had indeed harbored magic—and that maybe his aunt Sophie really was a witch.

So to test his theory, he'd wished for a fortune. Money to pay his father's hospital bills. *A curious fortune,* eight-year-old Jack had dramatically chanted as he'd rubbed the glass ball.

The next morning Donnell Harris had never opened his eyes. He'd died in his sleep.

So traumatized by losing his dad, Jack had not associated his wish with his father's death until a week later. His mum had let out a squeal, which had got Jack into the kitchen in two licks. A check had arrived by post. Donnell Harris had left his family a fortune.

"Such a curious fortune," Mum had whispered, for she'd not known her husband had invested in stock. He'd never once mentioned the money when they'd worried over how to pay the hospital bills.

A curious fortune had arrived in the Harris household. Jack really had wished his father dead.

And now, because of that damned ball, he attracted demons. Him, a familiar?

"What's the way?" Jack murmured now.

He must confront the truth of himself. To keep his brain from seeking the darkness of his past. Darkness that swelled about him, seeking to infiltrate the last bits of light. Was there any light?

"To know if you're a familiar? Well—"

"No." He thrust up a firm hand between the two of them. "I don't want to know." A few paces placed him before the window. Outside, the lights draped across the Westminster Bridge cast wavery streaks of fallen starlight across the Thames.

Did he already know the answer to Mersey's question? Is that why he had trouble even thinking about it? Could he be…?

Jack placed his palm over his chest. *Mine.* What had the demon Beryth meant when it had murmured that word to Jack after pressing its tongue into his chest while the scent of Monica had filled the air?

He bowed his head and fisted his hands, summoning the courage to allow this to happen. To not only seek the truth, but to allow Mersey to see that part of him he most wished to secret away. The soft part, that little boy who still embodied him, the demon frightener who held the glass ball high and thrust it toward the monster he knew to be real. The boy who believed.

Exhaling heavily, he released the anxiety from his lungs. "Fine."

He leaned over the chair Mersey sat in, fitting his hands to the arms and putting his face right before hers. Why did she have to smell so deliciously sweet?

Because she is sweet. If a bit off-kilter. You can trust her.

"Tell me. Go ahead. I won't stop you. There's a way to know if I'm a familiar?"

She nodded. "It's what I was trying to do just now. Kissing you."

He had to smile at her innocent eagerness. "You were trying to give me a tonsillectomy, love. That was some pretty urgent kissing."

"I'm nervous. I never act like this. It's not me."

He stroked her cheek, liking the soft, pale skin. Her kohl-lined eyes spoke to him of sultry mysterious women, intent on seduction. To touch this marvelous, eccentric, gorgeous woman felt wondrous. Made him feel like that eight-year-old boy who could defeat any monster.

"Mersey, I'm very attracted to you. You don't have to prove anything to me."

"Jack, you don't understand. There is one way to determine if a human is tapped by a demon, and that is to have sex with them."

Chapter 13

Oh-ho? They needed to have sex to determine whether or not he was a demon's sodding familiar? Jack hadn't expected that one.

"Really." He stepped back from Mersey's chair and swung his arms freely.

Have sex? Now he liked that idea. Hadn't been able to think of much else since running into this bird. "So how does that work?"

"According to texts—"

"Texts? What, have you been reading up in the library?"

"Yes, the archives—"

He narrowed a brow at her. "And where are the archives?"

"In—" She stopped and gave him an oh-no-you-don't look.

Well, he had to try or the night would be a complete bust as far as fulfilling any orders from P-Cell.

"None of your business, demon hunter. Now, will you pay attention? To determine if you are a familiar, I need to have sex with you. Then, during climax, when I look into your eyes, I'll see the image of your demon master reflected there."

"Huh." Leaning over her again, Jack dug his fingers into the chair arms. "As simple as that, eh? Sex, climax, demon image?"

Mersey beamed a hopeful smile up at him.

This was not keen. It sounded too…clinical. Get hot. Bring the girl to climax. But wait—pause—let her peer into your eyes. See a demon. Spoil the mood.

Not.

"Can't you, as a familiar, recognize another?"

"Nope. Even if you were natural born," she said, "I'd have to witness you shift shapes to know for sure. Sex is required."

Shrugging a palm over the short stubble on his scalp, Jack again paced. She was just so sanguine about it. As if suggesting they take another round on the dance floor at Monkey Chews, and what was wrong with that?

And yet, what would it hurt to humor the poor thing? At the very least, he'd get the shagging he desired. And once he'd made love to her, and she saw nothing in his eyes, well then, she'd perhaps consider taking him home with her. To base.

"All right, then."

Jack lifted Mersey up from the chair and planted a hard kiss to her mouth. Sliding one hand down to cup under her derriere, he drew her to him. She obliged by wrapping her legs around his waist.

"Does this mean we're going to have sex?" she wondered gleefully.

"I haven't decided yet." Because part of him knew this was very wrong. Still, another part, the manly macho part, wasn't about to resist.

Just give a tug to one of those bows at the top of her thighs, yes?

"Who says you get to decide?"

She kissed him again. Each time they connected she grew more confident, almost demanding. She felt so good with her silky corset sliding over his bare chest and her moans tickling like cat purrs inside his brain.

Jack kissed his way up from her wrist, along the sweet, silky inner flesh of her elbow, and to the narrow pinnacle of her shoulder. Lemons led him higher, to trace his tongue along the curve of her neck and skate the jut of her chin.

Did he want this? He needed this. But did he *want* it?

Or had the hunter fallen too deeply into the trap of vengeance? He wanted to kill that bastard, Beryth. Mersey was his key to again making contact with the demon.

And she wanted to help him. To determine if he'd been tapped. For her own purposes, of course. Which likely had something to do with the group she worked for.

Her moans tempted him back to the kiss. To the soft curves pushing up from the corset and snugging against his chest. He could dip his head and lash out his tongue across a nipple, and yet... This sweet, beautiful woman wanted him—for all the wrong reasons.

Jack set Mersey down.

"Jack?" Breathy and startled, the tone of her voice made him regret his indecision.

"What are we doing?" he asked. "You don't know me."

"We—we were going to have sex!"

"Precisely." He paced to the wall and then spun on her. "But for what reason? Give me one good reason."

"I..." She trailed two fingers down the loosened corset ties. When had they become untied? Her breasts were the perfect handful, and the corset pushed them up there like treats to be savored. "I thought we agreed to this, Jack?"

He paced. "This is not a business arrangement. People don't *agree* to shag—it should just happen. Christ, you're beautiful, and sexy and you smell like an orchard, and I want to bury myself inside you and forget the world."

"Sounds good to me."

"Does it?" Yes, it did. Yet no matter how much he talked the talk he couldn't force himself to relax and go with it. "Look at you. You're ready to have sex with a virtual stranger merely for business purposes."

"You need this as much as I do."

"And why is it that you need it? I can't believe I'm even arguing this. Oh, hell, don't pout like that, Mersey." He pulled her back into his embrace. Silken hair slid over his nose and he bit at it, taking the sweet-smelling strands across his lips.

Her fingers skimmed his nipple and the sensation rocketed to his groin. And there, she accidentally touched his scar. Fire burst through his chest. A deep, wanting flame that made him toss back his head and release a needy moan.

"Oh, Mersey." He studied the depths of her green eyes. Would he break her if he continued to touch her?

You didn't protect Monica. What makes you think you can protect this one?

A crash sounded from down the hallway, obliterating the heavy beats of Jack's heart. The loo?

"What was that?"

"I don't know, but I'm going to find out." He pressed her against the wall. "Promise me you'll stay here?"

"But—" A quick kiss silenced her.

Jack took off around the corner, retrieving the .45 from the cubby as he stalked purposefully down the hallway.

Giggles echoed out from the loo. Pressing his shoulder to the doorjamb, he listened. It had been empty earlier, which could only mean—

He kicked in the door and aimed. A skinny blond woman perched on the toilet. A shrill mewl pierced his eardrums as the thing sighted in his weapon. Not human; that mewl was demonic.

Jack curled his finger around the trigger.

"No!"

The gun fired into the floor, taking out two ceramic tiles near the base of the toilet. The demon squeaked and pressed itself to the wall, compressing its body grotesquely to fit between the shower and the window.

"I told you to stay in the living room." Mersey had slapped

down Jack's arms. He quickly re-aimed at the trembling OE. "Stand down, Bane!"

"I don't think so." She slithered beneath his arms and popped her head up between the barrel of his gun and the now giggling demon. "It's not going to hurt anyone. It's a lust demon."

"A what? Get out of here. You're standing in the path of a bullet, I'll have you know!"

"I wouldn't be if you'd put that nasty thing down!"

Violet bubbles floated up from behind Mersey. Bubbles?

Jack lowered the pistol and turned in the doorway to lean against the frame. He searched the ceiling for—God knew what. When he looked back down, the target was acting like something out of a Saturday-morning kiddie show, yet looking like a Saturday-night peep show.

"She's cute, don't you think?" Mersey asked.

The demon slinked onto the floor and stretched against the wall, shaking out her hair and fluttering her lashes like some kind of sex kitten. It was a skinny human-shaped thing in purple lamé and with curls of white-blond hair. Ultra-long lashes dusted its brow with each nervous blink.

Jack watched from the corner of his eye. This was not bloody right. Demons were not cute. Bet its tongue was long and forked.

"What did you call it? A lust demon?"

"Yes. Lust demons are attracted to well, lust, and can increase desire."

Things started to click and fall into order. "So that's the reason you've been all over me."

"No, that's—" Mersey flicked a glance over her shoulder at him. "You arse."

Wasn't the first time a female had named him the sort. Yet this time it tweaked at Jack's heart. So to avoid the weirdness of the moment, he pushed away the tendril of emotion and again took aim. "Let me blast it."

"No, Jack. I'll send it away."

"Are you—"

Mersey said a few Latin words…

"—nuts?" Jack finished.

…and the thing dissolved from the toilet in a shimmer of violet.

"How'd you do that?" he said.

She turned, hands at her corseted waist. Kohl-lined eyes narrowed defiantly. Goth witch personified, and she'd just used some kind of chant, so the whole look fit her to a *T*.

"Simple deportation spell, hotshot. It doesn't send them back to the dark realm, but merely relocates them."

"So it can torment someone else with lustful thoughts?"

"You consider lustful thoughts torment? Jack, you're more frigid than I am."

Ouch. She had no idea how he struggled with right and wrong.

"Now. Explain to me how you've got a demon in your loo?"

"It wasn't there when I checked earlier." He strode down the hallway, determined to hide his rising anger from her.

"You…checked? That's what you were doing? Demon check?"

He should have shoved Mersey out of the way, blasted the thing, and then drawn her into a victory kiss.

Right now? He needed her to leave so he could shuffle into order the remnants of his pride. Alone.

Jack settled onto the couch and set the gun on the cushion next to him.

"Which means…" She stepped before him, hands gesturing in mad admonishment. "You *expected* to find a demon in your flat."

"That's not the point!"

"What is?"

"The point is, earlier, the only reason you were kissing me was because that thing made it so."

"You were kissing me back, Jack."

"Exactly!"

"Don't change the subject," Mersey snapped. "The only way

a demon can appear in a mortal abode is if their familiar calls them there, or if a ritual is chanted. I didn't hear any ritual, did you?"

"Before or after you did your witchy chant in my loo?"

"Ah!"

"I know what you're implying." He leaned forward and tapped the glass coffee table for emphasis. "I. Am. Not. A. Familiar. I know a bit, little girl, and one thing I do know is that familiars bridge the demons here only with great pain. I didn't feel a thing just now."

"Because there's a leak. An unclosed passage that you obviously left open!"

"I didn't open anything! Christ, I wouldn't know how!"

Mersey breathed in through her nose and tapped her pointy boots on the hardwood floor. Jack followed the slim silhouette of those ribboned boots up the long length of her legs, glided over the leather and got lost somewhere in the corset laces that stretched loosely over her please-touch-me-again bosom.

Christ, he still wanted her. No denying his lust hadn't decreased one iota. Had that bloody purple thing returned?

"Fine." He stood. "If you must know, I've had…more than one demon visit me lately."

To her credit she didn't lash out verbally at him.

"Don't know how to keep them out. They just…show up."

Exhaling heavily, she nodded, and then offered, "You need to ward your home. Where did you study demon hunting? Didn't they teach you anything?"

"You tell me about your base, I'll tell you where I learned."

She slammed her arms across her chest. Nope, no matter how pissed she tried to look, he still wanted to cover those pouty red lips with kisses.

"I've heard of warding." He never thought he'd need it himself. Where to find a wizard to perform the required task?

"There's no other way to discover the truth?" he asked. "About being a familiar?"

"Far as I know. We've got to have sex. You still in the mood?"

He wiped a palm down his face and shook his head. "This is the least romantic date I've ever had."

"You think I enjoy it when a good make-out session is spoiled by a giggling lust demon?"

Much as he hated himself for doing it, he couldn't continue. "We can't do this! You don't even know me, Mersey. Hell, I could be your greatest enemy."

She chuckled. "Don't be silly. I'd never make it with a member of P-Cell—"

Sentence abruptly halted, Mersey grasped her throat. Her entire face changed. "Oh, my God. I didn't even consider... You hunt demons. You carry a nasty gun. You're big. You're tough. Why didn't I—? You are, aren't you? P-Cell. I was kidding before, but you really are...a freakin' death merchant!"

"Mersey, I—"

"Oh, my goddess, all this time. It makes so much sense! That big, nasty gun. Your utter lack of respect for the *para* nation. Your quickness to violence."

"Mersey, now don't get so upset."

"I can't believe I didn't suspect you right away. But I've never met a P-Cell agent before. I've always been warned... Oh! You've been trying to follow me to my base. I thought it was fun and flirty, like you couldn't get enough of me. What an idiot I've been. You're trying to infiltrate the Cadre for P-Cell, aren't you?"

Jack sucked in a breath. She'd just revealed exactly what he needed. The Cadre existed. And she was a part of it. Bingo.

He sensed Mersey's deep disappointment in him. His shoulders drooped and he nodded. "Yes, P-Cell. I'm following a direct order."

"Which means you have no interest in me romantically—"

"I didn't say that."

"You didn't have to." She flinched as he reached for her. "You betrayed me, Jack."

"Oh, look who's throwing daggers. You're the one who wants

to have sex for reasons beyond emotion. If you did learn I was a dangerous OE, what would you do? Capture me in one of those fancy little crystals?"

"You deserve it, Jack Harris, for lying to me." She stomped toward the door. "You call them OEs?"

"Otherworldly entities. I didn't lie to you, Mersey. You never asked the right questions. You assumed I was a hunter. I am. I hunt demons."

"For a twisted, patriarchal, maniacal—"

"Don't forget fanatical."

"—*fanatically* militant group that wouldn't know kindness from madness. You're pitiful, Jack Harris."

She'd called it right there. He bent forward, catching his palms on his knees. A breath to stop him from spewing out reactionary replies to her accusations was needed.

She grabbed the doorknob, and sighting his weapon, shook her fists and stomped the floor. "How many have you harmed for the greater good? No, don't tell me. I don't want to know."

"The greater good? You mean us mortals? Mersey, you can't even compare the two."

She opened the door. "What makes you believe mortals are the superior race?" And with that she stormed out.

Jack slammed his fist against the door frame as she marched down the stairs. He didn't go after her. She was in a marvelous rage and would not be calmed. Maybe it was better this way. He couldn't have had sex with her without guilt. And he had enough guilt on his plate, thank you very bloody much.

"Sorry," he muttered and pressed his forehead to the wall. "Didn't mean to hurt another female. Seems to be my MO lately."

Was this what he had become good at? Hurting women unintentionally?

What makes you believe mortals are the superior race?

No, she wasn't a mortal. But that wasn't the bad part.

This thing he and Mersey had going between the two of them

was wrong. Very wrong. The sex and attraction should not be twisted in with their true goals.

From now on Jack had to stick to the plan.

He must convince Mersey to show him to Cadre headquarters. And if Beryth followed him there?

Brilliant. He couldn't wait to get the demon in firing range.

Chapter 14

The infiltration was moving too slowly. He had hoped to land this mortal realm and ransack the Cadre immediately. Too much time had passed. Weeks, perhaps? He was not a good judge of mortal time, but it felt far too long.

He'd once had access to the Cadre—had actually worked for them for a short stint. Now there were supernatural barriers keeping him back. To be expected. Their kind were unthinking, cruel and not to be suffered lightly.

This mortal love, it dug so deep and it never left. She was not alive now, but he would never forget. Never forgive.

Do no harm? Even after his capture and false accusation, he'd been assured that the Cadre were benevolent and would see him returned to his own realm before any sort of physical punishment was inflicted upon him. Liars. To be sucked into one of those insufferable crystals—ah! They had no idea!

And now, the entire order of demonologists and torturers and trackers would suffer.

An access vessel had been procured. A mortal he had tapped and now remained connected to for the man's dread was vibrant and ever present. He would lead him into the Cadre. Soon.

He should send a reminder to Jack Harris.

It hurt Jack's heart to recall Mersey storming away from his flat, angry because he was something she had obviously been trained not to trust. If it came down to serving P-Cell or winning Mersey's trust, Jack knew he would not easily choose P-Cell's side.

But was he ready to sacrifice for a woman he'd known only a few days?

Either way, an apology was in order.

This time Mersey wasn't aware of him following her. Jack had searched the MI5 database and located her address. He was in the Bloomsbury neighborhood close to London University. Made sense that Mersey would live close to the university if she had gone to school there.

He'd cruised the roadways for less than twenty minutes when he spied Mersey walking the pavement. Stopping five buildings up from his parking spot, she punched in a code to an apartment building and entered.

Would she let him up? Probably not. She'd made it clear she wasn't interested in befriending anyone from P-Cell. But if he was lucky, he could catch the door when a resident entered or exited.

Allowing her a few minutes to get inside, Jack then slipped across the street, taking in the peripherals as he did so. The apartment building sat in the middle of a block, a dark alley to its left. Residential, upper-income housing. Houses stacked too close for more than a sliver of yard or a thin old oak tree. A safe, benign neighborhood.

Good. Now he wouldn't worry about Mersey living in a crime-ridden hovel. Because he did. The woman should be living with a man—someone who could protect her from the big bads.

He buzzed the Bane button and she answered. "Mersey, it's me Jack, don't hang—"

NO POSTAGE
NECESSARY
IF MAILED
IN THE
UNITED STATES

BUSINESS REPLY MAIL
FIRST-CLASS MAIL   PERMIT NO. 717   BUFFALO, NY

POSTAGE WILL BE PAID BY ADDRESSEE

SILHOUETTE READER SERVICE
3010 WALDEN AVE
PO BOX 1867
BUFFALO NY 14240-9952

Play the Lucky Hearts Game

and get...

2 FREE BOOKS and 2 FREE MYSTERY GIFTS... YOURS to KEEP!

Yes! I have scratched off the silver card. Please send me my *2 FREE BOOKS* and *2 FREE mystery GIFTS*. I understand that I am under no obligation to purchase any books as explained on the back of this card.

Scratch Here!
then look below to see what your cards get you...
2 Free Books & 2 Free Mystery Gifts!

338 SDL ENV9   238 SDL ENPX

FIRST NAME

LAST NAME

ADDRESS

APT.#

CITY

STATE/PROV.

ZIP/POSTAL CODE

(S-N-08/07)

Twenty-one gets you
2 FREE BOOKS and
2 FREE MYSTERY GIFTS!

Twenty gets you
2 FREE BOOKS!

Nineteen gets you
1 FREE BOOK!

TRY AGAIN!

DETACH AND MAIL CARD TODAY!

She hung up. He buzzed again. No answer. So he buzzed again. And again.

Finally, she replied. "Did you follow me?"

"It's what I do. Had some luck with it this time. So ah, can I come up? This is important."

"P-Cell business?"

"No, it's personal." Jack stepped back and peered down the pavement. Moonlight glimmered on the nearby freshly sprinkled micro-lawns. "Please, Mersey. I…need to apologize."

He could feel her apprehension through the speaker box. A sigh, a twist of her mouth, as she wondered exactly what she'd got herself into. "Fine. I'll buzz you—"

A fiery pain ripped into Jack's shoulder. His feet left the pavement. He didn't hear Mersey's last words. Instead, his body swung upside down, his head a pendulum over the cement. Strong talons gripped his ankles.

Clawing for something, anything to get a grip on, Jack's fingers slid across the rough concrete as the creature that had hold of him dragged him into the dark alleyway.

It had been five minutes since she'd buzzed the entry door. Was this Jack's idea of a joke? Make a play for her sympathy and then take off?

Mersey opened her front door and surveyed the hallway. Listening, she didn't hear anyone stomping up the three flights of stairs required to reach her floor.

Reaching back inside, she buzzed again, but didn't hear the lower door open.

"What's his game?"

That he'd followed her did not sit well. And yet, she figured if he'd gone to the trouble of following her, then something must really be bothering him. He wanted to apologize? She would listen.

So where was he?

A tingle at the base of her spine wouldn't allow Mersey to stand there. Something was wrong. She charged out the door and headed down to the lobby.

It was a murk. Demon henchman, to be exact. Jack had blasted a few of them in his short stint at P-Cell. They usually flanked their demon master, being much bigger, musclier, gristlier and downright uglier. They were an easy kill *if* a weapon were handy *and* he could get a brain shot.

Flung bodily through the air, Jack's shoulders landed against a brick wall. Limbs splayed, he felt the impact against the back of his skull. Copper coiled in his mouth. He'd bit his tongue. He fell forward and landed on his knees. Cartilage crunched. Next to take the brunt? His face, as nose met concrete.

"Jack Harris," the murk gurgled. Murks always sounded as if they were cycling through a mouthful of rocks. "I've a message for you."

Oh, really? Jack lifted his forefinger because that was the only part of him that didn't ache or feel broken.

The murk's skinless foot crushed Jack's ear. His skull became a part of the road. "Get to work," it mumbled. "Ba'al Beryth grows impatient."

"Your master is impatient?" Jack managed to say. "Try putting off sex with a gorgeous bird for no reason other than morals. Get off me, you sodding bit!"

He grabbed the ankle portion of the murk, slimy and ribbed with visible arteries, but it was too quick. Running for the brick wall, the murk ran up it with ease, apexed and looked down to Jack.

Oh, sod it. Jack knew what was coming.

Lifting his battered body, Jack achieved a girlie push-up before the wind huffed out of him. The murk landed on his back, feeling like the proverbial piano dropped upon him.

"Jack!"

The weight disappeared from Jack's body and he rolled to his back. Tracking the walls and the sky, he saw no sign of the beastly henchman.

"That's right," he called. "You run! I was just about to kick your ugly arse."

"Jack?"

Mersey plunged to the ground beside him. The lightness of her presence, coupled with her gorgeous fruity scent did silly things to Jack's brain. His vision blurred, and he inhaled deeply, taking Mersey deep into him.

"I'm sorry," he murmured, and then passed out.

Chapter 15

When Jack had hit the wall, the jar to his bones had done no more damage than tear a few muscles. But when a murk stepped on your face, then things went pear-shaped.

He couldn't breathe through his nose. It felt like a goose egg, tender, the shell easily cracked if merely touched. The taste of tuppence trickled along the back of his throat—blood.

"I think you broke your nose."

"I didn't," he muttered to the soft, feminine voice that spoke outside the periphery of his pain. "A murk did."

"Why would a demon henchman be after you, Jack?"

He could make a guess. What troubled him was this woman's obvious knowledge of all things creepy. Yet, to move beyond the troubling feeling, he did like that she was in the know. *Of course, she would be.*

"Sit tight," she said. "I've some plasters in the loo."

Ah. So, he was inside, lying on something—Jack stretched his fingers across the surface—silky. A bed. *Her* bed. He was in Mersey Bane's bedroom. With a broken nose and a death wish.

Could opportunity have presented itself in a more twisted manner?

"I suppose a man who's killed any dozens of demons would bring their wrath upon him," she said, returning to his side.

Jack wasn't able to open his eyes. Or maybe he could, but even his eyelids ached, so he kept them shut.

"But the murk didn't kill you." Something cool touched his nose, making him flinch. "So it must have given you a warning. Or did I get there before it could tear you in half?"

She was determined to make him smile and then his nose would really hurt.

"I'm going to put some wadding in your nostrils. I don't think it's broken." She tentatively touched the bridge of his nose. "You'll have to stop by Casualty to be sure. Don't worry, Jack, I'll be your Nurse Nightingale," she pronounced much too gaily.

He may have blacked out during the procedure. All Jack knew was when next he heard a woman's voice she was standing farther away, perhaps down the hall, and was humming a tune. Clinks of metal against glass clued him his Nightingale must be gathering more supplies.

Pushing up on the bed, Jack opened his eyes, to find he lay entombed in a strange yet marvelous world.

Deep purple walls sparkled with iridescence and overhead a crystal chandelier provided more glamour. A stone gargoyle crouched disapprovingly over the doorway, its hollow eyes taking in the intruder on the bed. The bedspread was also purple and matched the many lavish pillows stacked before the black iron headboard.

Jack closed his eyes, wishing briefly that if he clicked his heels he would end up back at his own flat.

"You're up?"

He stretched his neck from side to side, testing the aches, and knowing most were minor.

"I thought I'd put some saline on all the scrapes," Mersey said, sitting on the bed next to him. Plopped herself right beside him like a faery princess lording over her inner chamber. Wielding a cotton-tipped swab, she examined his arm.

Jack opened his mouth to speak, but instead tilted his head down and nestled his cheek aside Mersey's shoulder. The tickling stroke of her fingers along his forehead appeased the aches. Here in her purple treasure box, the real world did not exist. That freaky, fickle world that shouldn't have been populated with strange creatures, and yet, was.

"You going to be okay, love?"

He knew it was an endearment used overmuch by his countrymen, yet for some reason, the word *love* really worked a number on Jack. It claimed the softer part of him that needed the tenderness she seemed very willing to offer.

He curled around and embraced Mersey, landing them both upon the stacks of pillows, and prepared to kiss her, when her horrified expression stopped him inches from her lips.

"What?" he murmured.

She pointed to his nose. "I find you sexy and all, Jack, but really, the battered look isn't working for me right now."

He prodded carefully at his nose. Ah. The wadding. And surely his face was black and blue.

"Sorry." He rolled to his back and stared up at the purple ceiling that sported a constellation of glinting diamantés.

"Ouch." He flinched as she began to touch a cotton swab to the wounds along his arms. Scrapes from sliding down the face of a brick wall.

"So is it true?" Mersey asked. She dipped a new swab into the bottle of saline. "That you tracked me down to apologize?"

He sat up and that allowed Mersey to tend his back. A glance to the floor spied his shirt, bloodied and torn, tossed over the head of a seated stone lion near the bedroom door. A quick exit felt necessary, if only to escape the woman's assumption. But he was surprisingly weak.

"I'm sorry for the way things went. Earlier, during our…date. You don't deserve to be treated that way, Mersey. And, I should have been up-front with you right away. Though, we are trained to be covert."

It hadn't been a date; he'd gone into it with the intention of discovering more about the Cadre, and now he had that info.

But it cut him to know it had been gained at Mersey's expense.

"That's enough, please, sweet." Right. Caution using that word *love,* no matter the context. "There's only so much torture a man can take in one sitting."

Mersey closed the bottle and set it on the dresser, which looked like something out of a medieval castle with dark stain and ornate iron fixings.

She leaned against the wall, arms crossed over her chest. Her thin grey T-shirt made Jack very aware that there was no bra underneath. Black sweats stopped just below her knees. And look at those bare toes.

How many times had they come so close to shagging? And now here he sat on the woman's bed!

She wanted to have sex with him? He was ready.

"So, uh…" He slid forward across the satin comforter.

"No." Mersey swung her arms down and marched out of the room.

"No? No, what?"

Jack jumped off the bed, and almost collapsed. So maybe he was hurting more than he'd suspected. His quads felt shredded, but with careful balance and wincing through the pain, he stood and walked out after her.

"What do you mean, no? You won't accept my apology?"

"Oh, I accept. And I understand you couldn't reveal who you

worked for. But I won't have sex with you, hotshot, so don't even ask."

"That's—you think I came here to have sex with you? Woman, you were the one gung-ho to get into my trousers just last night. What's changed?"

"Besides the fact that you're P-Cell?"

He shrugged a palm over his scalp. Stating the obvious wasn't fair. Nor were those big green cat's eyes and the defiant pout. Had she thought he was going to proposition her? His thoughts *had* strayed, but—

"It needs to be done for the right reasons," Mersey said.

Spying a thick, comfy sofa, Jack collapsed into it.

"Oh, no you don't." She grabbed his hand and tugged. "You're leaving."

"But— This is not what I intended to happen. Mersey, I came here to apologize, trust me."

"Fine. Accepted. Now you need to leave before I do something I'll regret."

She thought she'd do something she would regret? Christ, what kind of man had he become?

"Jack?"

He couldn't summon a genial response. He tugged out the wadding from his nose and crumpled it in his fist. Obviously he needed some rest, time to think, before he could stand his own against this indecisive Nightingale of the purple treasure box.

"I understand. It's not right…between us. I'll see myself out."

"Sure. See you…whenever," she said. The door closed.

And Jack stood in the hallway, swaying. What had just happened?

He'd apologized. He'd given her the truth, yet for some reason, his truth had put her off.

Or maybe it was the way he was delivering it?

Jack turned and pounded on the door. "I'm sorry, Mersey."

Pushing away from the door, he wavered and then caught

himself against the stairway railing. He didn't need Casualty, but what he did need wasn't interested—

The door opened and Mersey stood there with arms crossed over her chest. "Come back inside."

Chapter 16

"I didn't want to push you," Jack offered. "I know this situation is as strange as it gets. You asking me for sex. Me implying we could have sex. Not a hint of romance in the air. But...there should be. I like you, Mersey. *More* than like you."

"Really?"

Mersey was everything he had never expected to find attractive. So why, every time he shared the same air with her, did his better senses flee and his body parts take charge?

And yet, he couldn't bring himself to do anything with this woman without offering more. Like his real feelings. He did like her. Even knowing Mersey but a few days, Jack knew she was something special in his life.

"I like you very much, Jack. You accept me. And I feel needed by you." She touched one of the scrapes on his arm. "And you make me forget a lot of my worries, and just feel free. Freedom is all I've ever craved."

"You don't have freedom?" Anger stirred, warming his neck. Jack made a fist. "Mersey, is someone keeping you under their thumb? Has it to do with…" The Cadre? But she didn't know he knew.

"Not like that," Mersey said. "I've grown up in a place where I was watched after, guided and taught. I always felt as if I were being trained to serve. Which I was. But I'm not beholden to anyone. I took this flat a few years ago, thinking to gain independence. Yet, I always seem to gravitate back to what I know, because this place has never felt like home."

"This treasure box doesn't feel like home to you?"

"A girl can't sit alone in a treasure box, Jack. She needs… someone."

So she was lonely. A feeling Jack could relate to. If he allowed himself to move beyond duty and vengeance. There was a big open empty spot in his life labeled Relationships and Emotional Connection. He'd ignored it well enough—until now.

"You don't feel lonely now, do you?"

"A little." Mersey bowed her head and nudged it against his chest. He stroked his fingers through her hair.

"Do you think I'm a bit off?" she wondered. "I can't seem to make up my mind about you, Jack. I want to be this perfect, prim girl who wouldn't dream to invite strangers to kiss her in dark warehouses, and yet, a bigger part of me just wants to grab you and never let go. Like if I don't hold on, you'll slip away, never to be seen again."

Clasping her hand in his, Jack kissed her knuckles, remarking the rings felt like cool liquid stone.

"It's not a bad feeling to have," he offered. "Never letting go."

"I've been let go of a lot," she whispered. "I can never seem to hold on to anything meaningful."

Dipping his head, he kissed her forehead, then skated down to her dark, shadowed eyelids. Salty there, for he guessed that was a tear just at the corner of her eye.

"Don't cry, Mersey. There must be something in your life that gives you meaning. Your capturing demons, for instance. You must do it for a purpose, or else you'd never take the risk."

"It's just something I've always done. But I do enjoy it, and it does satisfy. But lately, I need to be satisfied on a different level."

"Such as?"

She fluttered her lashes.

Ah. Jack was no idiot, and that flirtatious look didn't need words to get its meaning across.

"Will you stay with me, Jack?"

The question was not innocent. She didn't intend to get out the blankets and make a nest for him on her sofa. The woman sought *satisfaction*. And for all they had gone round and struggled and fought about, he couldn't think of a single reason to deny her now. Or himself.

"I thought the battered look wasn't working for you?" he whispered.

She smirked and began to unbutton his shirt. "I've changed my mind. There's nothing about you that could turn me off, Jack. It's like you're this huge magnet, and even if I get brushed away, I end up snapping right back to your side."

"I don't know what to say to that."

"Don't say anything. Just get this shirt off. It's in the way."

Mersey led Jack back into her bedroom and they plunged half-dressed onto the slippery purple satin. The stone gargoyle observed stoically as their kisses and murmurs blended into the twilight.

The gray T-shirt completely removed, it slid to the floor. One moment Jack was at Mersey's mouth, kissing her, learning the shape of her lips upon his, the next he explored the faint lemon trail down the curve of her neck. Her breasts sat heavily in his cupped palms. They tasted like Mersey, sweet yet spiced with a wicked tease. He lashed the bead of her nipple with his tongue then played his lips across the hard, slippery nub.

Mersey reacted with sighs and mewls and—the strangest thing—the heels of her palms kneaded against his shoulders in a steady pace.

When he neared the edge of the red, crescent-moon mark upon her left breast, it momentarily drew him up from the heady enchantments that threatened to blind him to reality. The mark wasn't raised, but sat flush on her pale skin at the apex of her breast, and was red like a brand.

"Were you…born with this?"

"Yes." She gasped and blew long hairs from her face. Cheeks flushed deeply, she fluttered her lashes and the tip of her pink tongue dashed out to taste Jack's last kiss. "All natural-born familiars have it. It's a remnant from our feline ancestors who served witches."

"Does it hurt?"

"Not at all. Feels good when you touch it."

He breathed softly over her breast and touched his tongue to the crescent mark. Mersey gasped and arched her back. Her entire body reacted to the touch, much as if she'd just had an orgasm.

"Oh, Jack." She slipped her fingers over his scalp and coaxed him forward for another lick. "It's like we've found each other."

"Two strangers, yet familiar to the touch." He kissed her breast and pulled down her hand to trace his scar. "But I think you're the one who found me."

"You have a mark, too?"

"It's from when I was a kid. But I can feel the demon in it now. When you touch it—oh!"

"I think it works the same way mine does," she said on an elated huff. "Does it feel like I'm stroking you…?"

"You mean my cock? Pretty bloody similar, if not—oh, mercy—*better*. Mersey!"

It seemed a ridiculous idea, but when the orgasm streaked through his system at the same time it captured Mersey in a shuddering quake, Jack knew he had found something made only for him.

He hadn't even put himself inside her, and he'd just had an orgasm. By mere touch. How was that possible?

Mersey sighed against his chest. Her smile curved above the

scar. A dash of her tongue drew up another shudder to scintillate across his flesh.

"What the bloody gorgeous hell was that?" she asked on a breathy exhale.

"Haven't a clue." Jack kissed her mark and then licked it. "Want to do it again?"

"I'm all yours, hotshot."

Her leg twined between his and nudged gently against his cock. So hard, and still concealed in his trousers.

"Let's get naked," Mersey suggested, "and see how far we can push it."

"You are reading my mind, little girl."

"I'm not your little girl, Jack."

He nuzzled into her soft dark hair, pooled about her collarbone. "I like you that way. Small and girlie and something I can hold in my arms to protect. I know you don't need protection—"

"I like that you want to protect me." She unzipped his trousers and slid them down his hips. "But you know I can handle myself."

Her fingers clasped firmly about his cock. "You can certainly handle something."

"I can't close my fingers around it. Am I doing this right?"

Sweet little girl. Jack closed his fingers around hers to teach her the pace. "Slow and steady, love. That's good."

"Jack," she whispered in his ear. The hint of a giggle tickled his cheek. "You're very big. I don't know if we'll fit."

"We can stop?" *Please, don't take me seriously.* "If you're not sure?"

"No." A lash of her tongue under his jaw steered his mouth back to hers. She nipped his lower lip, all the while never losing pace with her strokes. "I want you. All of you."

Mounting him, she took charge, directing him there, to the unreal heat of her mons. He knew immediately they would be a tight fit, and so held her by the hips to slowly direct her onto him.

Shudders, as uncontrollable as her sweet kitten purrs, racked his body as she enveloped him completely.

"Jack," Mersey gasped. One hand kneaded against his shoulder, while the fingers on her other dug across his scalp, pulling as she pushed herself up his length and gave herself over to him.

Drawn deep, the world grew silent and vast and began to glitter with all the enchantments he had imagined to live within Mersey Bane. And together they touched that dark magic.

"You smell like Morocco," Mersey said as they lay twisted in the sheets and within one another.

"A country?"

"Yes, like incense, musk, and a bit of cinnamon."

"My aftershave."

She stretched her arms above her head and made a satisfied noise as she snugged her body up against his. They'd shagged for hours and a scythe of white moonlight crept through the blinds to light her flat belly. "You have shown me the world, Jack."

An arch of her back slid her breast across his chest, the soft, heavy globe nestling against his arm. Jack sucked in a breath and let it out as a sigh.

"And you have shown me that a world I once found dreadful can be just as gorgeous as my own."

"You mean because I'm a familiar?"

"Yes. But you're just like me. Real, warm, loving."

"Satisfied." She snuggled her head against his shoulder. "No man has ever treated me so well, made me..." She giggled and said, "Come so much."

"My pleasure." He reached high and drew down one of her hands to kiss the knuckles, one after the other. "So tell me why you wear all these rings?"

"Protection for my future." She splayed her hand to show two rings on the littlest finger and two on the ring finger. "Dash, I lost another."

"Why on just the one hand?"

"My left hand represents my past—which doesn't need protection. These rings on the right are protected by a spell." Mersey sighed. "So many have broken in the past few days."

"You can get more."

"Not like these. They are common, but… Well, it doesn't matter right now." Curling closer, she blew softly along his collarbone. "Tell me about these scars on your shoulder. Demon attack?"

"Rifle kickback."

"Better than a demon, I guess." She glided her palm across his pecs, drawing out the hard curves, and down his tight stomach. Not nearly as satiated as he felt, Jack's cock reacted, tightening. "How does a man get abs like this?"

"Upside down pull-ups."

"I'd like to see you hanging upside down. Naked."

"That could be arranged."

"Wicked." She traveled lower. "And this big boy? I've never studied one closely before." Her hair sifted across his stomach as she took the study of his cock to heart. Each trace or touch zinged at his pleasure core, strumming him tightly. "It's thick and strong, and I do love it."

"You know you can't touch me without then expecting to pay the price."

He slid his hands down to curve over her buttocks and lifted her onto him. They moved silently, masters of the rhythm that had become theirs exclusively. There was a lot a man could learn about a woman during hours of sex, but the most basic, her natural rhythm and that moment when she was ready to fly, were paramount.

Curling a palm around her neck, Jack coaxed Mersey forward, sharpening the angle of their exquisite connection. This way, every time she slid along his cock, her clitoris would also receive the benefit of the motion. And that contact quickly brought them both to climax.

"Oh, Jack, that was so good." Mersey's shoulders tilted back and her body arched upon him. Shuddering with orgasm, she bent forward and met his gaze, deepening the moment with a stare that reached into his soul. "Oh, my goddess. There!"

She peered at him intently, while her body contracted and hugged him in the wake of the orgasm.

"I see it," she said, clasping his face to hold his head still. "Jack, it's there, in your eyes."

He'd almost forgotten the reason they'd come together in the first place. Who could think when shagging? "You're serious? What does it look like?"

"I've seen it before in books. A...dread demon?"

"Ba'al Beryth?"

"You know it?"

"Sod it."

The truth stymied him, but he could believe. Had he been expecting this result? While amazingly easy to accept, it didn't make the news any more welcome.

He, a demon hunter, had been tapped by the very prey he stalked.

Chapter 17

"Don't worry about it, Jack." Mersey stroked his cheek. "It obviously happened without you being aware. Demons can tap innocent mortals without them ever knowing."

"You know a lot about demons."

"Training. I don't understand how you couldn't have noticed?"

"I get it. All right?" What to do with a gorgeous bit of naked perched upon his cock, and he—blimey, what a way to spoil a good shag. "Fine, I believe you. And I know the exact moment it happened."

There had been pain, but he'd never associated it with being tapped. How could he? It had never happened to him before. When he was eight? That had been different.

Mine.

What a fool he had been.

"So now what do I do?"

He wasn't sure he wanted an answer. Hell, just looking at Mersey's body, glowing with perspiration and her breasts rising and settling heavily with her breaths tested all restraint. So he plunged forward for more of the good. The woman purred like a cat when he licked her nipples. Could he get it back up? *Come on, Jack, avoid the truth. Take more of the good!*

"Though you're tapped," she murmured, adjusting her shoulders to direct his attention to the other breast. "I believe you didn't open the passage that's admitting the demons to this realm."

"Like I said before, wouldn't have a clue how to do that."

"And because I believe you, I have to assume it was opened from the dark realm. Perhaps by the very demon who then tapped you, in order to remain here in the mortal realm. It will require a skilled adept to close the passage, but it's got to be done."

Jack paused, settling his head back on the pillow, and peered into her gorgeous green eyes. Mixing business and pleasure was never easy, but the more she mentioned bits and snippets of things he decided were Cadre related, the more he needed to know.

"You're not making this easy, Mersey." He couldn't avoid the truth. And he did have a mission to consider. "I want to dive inside you again and never surface, but there's a very obvious white elephant splayed out on the bed, and it's me, the bloody familiar."

"There's nothing wrong with being a familiar, Jack."

He sat up, putting space between himself and Mersey's body. Tugging the sheets around his waist, he caught his forehead in his palm.

"Except now," she said, "maybe you'll start to acknowledge that there is fallout."

"I still don't know what you mean by that."

"I'm the fallout, Jack." Her tone wasn't soft and sex-tinged; now it had become resentful.

"Don't you know that every time you blast a demon, you take out the familiar, too?"

"That's not true."

"Oh, please, you can't be that naive. Kill the demon, and you obliterate its familiar. Some demons slip through open passages, so they may not be connected to a familiar."

"But I couldn't…"

He'd killed familiars? Others…like Mersey? Why hadn't he learned this in training? Did P-Cell know that familiars were collateral damage?

"No. I only hunt demons."

"Get a clue, Jack. Just because you don't witness the familiar die doesn't absolve you."

He glanced over her naked body. High breasts with pointed cherry nipples. Flat stomach and the sweetest dark curls. Every inch of her looked normal. Human.

But not human.

"Does that make me…" he wondered, "not human, too?"

"What? Jack, I can't believe you're still hung up on that! I thought we'd moved beyond our differences. And no, you're still a bloody inconsiderate human—who just happens to be tapped by a demon."

With a huff, Mersey slid out of bed and began to shuffle the knee-length black pants up her legs. She tugged the T-shirt back on. "You're an arsehole, Harris. I can't believe I had sex with you."

"You were doing it because someone ordered you to."

"What?"

"Admit it," he said. "This was a job tonight. The Cadre and P-Cell have been after each other for decades. They saw opportunity for you to…"

"To what, Jack? To sleep with P-Cell? That is so idiotic. You followed me. This is *my* home. You think far too highly of yourself, you know that?"

She stomped out of the bedroom. "On second thought, yes it was!" she called. "It was business. And now I've the information required. You are a familiar. And you're the cause for the leak. You *will* be dealt with."

Dealt with? Grabbing his boxer briefs and trousers, Jack slid them up and stalked out after his angry familiar.

"What are you going to do?" he asked as Mersey struggled to release the chain lock on the door. Was she going somewhere?

"I need to get back to that warehouse."

"Mersey, you're not going anywhere." Jack pressed his palm over the door to keep her from opening it.

"Oh, I know I'm not going anywhere." She tramped back into the bedroom and returned with his shirt and shoes, which she shoved at him. "Don't let the door hit you."

"Right then." No sense in arguing this endless merry-go-round of emotions. He'd been on this ride before and knew the drill.

Jack clattered down the stairs to the foyer of Mersey's building. The night was cool and he tugged up his shirt and buttoned it. Sitting on the curb, he pulled on his shoes.

You continue to label her something that isn't right, undesirable to you, and yet you want her even more now that you're away from her. "Bad, Jack."

God, he was an arsehole of the highest degree. He should have never said anything about P-Cell and the Cadre. He'd blown his cover. A cover he should have never wielded before crawling into bed with Mersey Bane. He'd been so concerned that they have sex for the right reasons, and then it was he who'd pulled business back into the mix.

"Bloody idiot," he muttered as he stalked down the pavement to his Range Rover. The night was dark and the roads were empty. But instead of driving away, Jack waited.

He didn't have to wait long. Mersey slipped out of her building and into the stairs leading down to the car park.

Where was she headed so early in the morning?

Chapter 18

The forest wrapped thickly along and over the road. Mersey liked entering the protected borderlands surrounding the St. Yve manor. This ancient land was magical and steeped with myth. She had grown up here, and had known nothing of the busy city until she'd taken a flat in London. To her, London was the unreal, paranormal world.

Returning to the Cadre gave her peace and it managed to settle her ire over that impossible man.

Jack was upset? He was the one who had lied to her and was responsible for the leak of dozens of demons. He should be apologizing to her, not cringing.

"The nerve," she muttered through a tight jaw.

So the forest hadn't settled her anger quite as much as she'd thought.

She was endowed with the frustrating ability to bridge demons here from the dark realm. And to shift shapes to a cat. Other than that, she was completely normal. Depending on whose viewpoint.

And if she were completely honest with herself, she couldn't remain angry with Jack. He was being truthful; he hadn't opened a passage, and could have nothing to do with the flow of demons into this realm.

But that didn't mean she wasn't going to be angry with him for his reaction to her.

Five miles from the entrance to the Cadre, she decided enough was enough. Headlights followed closely. Jack had followed her out of London.

Didn't they teach P-Cell methods of trailing cars? Rule number one. Never trail a suspect in a vehicle you've previously given them a ride in. And rule two? Never stalk a dissatisfied date!

Mersey slammed her palm against the steering wheel. "Oh!"

The pieces of another ring fell between her knees to the floor mat. She now had but three left.

"I can't believe they're breaking. I've had these so long."

It had to mean something. But what? Was something destroying the spell? Could her relationship with Jack be the cause of it?

It didn't make sense, but then her life didn't make sense, either. Falling for the enemy? That was akin to mooning over bad-boy faeries even after they'd given you the snub.

Pulling over to the narrow gravel verge that sloped into a deep ditch, Mersey slammed on the brakes, put the Beetle in Park and stepped outside.

A chill fall breeze tickled up under her long coat. She reached inside and retrieved the aviator cap and pulled it on. A gift from her father. He'd gone his way, and Mersey understood he was a man who could never be content in one place. The world was home to Caractacus Bane.

Yet before venturing off, he'd neglected to show her how to find her own home. Was it a place, or, as she'd being thinking more and more, a feeling?

The Cadre provided family. A family that felt as absent as her father had been. But if the Cadre got wind that she'd led a P-Cell agent this far… Well, they would never find out because she'd put a stop to it right now.

The Range Rover stopped fifty yards up.

"Yeah, I can see you, hotshot."

But Mersey smiled, despite herself, and rubbed her arms against the chill. What had happened back at her place had been unavoidable. The sex had been amazing. He'd said things to her she'd always dreamed of hearing from a man. That he could be true to her.

"Can you be true to a familiar, Jack?"

Deep inside, her feelings toward him had not altered, and their making love had only made her…

"Want more," she said on a sigh, her breath misting into the night.

The Rover slowly approached, until Mersey had to shield her eyes from the bright headlights. They didn't blink out as the car stopped. Jack stepped out and leaned against the bonnet, arms crossed high on his chest.

Waiting for her to go to him.

"Oh, I've got your number, Mr. Macho Familiar."

How could a demon hunter *not* know his violence also affected the familiar?

Stomping purposefully over to Jack, Mersey stabbed him in the chest with a fingertip. He reacted by rubbing the spot and groaning, much too loudly for the poke.

"You have a thing about following me. And none too sneakily, I must say."

"It's a free country. I figure you got what you wanted from me, now it's my turn, little girl."

"Stop calling me a little girl."

He bent a look down at her, and Mersey avoided looking up at him.

All right, so he was tall. She was short. In the grander scheme of height he won.

She stopped herself from reacting to the affront by stomping back to the car and peeling away. Little girls did things like storm off in a pout. She was a grown woman who could take care of herself, thank you very bloody much.

So maybe she had been overly emotional with him. Was it because he was such an arsehole? Or maybe it was because he'd stirred something awake inside her. Stirred it up and he'd entered her, filling her, becoming her...

He's not an arse. But right now the defensive accusation worked for her.

When was the last time she'd cared what a man thought of her? Taken the time to dress to seduce? She was acting like a teenager with a crush!

"You going to lead me onward?" he prompted. "I don't have all night, and I'd really hate to return to P-Cell with nothing."

So that was all she meant to him now. "Just where do you think I'm leading you?"

"Cadre headquarters."

"Well isn't that rich." She toed the wheel of the car, still avoiding his gaze. "P-Cell sending in a man to seduce his way inside the Cadre."

How to read him? Was he using her, or fighting the attraction as much as she should be?

"You were the one doing the seducing, Mersey. And you admit it, then? You're with the Cadre."

"I'd be stupid to deny it. Unlike you, who insists upon lying about being tapped by a demon."

He clenched his fingers into his chest. "I'm still trying to wrap my brain around that one, but give me credit for not freaking about it. I can go there. I can accept that it may have happened—"

"Did happen."

"*Did* happen while I wasn't aware."

"To be tapped by a demon is very painful, Jack. Your whole musculature clenches and you can feel the demon enter your body with its tongue."

"Yes, it happened," he said quietly. "But that's not what I'm focused on right now. Why do you keep running away from me?"

Mersey shrugged her fingers through her hair and tugged. "I don't know! I need to think, Jack. So just go. I won't show you the way, even if you ask nicely and made love to me again."

He slid up close and whispered in her ear. "You want to make love again?"

The touch of him, his arm dusting her nipple, instantly aroused. "Not tonight." Liar.

"But you're not ruling it out for the future." He gripped her fingers, and despite her struggles, kissed her knuckles. "These rings aren't protection from me?"

Mersey tugged away from him and shoved her hand under her opposite arm. The protection spell should put up her hackles to danger, yet the rings hadn't so much as tingled since meeting Jack Harris, death merchant. Which was an odd realization, now she thought on it. And yet, her protection was slowly, methodically breaking away.

Was the demon doing it through Jack? Beryth. She knew that name. Could it be the very same one that had tormented her mother?

"Oh, goddess," Mersey said on a gasp under her breath.

"Listen, Mersey, I know you think I'm all about the blasting and killing."

"And you're not?" It was difficult to concentrate now that the demon's name hummed in her brain.

"Mostly, yes. And that I'm following you because I've been ordered."

"You've made that clear."

When he took her by the shoulders, the scent of him, overwhelming and spicy and tainted with remnants of their lovemaking, wouldn't allow Mersey to step away. Her tough act faltered.

"I'm concerned about you," he said. "Every time we get together it's like fireworks but then it leads to misunderstandings and someone storming out."

Plunging into him, she wrapped her arms about his chest. "I'm so confused," she said. "There's so much happening in my life right now. And we've only just met. But it feels like you've been waiting for me forever. I like you, Jack. But you keep sending me mixed signals."

"Me?" He stroked her hair. *I possess you,* the move said, as if she belonged to him. And that wasn't a horrible thing to imagine. "I've been confused, too. What are we going to do?"

"Truth only, Jack."

He nodded against her head. "I agree."

"You're not hiding anything else? Because truth means putting it out there."

"Cross my heart. I'm a familiar. There, I said it. Feels weird though. Is there any way to control it? To get away from the demon's influence?"

"Not until the demon that tapped you releases you. I'm sorry, Jack."

"Take me home with you and we'll work everything out."

"I can't invite you into the Cadre, Jack. It's against the rules."

"I understand. Really, I do. And I won't force you. But would you…" He spread his palm under her breast to press flat to her ribs. "*Could* you invite me in here?"

It must have taken a lot for him to ask such a thing. To expose himself like this to her. It felt good. It mirrored Mersey's feelings. But that she'd snagged such a confession from the one man whom she shouldn't have contact with disheartened her.

She should not have anything to do with a P-Cell agent. But she'd meant it when she'd said it felt as though he'd always been waiting for her.

"I…" How to completely give herself to him? She wanted to. But she couldn't. Not when everything in the world currently plotted to put them at opposite sides.

And not when she knew he could never truly be *the one.*

Why hadn't the rings tingled upon their first meeting? What was it about Jack Harris that she *didn't* need protection?

"I should go."

She pulled away from him, and in doing so, saw the crestfallen look on his face. *Don't look back.* Turning, Mersey strode purposefully toward her car.

"And don't follow!" she called back. "Because if you do, you'll get lost, and these woods are thick. Difficult to find one's way out without a guide."

"We can't avoid the truth forever, Mersey!"

So now *she* was the one running from the truth?

He'd follow. And he'd get lost. Jack was as stubborn as she was. Well, she had warned him. "I'll see you…soon."

"I'm right behind you."

She returned to her car and slid behind the wheel. Jack revved the engine as she sat there. "Be gentle with him," she said to the guardian demons that protected the borderlands from unwelcome visitors.

This exposing-his-feelings thing was so new to him. He couldn't be doing it right. Every time he opened his heart a little more for the woman, she ran. What was he doing wrong?

Jack slammed his palm against the steering wheel as he shifted into gear and began to follow the white Volkswagen.

"Cheeky bird." He tracked Mersey easily as they traveled through the forest.

She had said she'd liked him, too, and in doing so, had reached into his heart and pulled out the truth. Mersey would not allow Jack to shrink back from his emotions. She had earned his respect.

Now, he hoped to earn hers.

The fact they worked for opposing organizations? A trifle. Of course, any and all reports Jack brought back to P-Cell about the Cadre would ultimately affect Mersey. He didn't want to get her in trouble; yet, he had never in his career turned his back on a direct order.

What he needed was more information. What was P-Cell's reason behind locating the Cadre headquarters? P-Cell wasn't against humans studying OEs, unless those humans were aiding the denizens of the dark realm. If P-Cell believed the Cadre to harbor dangerous OEs, then of course, he would enter and eradicate the situation.

The road was lined to the verge with tall, flaky birch and twisted oaks. Very little moonlight passed through the leafy canopy. A few thick snowflakes buffeted his windshield.

Jack braked gently. Snow? This time of year? It had snowed in September before—when he was a teenager—but more like a light flurry than actual flakes.

"This is unusual."

Maybe it was ash flakes? Was there a fire in the forest? He bent to study the sky above the treetops but the dark canopy did not emit moonlight.

The snow began to pick up. The glare of Mersey's red taillights flickered as she turned a curve in the road.

Reaching to flick on the heat, Jack couldn't believe how quickly it had become cold. He hadn't had the heater running since last winter and the thing huffed and hissed out musty air. "What the bloody…"

Clicking on the wipers spread the thick, wet snow across the windshield. It quickly became a blizzard. Except that blizzards were usually small, icy bits of snow, not this huge fluffy stuff forming on the car's bonnet even as he drove a good clip.

Said clip rapidly slowing. Jack slowed the Range Rover to twenty miles per hour and scanned the road. No sign of Mersey's VW.

He stepped on the gas. The car swerved and the tires couldn't find traction. Before he could turn back into the skid, the back tires slipped and the car slid off the road. His door hit the line of trees with a forceful crash. Jack plunged to the passenger side to throw off the impact.

He pushed open the passenger door and scrambled outside. Snow pelted his shoulders and head. He wore a thin summer sweater, and tugged down the three quarter–length sleeves, but it did little against the insistent chill.

His research on the Cadre had turned up something about the woods being enchanted. Outsiders could never access the Cadre, no matter their methods.

"So this is the best you can do?" he called out to the sky. "You're not scaring me off. I can wait!"

He got back inside and closed the door. The atmosphere had changed. The heater couldn't have warmed up the car so quickly, nor made it feel so…humid. Jack twisted about and peered into the backseat.

"Thought I smelled something niffy."

Two red eyes materialized in the backseat and offered Jack a deadly yellow grin.

Mersey tossed the wet towel she'd used to dry her hair into the laundry basket. Plopping onto the bed, she stared up at the ceiling. A shard of amethyst sat on her nightstand and she placed it upon her forehead, over her third eye. It was a catalyst to meditation, a method she'd learned during her studies on how to utilize crystals in healing and healthful living.

Tomorrow morning she would have to confess to Lady Aurora that she had picked up a curious P-Cell operative. It was the right thing to do. It would probably result in Mersey being taken off the London retrieval job, or worse, expulsion. The Cadre was very firm on its secrecy.

Could she risk not seeing Jack again?

Would you invite me in here?

Touching the spot below her breast where he'd made an indelible impression, Mersey closed her eyes and sighed. It still lived there, the dark glimmer that had surrounded her heart the first night she'd met Jack Harris in the warehouse.

And now he'd asked her to open her heart to him. It all sounded so romantic, and certainly she wanted romance and to have a man care for her. And to make love to her. *Again*. It was what she needed—a hero. But he wasn't *the one*.

She held up her right hand and moved the remaining rings up and down her fingers.

Why couldn't she simply fall to her desires? It wasn't as though she believed her mother's portent would come true. If there was a man out there looking for her, surely he would have found her by now.

Catching the amethyst in a palm, Mersey slid off the bed and leaned before the vanity where the etched mirror held a snapshot of her mother and father, always witness to her moods.

As green as emeralds, her father had once remarked on the color of her and her mother's eyes. Reflecting all the treasures of the world.

Straightening, she hooked her fingers at the neck of her T-shirt and tugged it down to expose the top of her left breast. There, the crescent-shaped witch mark she'd had since birth beamed a bright red. When Jack had touched her there, she had flown.

She wanted that experience again. And only from Jack. Because she did feel safe with him, protected. Desirous. Giddy. Angry. Intrigued.

Enchanted.

"Oh, my goddess, is this love?"

Jack woke with a shiver. He sat up quickly, his limbs shooting out for balance and not hitting any obstructions. He wasn't in the Rover, buried bonnet-deep in a freak snowstorm. It wasn't cold, nor did a demon sit in his backseat, gnashing its sharpened grimace.

He touched the cotton sheets. Warm, slept in. This wasn't a dream.

He wore but his boxer briefs. The clothes he'd worn earlier were neatly folded on the dresser to his right.

Folded? Had he? Or someone else? Some*thing* else?

He glanced to the floor where his toppled boots sat. A dark puddle of dirty snow seeped into the carpet. Beside them lay his car keys.

He'd driven home?

"Why can't I remember?"

He twisted to eye the digital alarm clock—7:00 a.m. He'd last been in the forest after midnight. There was no date function. He sure hoped he hadn't lost any days.

Scrambling out of bed, he dashed into the living room to check the date on the answering machine, but he didn't make it that far.

Seated on his couch, and brandishing the M4 carbine rifle, sat the dread demon.

Beryth grinned a decadent sneer. "We've some talking to do, Jack."

Chapter 19

This was the demon Mersey had seen in his eyes. Brave woman. To not have fled at the sight.

Certainly, as a familiar, Mersey must have seen many in her days.

Brimstone suffused the room. Beryth appeared in human form, though the limbs and face were hardly humane. The flesh remained leathery red and the tight red muscled brows protruded over blackest eyes without a hint of white in the orbs. Though it wore a black suit, the shoulders bulged along the seams to the thick neck. Horns along the shoulder bone? Razored spikes? Likely both.

The demon sat with crossed legs. Thin legs ended in overlarge brown leather shoes, the toes bulging as if stuffed with appendages not meant to be enclosed.

A woozy trickle rode Jack's scalp. He tried to keep his focus on the M4 in the demon's grip. No disguise there. The red fingers were multijointed and tipped in long black talons. One clawed appendage tapped the trigger.

The scar on Jack's chest burned. He didn't want to react, to slap his hand over the itching reminder of his bond to this creature, so he clenched his fingers into fists near his thighs.

Closest weapon was down the hallway in the cubby. The demon might blast him to bits before Jack could dash out of the living room. Worth the risk. Besides, what could a salt grenade do to mortal flesh, beyond tear it? Unless the demon aimed the shot right for Jack's heart.

"So talk," Jack offered. "What do you want from me?"

"I've already explained, I need you to gain access to the Cadre. Thus far you have failed miserably. Is this the skill and cunning that saw you inducted into the spook trade?"

"If you know so much, why not apport into the Cadre yourself?"

"There are supernatural barriers about the insufferable place. A glamour to keep the uninitiated out—or rather, the ostracized. Though the forest does provide a neutral ground, I can only enter if my familiar is there first."

"Ostracized?" Jack questioned.

The demon jerked its head dismissively. "I was once a favored consultant to the bloody ingrates. Until I was falsely accused of murder."

"False? I've witnessed your crime, Beryth. There was nothing whatsoever false about it."

"Ah, my unknowing familiar. You've just now figured we're attached?"

Why answer the obvious?

"Want to kill me, Jack?"

"More than I wish to live."

"Ah, so heroic."

"I'm no one's hero."

"Ooo, a *hero*. Is that what she thinks of you? Poor girl. She'll be tragically disappointed. I suppose you're biding your time, marking the perfect moment when you'll have the kill shot." Beryth lifted the gun and aimed.

Right for Jack's heart.

Jack stretched back his shoulders, lifting his chest. He avoided the demon's gaze—there lay madness—instead focusing on the glisten of black talon that tapped the trigger.

Against all better judgment, Jack took a step forward. He didn't want to move and yet his left foot stepped again. He moved until he pressed his chest right into the gun barrel. He winced at the cut of hard steel into his flesh.

Much as he wanted to slap away the danger, to step back, he could not. His fingers clenched, shaking as he tried to resist. Sweat pearled down his scalp.

"You. Are. Mine," Beryth said in a deep, hollow voice, void of humanity. "It is dread you crave, and dread you shall have."

"I don't crave it," Jack spat out.

"Ah, but you do. It is what called me to the warehouse. Your dread over the woman."

"I didn't feel that dread until I saw you rip out her heart. You were there first."

"Just so." The demon grinned. "You know it cost a fortune to have a passage opened. Had to trade a pact of never-ending malice to get those ridiculous sidhe to work the spell."

"So I didn't lead you here."

"Yes and no. I've had my eye on you for a long time, Jack the Demon Frightener."

The only other time Jack had heard that moniker was from the woman in the field when he was a child. And yet, he'd thought of it ever after.

"You know, Jack, I can make you reach down and pull the trigger, if I so wish."

Cringing against the movement of his hand, up, toward the rifle, Jack spat out, "Go ahead! Blast me to bits. Then who will lead you into the Cadre?"

"You'll do it?" The gun barrel fell from his chest. The persuasion released, Jack stumbled backward. The demon set the M4 aside on the couch, picked up the glass ball and tossed it a few times. The glass hit its red leathery palm with a smack. "No more mistakes?"

"'Course not." Catching his palms on his knees, Jack heaved against the exertion that had been required to keep from touching the trigger. "Whatever you want." Arsehole. "But it'll take some time. She's not going to lead me in."

He didn't mean a word of it, but appeasing the beast required the lie.

"She will, Jack. You just have to step up the seduction. Shall I send another lust demon?"

"Sodding hell, that was you?"

"One of my many minions. Though you didn't seem to have difficulty yesterday evening. She does purr sweetly when she comes." The demon held the ball up to the lamplight, considering. "You are aware this thing has no power, Jack."

"Fuck off."

"Oh, I'll fuck something. Something that means the world to you. Like she did."

Fighting the rising dread, Jack tried to remain impartial, to not give the demon any fuel. Is that how it held its connection to this realm? By committing heinous acts and feeding on the dread of tapped familiars, like him?

"Our coming together wasn't coincidental," Beryth said. "It's never random, Jack. You led me to her."

Jack shook his head vigorously.

"You once gave up on believing. Remember that, Jack, boy? When you thought to cause oh, so many horrors? But then this thing brought back the belief." It tossed the ball high, almost touching the ceiling. It landed in Beryth's palm with a hollow smack. "You remember now, what it's like to believe. To know? To feel? To believe in dreadsome nightmares and all that cannot be altered? I merely followed that belief. Her heart was…delicious."

"Damn you!"

"Good, Jack. Let it all out. Soon enough you won't need me."

"I never asked for you. I didn't call you to me!"

The demon tilted its horned head. It had begun to change, to become more grotesquely exaggerated in every portion of its structure. The suit seams began to rip away over the expanding red muscles.

"You did, Jack. I have breathed in your dread, and I find it most tasty. Catch."

It tossed the ball and Jack caught it. His flesh smoked and he dropped the thing onto the carpeted floor. Welts formed instantly on his palms.

"I'll be watching you." A talon snapped out and tipped Jack beneath the chin. He felt his flesh open and out oozed the dusty scent of blood. "If you do not please me, Demon Frightener, well then…I shall have to break the lovely Miss Bane's neck."

The beast twisted its claws to demonstrate the breaking of a human neck.

"You're not thinking this through correctly, Beryth. With both Mersey and I dead, then how will you get inside?"

"There's more than one mortal in this world. Dread abounds. I've merely to tap into it."

"What is it inside the Cadre that you need?"

"What I *want* is revenge. What I *need* no longer exists. The Cadre is responsible for that. They will suffer, one and all of them. Including your Mersey."

Muscles tight and pulsing, the sweat rolled from Jack's head and chest. Again, the response was uncontrollable. He really was the demon's bitch. *Better that way.* That meant there was not an innocent mortal having to deal with this monster.

"You harm her, I'll kill you."

Beryth chuckled. "I would adore the pain, Jack boy. But I cannot harm the bitch so long as she wears those rings."

Rings that were shedding from her as if layers from an onion. Did the demon know that? Was it causing them to break?

Beryth misted above him, half formed, half dark smoke.

Jack grabbed the glass ball, still molten hot, and thrust it. The demon took the projectile at the back of its head. A wicked burst of brilliant white light ignited in a star design out from the target. It yowled. The ball dropped to the floor.

Beryth disappeared.

"Bloody hell," Jack muttered.

He swiped up the ball and, now cooler, held it firmly. "There's something to this thing that frightens demons."

Had to be. He just felt it.

Swiping away the dribble of blood from under his chin, he then curled the ball against his chest, his fingers wrapping it securely. "Think I'll hang on to it a while longer."

Dashing down the hallway, Mersey headed to the Cadre archives. A vast library was housed in the center of St. Yve manor and was capped with a gorgeous stained-glass cupola that Mersey had many times climbed up into and had got lost in a book.

She knew all the volumes on demon lore and faeries—she'd developed a keen interest in the sidhe at the age of sixteen, after she had first noticed Raskin.

Now, she went directly to the volume she considered an omnibus version of some of the larger demon directories. Bound in red leather and printed with ornate gilt lettering, it contained pictures and brief descriptions of both the *daemon sapiens* and *daemon incultus.*

There must be a picture of Beryth in here somewhere. Her mother had only once described the demon, but it had been a vivid description. Mersey had been nine, so she wasn't too clear on the name, or if her mother *had* even named it.

Tucking the book under her arm, she walked right into Lady Aurora. Ever a shock to run into the sterner of the twins, Mersey always knew immediately it was Aurora for her straight mouth. Lady Dawn's greetings were usually accompanied by a bright smile.

"Lady Aurora, I didn't hear you come in. I thought I was alone."

Taller than Mersey by a head, the auburn-haired director tilted aside the book Mersey held to read the spine. "Research?"

"Always." She made to pass by Aurora, but the woman stepped to block her.

"You in a hurry?"

"On my way to London. Er…I think I've a lead on the leak at the warehouse."

"So the retrieval is coming along well?"

"I've determined the passage was opened from the dark realm."

"You'll have to employ an adept to close it."

"Yes, tomorrow night, the moon will be full. Perfect time to close up a passage."

"Do you want me to do it?"

The only other option was the earl, and Mersey didn't talk to the old man unless she met him while out jogging the trail—and then it was merely a *hello* and *good day*. "Would you?"

"I can." The ruby-and-gold ring Aurora wore flashed as she stroked her hair away from her face. Mersey knew that ring had history, something about it containing a demon—yet she also knew Aurora hated demons. "So, anything you want to talk about?"

Since when did she care? "Nope. I'm good."

Still, Aurora blocked her escape. The overwhelming sensation that she was being assessed and measured spilled across Mersey like spiders creeping over her flesh. "Are you happy here, Mersey?"

Mersey toyed with the leather spine of the book. What an exact question. She'd never been close to Lady Aurora, finding her sister much more amiable and even on occasion fun during sidhe parties in the woods.

"Why do you ask?" And why now? After all this time, and when Mersey was so ready to leave this place behind.

"I sense your discontent. It waves off you like an aura."

Mersey lifted her eyes to met Aurora's. "Honestly? I'm not sure where I belong lately. The Cadre is my family, but…I think I want more."

Lady Aurora nodded. "*More* is one of those indistinct words that really means you're not sure how to deal with what you have."

Right then. Mersey tapped the book spine, avoiding the woman's seeking gaze. What did she have? Besides one messed-up life?

"I've watched you grow up, Mersey. Your skills in the field are to be admired, and you're smart, not about to fall to demon influence. Your contributions to the Cadre have been invaluable. We'd really hate to see you leave."

"Oh, I…" She suspected Mersey might leave? *Would* she?

Only if the hero snapped her up and galloped off into the sunset with her.

"Like I said, it's just something I've been thinking about. Not decided, or anything. I um…should be going."

"Tomorrow night, then?"

"Er, yes. I'll…" Pray Jack was no longer the dread demon's familiar by then. Which should require a bloody miracle. "See you then."

Chapter 20

Miss Accidental Goth stood before him, wearing a tight black-and-gray striped shirt that had dangly lace stuff around the wrists, à la pirate gear, and the cargo pants were actually a skirt now he looked, though it seemed like pants that had been pulled apart and sewn open.

To top it all off, she smelled like lemon pie and cozy afternoon tea.

She'd come to his flat, toting along a heavy book, which she now splayed open upon her lap as she sat Indian-style on his couch.

"Ah, you pried out the ball," she commented, tapping the glass ball that rolled to her thigh on the couch cushion. "You could hang a picture over the hole in the wall."

"Good idea." Jack hadn't considered that. What a woman's touch couldn't do to a man's flat. He sat on the arm of the couch next to her and kissed the crown of her head. "So you're not angry with me today?"

"Nope. I've decided it's stupid to remain angry, especially

when you have every right to be cautious about me. But I do know how I feel about you, and that won't change."

Her smile did something to his insides. Jack felt his heart open wide and grab out for Mersey. She fit him well. They were two alike, despite working for opposing teams. This bit of all right he wanted to keep in his life.

So don't mess it up, Jack boy.

That was not the demon's voice. Couldn't be. Could it?

Jack searched the room, but didn't see or smell demonic presence. But he wouldn't let down his guard.

Wrapping an arm around Mersey's shoulders, but keeping his senses alert, Jack leaned over the book. "So what are we looking for in the book?"

"A picture of Beryth," she said. "These rings." She fluttered the fingers on her right hand. "They were bespelled to specifically protect me from a demon my mother described to me when I was a child. I don't think she ever named it, but I have a creepy feeling that your demon might be mine."

"Slide over." She did, and Jack settled in next to her and nudged his nose up to the sweet lemon darkness of her hair. "You always smell so good."

"Jack, will you concentrate? Find the picture, then we'll snog."

"Promise?"

"You won't be able to keep me from your lips."

"Right then."

While he paged through the book, Mersey tossed and caught the ball in her palm. "This is crystal, isn't it?"

"No, just glass. A gift from my aunt when I was eight. She might have been a witch."

"Really? Well. It's filled with wonder." She pressed it to her forehead and smiled. "Lots of wonder."

Jack had to smirk at her mystical attempt at figuring the thing. "What makes you say that? You got some woo-woo powers?"

"I'm a familiar, Jack, not a witch."

"I'm not as up on all the paranormal creep—er, sorts—as I should be. I specialize in demons and leave everything else for the gray seekers."

"The gray seekers?" she said in a marveled hush.

"Yeah, er, forget that. I didn't tell you what I just told you."

"Right. P-Cell secrets. I can play the game."

Another toss of the ball and she held it out at arm's length, squinting as if to peer into its center.

Wonders, indeed.

Oh, that he had ever shown her his initial reaction when learning she was a familiar. But he knew better now. And the demon was right. Belief had returned. He'd once possessed childhood marvel. Adulthood robbed a man of the mystical, the enchanted and the wondrous. Only now could Jack begin to acknowledge the wisdom of a child's intuition.

"Mersey, I'm sorry. I know I continue to offend you, but you've got to understand, this is all very new to me. Until a few months ago I never believed in demons and faeries and familiars and all that woo-woo stuff."

"That's another lie."

"What?"

"This," she said, holding the ball between the two of them. "You once believed."

"You think you know me so well?"

"Well enough. And don't give me the 'I've grown up and know better now' response," Mersey said. "You would have tossed this long ago if you didn't harbor some belief."

It wasn't fair that she knew him better than he knew himself. But he kind of liked it. As much as he enjoyed kissing the crease of her inner elbow and nestling his body up against hers as they made love.

Could they drop the pretense and the fact that they should be enemies and spend the afternoon making love between warm sheets?

"Fine. I once believed, until bad things started happening and

I decided I wouldn't believe an more. Now that I've been living the proof every day, it's slowly sinking back in. I've got a thick skull. So forgive me for my insensitivity?"

Thrusting a finger to her lips, her all-seeing green gaze took him in. A woman ought not to pout so sweetly; she could lure in all sorts. Like a lovestruck demon hunter.

Lovestruck?

"Forgiven."

"What?"

"You heard me," she singsonged.

Right. But he was still stuck on the lovestruck part. Was he?

"As for this ball of wonders—" Jack leaned forward onto the open book, but didn't touch the ball she still held "—I think it has some power."

"I'm sure it does. It was infused with very strong childhood magic. Nothing can overcome the innocent belief of a child."

Mersey made the strangest sense in a world of strangeness. "Whatever it was, it did a nasty to the demon Beryth," he said.

"You saw it again?"

"It was waiting for me in my flat this morning *after* I woke from being lost in a snowstorm. In the middle of September. You have something to do with that?"

"There are guardians who inhabit the bordering forest and protect the Cadre from unauthorized access. I did warn you, but you had to try, didn't you?"

"It isn't like me to give up easily."

"I wouldn't expect otherwise. You're safe though?"

"A lot better condition than my car. The front end is smashed. About the same as Beryth's skull. I used that ball. That's the second time I hit the thing with it."

"Second? When was the first?"

"When I was a kid."

Mersey tilted her head. "So, you've seen it before? And you know it to be the same dread demon?"

"Yep. And…" He studied the woodcut of the dread demon on the page before him. "I do believe this is the bastard, right here."

Mersey tossed the ball to the couch and grabbed the book to twist it and inspect the photo. She ran her fingertips across the page, taking in every part of the demon's structure, and then tapped it. "It could be the same. Red and muscled, and lots of horns. I remember my mother telling me about the horns."

She twisted a ring on her finger. "Why are they breaking? If this is the same demon, and it's connected to you?" She looked into his eyes. "Do I need to be wary of you, Jack?"

"Mersey, don't say that."

"I don't mean it like that. I trust you. But, if this demon is attached to you, and you've no control over it, it could harm me?"

"I won't let anything harm you Mersey. You can believe I won't rest until Beryth and I have come to arms again."

"You intend to kill it?"

"Hell, yes."

"Bloodthirsty crew of hunters you work for."

"Bloodthirsty is fine with me when it serves the greater good. We protect mankind from the terror of a demon invasion."

"I do the same thing, Jack. Without violence. Besides, I can't believe you buy into that. Demons are not going to *invade*. They're simply here because they've been called."

"Beryth said the same thing. That I called him here. I did no such thing."

"It's not as if you holler out an invite. Demons are attracted to human emotion, to a strong need, loss or desire. Dread."

"I know that. But if your mother wanted to protect you from Beryth, then shouldn't you be glad I'm going to take care of it?"

"At the risk to harming another? Jack! You're the demon's familiar. You kill it, you kill yourself."

The silence stabbed at Jack. Hell, he hadn't thought of it that way. His own death to set a small portion of his world right? It should make him pause, but all his life Jack had stepped to the front, determined to protect, and never mind his own life. If he could make a change, then it was all worth it.

"If it'll save you, then that's a risk I need to take."

"Don't talk like that. I don't need you to die for me. In fact, I'd prefer you stick around. I'd miss your kisses."

"And I'd miss the taste of you." He kissed the side of her neck, but Mersey wasn't into it so much.

"How to make you see the other side of the dark realm?" she said. And then her eyes alighted. "What if you met my friends? I work with a number of *paras* every day. They're wonderful. They are as determined to understand their more violent counterparts as I am. If only you could come to the Cadre."

Now there was an opening he couldn't refuse. "So it's a date?"

"Oh, no you don't, hotshot. I see what you're trying to do. I'd be expelled from the Cadre if I ever allowed P-Cell inside. It's bad enough I'm carrying on with you."

"Yet you want me to learn empathy toward the OEs. Well, it isn't going to happen out here where they pop out from my walls and attack me."

"It's because you're a familiar; you're attracting them to your home."

That had not occurred to him. He really must get Beryth off his back—without leading him to the Cadre, where he might then go after Mersey.

"I can get you that ward," Mersey said. "Something nonviolent to protect your flat from intrusion."

"Of course, no violence. Invite the demon in and offer it some tea, will you? I think it's all about perception. Trust me, if you let those OEs out into the real world, they show their real colors. And those colors are bloodred. You haven't seen anything until you've watched a demon tear out your best friend's heart and consume it before you."

"Your best friend?"

Now he stood and paced to the window. Easier to avoid

sentiment when he didn't have to look at another person's face. The conversation had taken a turn down a road he had tried to avoid. Did he want to pull onto it completely and make the drive?

"A buddy you worked with?" she prompted.

Buddy. Friend. Would-be lover.

If only he had been honest with her.

"My partner, Monica Price. We were together for two years at MI5. We were on a stakeout, she had insinuated herself inside. I should have gone into the building sooner. I knew something was wrong when she didn't answer me. Bugger!"

He clamped a hand over his chest. Still he stood with his back to Mersey. "I felt different afterward, but not as if I'd been tapped. I thought it was grief, and of course there was the whole 'they exist' thing to deal with. I hadn't thought about things like that since I was a kid."

"I'm sorry."

From behind him, Mersey spread her hands down his arms. This touch he took easily. Or maybe resolutely. He didn't know how to react to her anymore. Because if he followed his heart, he'd turn and pull her into an embrace, and seek to shield his dark memories by diving into her sensual pull.

"Did you love her?" she asked.

"I…respected her. Yes, I loved Monica." Not until now had he put it out there in the open, for anyone to hear and know. It felt…odd. Was he lying to himself?

Mersey deepened the embrace and her cheek snugged against the back of his shoulder. "To be loved by a man like you must have meant the world to her."

"I never told her." Throat dry, Jack swallowed. This was it; he was exposing the softest part of himself to her now. "I'm such an idiot. Telling her wouldn't have stopped her from thinking she could do the undercover assignment on her own. It wouldn't have stopped that damned demon— I can feel Beryth in the scar on my chest. Twice now since her death, Beryth has come to me, but I've been literally paralyzed, so I couldn't blast it. I've failed."

"It's an air demon. It can utilize human breath to draw in power and the human's thoughts and emotions. You need merely breathe and you fuel Beryth."

"So I need to stop breathing? Which could be solved with Beryth's destruction."

"Jack, no."

"I want you to be safe, Mersey."

"The hunter wants that. But what about the man? Don't you want to be around…for me? Show me how you feel about me, Jack." She reached for him, but he flinched and tilted his head away from her touch. "Please?"

Indecision warred with Jack's features.

He bowed his head and fell to his knees before Mersey, encircling her waist with his arms and pressing his head against her ribs. She smoothed her fingers over his short-cropped hair.

"This is how I feel about you, Mersey Bane," he breathed against her body. "I want to lose myself inside you. You make me believe in good things, that maybe I should give the world a second glance."

Closing her eyes, Mersey nodded. "It's worth another look."

She bent to kiss him, and Jack pulled down the front of her shirt to kiss the crescent mark on her breast.

"You think so?" she murmured, eyes dancing in challenge.

"I know so, little girl. Let's shag."

"How can I resist a romantic come-on like that?"

Jack sat on the curb outside his building. It was barely seven in the morning. The roads were empty of traffic and a light mist shrouded the city. Cool rain dusted his face. After making love until the wee hours, he'd woken to find Mersey's side of the bed cool. Shards from yet another ring had been tucked in a fold of the sheets.

She'd just left? Without so much as a note. She had to be the singularly most frustrating woman he'd ever met.

A black cat curled its tail along Jack's back. The thing purred so loudly, Jack took the hint and reached out to scratch under its chin. That, it loved, so much so that it climbed onto Jack's lap and put its paws up on his chest.

More, it seemed to say with a *meowr.*

"You like affection, eh, pussycat?" He obligingly scratched, slicking away the jewels of rain tipping the cat's fur, and the purrs hummed against his chest, chasing away his frazzled thoughts. Breathing deeply the misted air, Jack drew in calm, and nodded. "Gorgeous black fur. And you're talkative, aren't you? Just like a woman I know. She purrs when she comes. It's amazing."

Jack bracketed the cat's head and peered into its vivid green eyes. "There's something familiar about your eyes."

The green eyes glinted and smiled. The cat did not stop purring, in fact, its noise increased, as if pleased.

"Mersey? Nod your head if this is you."

The cat tilted its head, purring even louder.

"That could have been a nod. Blimey. So it's really you?" He gave her neck another scratch. "Why'd you leave? Need to do some prowling? I guess I can understand. Don't worry, it doesn't bother me."

And it didn't, for reasons he couldn't even touch. All Jack knew was that Mersey sat on his lap purring, and nothing felt more right in the world. He stroked her fur and coiled his fingers down her sleek tail.

"So this whole familiar thing is a little weird. Maybe you can teach me things?"

"Sure," a voice said from behind him. Mersey, the human-form woman Jack knew, squatted beside him and patted the cat on the head. "First lesson? Sometimes a cat is just a cat."

"Oh, Christ." Jack shoved the cat away and it mewled in protest.

Stretching out her legs and heeling her boots into the tarmac, Mersey shooed away the curious cat. She wore striped tights beneath the long skirt and combat boots. "Did you think that was me?"

"Of course not. Er, where did you come from?"

"That way." She pointed down the roadway and then settled closer to him on the curb. "Should I be jealous that you're cozying up with other kitties?"

Relieved she was teasing, yet still embarrassed that he'd been holding conversation with a plain old cat, Jack leaned forward, elbows to knees and shook his head.

"I just thought… I know familiars change to cats and vice versa. Why did you leave?"

She hefted a grocery bag. "Thought I'd make breakfast. Were you looking for me?"

"Yes."

"Sorry, I should have left a note. So you know about a familiar's ability to change shapes?"

"Actually, I've known since I was eight."

"Ah. The same year you received the ball of wonder from your aunt?"

"Yep. I used to live in the countryside, west of Shrewsbury. A big oak forest backed up to our land. I played in it every day."

"I love forests. They're so magical."

"So it would seem. Your St. Yve wood isn't particularly normal."

"Normal is so dull."

"Since knowing you, that is a philosophy I can completely get behind."

He kissed her mouth and rubbed his cheek aside hers, catching a low-toned purr. God, he loved her purrs.

"Anyway, I was out one night, lurking along the borders of the forest, as I usually did. I was a boy. That's what we did—lurk. Had my trusty wishing ball with me."

"A symbol of mystical and dark enchantments. Were you trying to conjure magic?"

Jack shrugged and swiped a hand over his five o'clock stubbled chin. "I suppose so. I don't remember what I said exactly, or how it happened, when suddenly this cat padded right across my chest and scampered off and into a clearing. I was about to throw a stone at it, when it changed."

He had never recounted the happening. Not even to his parents. It felt right now; he trusted Mersey. A child's curious excitement stirred in his belly.

"The cat changed into a woman. A naked woman. And she was fat."

"Jack!"

"Though, to look back now, I know that she was pregnant. She was glowing and had long black hair, same color as the cat. She scampered across the field, and before she disappeared into the forest, she turned and looked right at me and winked."

"You witnessed a familiar changing. Jack, that's so awesome."

"Awesome? I was scared out of my gourd. And not so much at seeing a cat change to a lady, but for seeing a naked lady, you understand? I wasn't yet at the age where I could appreciate a naked woman."

"You've grown into a very appreciative man."

"I have." He nuzzled into her palm and kissed it, finding her heat delicious. "Anyway, that's when the demon appeared above the woman. It was going to hurt her, I knew it. So I threw the glass ball and hit it."

"Really?"

"I pitched for my school's cricket team. I thought I'd defeated a monster, you know? Then it came after me and touched me with its long tongue."

"Tapped you?"

"I don't think so. It wasn't painful, just frightening. There was a burn on my shirt for which I got switched later—but it didn't hurt."

"Interesting. Demons usually don't tap young mortal children. If anything, they usually go for the pubescent girls."

"You mean *Exorcist* kind of stuff?"

Mersey shrugged. "Never heard much about them."

Interesting that she didn't know about exorcisms. P-Cell had trained him in the rare event he came upon a possessed human. Exorcisms were one thing Jack hoped never to have to perform.

"Anyway, I ran straight home and locked myself in my room. I shoved that strange glass ball deep into my sock drawer."

"And you never tried your magic again?"

"It wasn't *my* magic. It wasn't even the gazing ball. I know now, it was being in the right place at the wrong time. Though at the time I believed it magic."

"You still do. Admit it. You need to begin to recognize that belief, Jack the Demon Frightener."

"What did you say?"

"I called you Jack the Demon Frightener. Because you are."

"That's the same thing the lady said after I'd scared the demon away. And then later—"

"She came back to you?"

"Yes, and…yes. It was weird, and at the time, scared the shivers from me. Later that night, when the moon was high and my folks were snoring in the next room, there was this awful scratching noise at my window. I knew right away it was that bloody cat. I pressed my nose to the window, but wasn't about to open it."

"You thought you'd be inviting a naked fat lady into your room?"

"Oh, you know it!" He clasped both her hands and held them to his mouth a moment, as he hid his guilty smile, "So, the cat sat there, incessantly scratching, then finally it opened it jaws and out dropped a black ring onto the sill. Then it leapt to the ground and scurried away."

"A black ring?"

"Yes. Like the ones you wear. Anyway, I didn't dare open the window, and by morning I had forgotten all about it. I didn't remember until days later when I was chasing a cricket around the house and saw that ring. I thought it was cursed, so I took it and buried it— Mersey?"

She stood up beside him, her fingers working in balls clasped before her.

"What's wrong? Did I say something?"

"Huh? No. Er, you buried the ring? Did you ever dig it up?"

"Hell, no. It's probably part of a grand old oak tree now. Right at the edge of the forest where I used to go to hide in the branches when Mum called me to take a bath."

"I've got to go." She shoved the groceries into his hands and took off. "Sorry! Rain check on breakfast."

"But, Mersey, wait!"

She was already running—*running*—away from him.

For the life of him, Jack couldn't figure what he'd said wrong.

"Not this time," he muttered as he stood and raced after her. "No more running. We're going to start talking, Mersey Bane. If it kills us."

Chapter 21

After running up to his flat for the keys, Jack commandeered the Range Rover and quickly tracked Mersey's white Volkswagen.

This time he wasn't concerned so much with losing her because he remembered the drive. At least, until he got as far as where the snowstorm had struck. So far, the sky looked clear, no flakes in sight.

On the passenger seat, the glass ball rocked with the motion of the car. He didn't think about why he'd brought that along. It had been a feeling that Jack reacted to, so he'd grabbed it as he'd left his flat.

He wasn't prepared when the road came to a complete end. No left turn. No right access. The road just ended. And yet he could still see Mersey's taillights straight ahead.

"Lovely. Just bloody rich. Now what, wise guy?"

Mersey ran down the hallway to the private residents' quarters. She didn't stop until the bed in her room caught her body. She slid across the old handmade quilt spotted with tufts of faded red yarn, her fingers landing on the drawer pull of the Louis XIV nightstand. Inside sat a small red glass box, no larger than a tin of breath mints.

Heartbeats pounding in anticipation, she sat cross-legged on the bed and huddled over the treasure.

Inside, one remaining hematite ring slid across the mirrored bottom as she tilted it. She took it out and held it before her, slinking backward to lie on the bed.

She had always worn eight of the rings on her right hand. Protection. But two remained. Her mother had had the rings bespelled before Mersey's birth. She'd gifted them to Mersey on her tenth birthday—three days before Mirabelle Bane's death.

A twinge of sadness tugged at the corner of Mersey's mouth. It was almost as if her mother had known she was not long for this earth. Mersey distinctly recalled how upset she'd been to see her mother packing up valuables and giving away her clothes. "Only the necessities," Mirabelle Bane had said to her daughter. "I don't need things. They're just clutter." Even Mirabelle's assignments with the Cadre had come to completion a week before Mersey's birthday.

An ache had grown in her gut, as Mersey silently stood by, not daring to ask her mother if she had plans to flee or run off. Something ominous was about to happen.

Mirabelle Bane's body had never been found. Mersey had cried for weeks.

She would never forget the portentous words her mother had given her that evening she'd gifted Mersey the red glass box. "Inside are nine, for you. But there are ten in total. Thanks to the spell, they will protect and alert you to danger—most especially to a particular demon—but they are not armor."

Mersey had nodded and tried on a few. The smaller rings had loosely fit her thumb. Not until her teens had she been able to wear them all. The right hand represented her future. As a palm reader, her mother had told Mersey her left hand represented her past, and one should cherish memories, but never seek to protect them. The past must remain as it was. Mersey had chosen to wear eight of the rings, thinking one must be preserved in case the others were lost.

"Or broken," she whispered now.

"Ten total?" Mersey had questioned her mother because her little box had contained but nine.

"There is one other," Mirabelle had said, with a twinkle to her emerald eyes.

Mersey rolled over on the bed now and sought the square of green calico she'd oft traced when younger. The brilliant emerald of her mother's eyes forever preserved in this palm-sized square of fabric.

"I've given it to the one whom I approve for you, daughter," her mother had said. "You will know him when you see a similar ring on his finger, and he will tell you a cat gave it to him."

The cat? Mersey's mother in feline shape. She had chosen Mersey's mate while Mersey yet grew in her belly.

She was a naked fat lady. I know now that she was pregnant.

"My mother approved Jack Harris?" Mersey slipped the ninth, and largest, ring down her thumb. "He must have been so young then. How could my mother have known? And how could she guess I would ever see him in my lifetime?"

But he didn't wear the ring.

They were fashioned from common hematite, actually mass-made and sold in huge bowls at festivals and shops. Mersey had seen them many times.

Jack could have been talking about any ring. Not necessarily the one ring Mirabelle Bane had bespelled and then had given to a boy. Any boy in this whole, huge world.

Of course, it would be an incredible coincidence that Jack had witnessed a familiar transforming to human shape as a child. And to have that same familiar then drop a hematite ring outside his bedroom window?

Had the one man her mother approved for Mersey actually found her?

"I must find out for sure—" she sat up on the bed "—if Jack is the one."

Jack peered through an iron gate and across the small flowered front yard nestled before a cozy cottage. Covered over with climbing vines and blooming white and pink flowers, the home looked like a faery-tale retreat where the princess always fled, yet found dark, growling evils waiting for her within.

He tried the gate, but it wouldn't budge. Two stone gargoyles guarded each post. Their wings spanned across the gate, touching in the middle. There was no sign of a latch.

He'd seen light from the road, a glimmer like a winking eye.

"Hello?" he called.

A pulse in his chest, behind the scar, alerted him. Was Beryth with him? He searched the sky, knowing he would not see the demon. A sniff didn't scent brimstone.

Something shifted in the garden. The swaying red-petaled flowers and lavender stalks couldn't disguise a garish orange frock. A little old lady?

"I'm lost!" Jack tried. "I need directions, if you please."

If he could get through this gate, he felt sure access to the Cadre would follow.

Both gargoyles silently growled at him, their wings canopied over his head, the talons digging into the stone pedestals. In preparation to attack?

Jack slid a hand behind his back, securing the gun tucked in his waistband. Another pulse at his scar made him wince. The gun was loaded with salt shells. If Beryth was lingering close by, he'd be ready.

"I've lost my traveling companion," he called. "Mersey Bane? She's a good friend."

The orange frock swirled about, and though the distance was

too far for Jack to get a good fix on the face, he did see the waving hand. But it wasn't a friendly wave. More…commanding?

A hush of hot air stole over Jack's scalp.

Instinct scurried a chill shiver up his spine. Beryth?

Stepping back and looking up out of the corner of his eye, he verified that the hot air had come from now-moving stone jaws. Wings spread, and a silent stony yowl took escape.

Not the demon Beryth, but something more startling.

"Right then. Not the friendly sorts, are you?"

Backing slowly down the pathway he'd come, Jack tugged out his gun.

The first gargoyle took to flight. The wingspan stretched ten feet and gushed the air with a mighty rumble.

Taking aim, Jack pulled the trigger. Stone exploded and scattered. Jack turned and broke into a sprint. The second gargoyle cut through the sky behind him. The noise of its wings was like rocks tumbling down the side of a stony outcrop.

He stumbled on a tree root. Lunging forward, but not falling, he twisted a look over his shoulder. The gargoyle had not entered the thick copse of white birch that lined the roadway. Couldn't stretch out its wings between the close-spaced trunks, no doubt.

Bugger it, he'd been chased off by a pair of rocks!

Climbing the ditch to the road, Jack pulled himself up and looked down the road beyond his car. A figure framed by bril-liant sunlight stood fifty yards away. Slender hair moving gently in the breeze, she beckoned to him.

Chapter 22

Mersey rushed to Jack as he neared the car and spread her arms around his shoulders. Lifting her, he supported her fey weight and kissed her soundly.

Had she returned to gloat that she'd yet again given him the slip? And almost to his detriment? This hug didn't feel at all wallowing. And the kiss was unfettered by reluctance.

He wanted to show Mersey he needed her. Craved her. Felt as if she were the only one for him.

He buried his nose in her loose hair and held her until the eerie shivers he'd gained during the flight from the gate dissipated. Together they sought sanity in the embrace. A kiss tore away Jack's final bits of reluctance. And then it was all good. Mersey in his arms. Mersey at his mouth. Mersey all over him—

"What are you doing wandering the road all by yourself?"

"I've had a change of heart," she said as he set her down. Reaching up, she corralled her long hair into a ponytail behind her head and then let the silken strands swish back down her shoulders.

"You need to see inside the Cadre, Jack. To learn about us. To know that not all *paras* are dangerous and worthy of your violence."

What was this woman up to? To completely reverse her stand? Had she been ordered by someone higher up to bring him inside? So the Cadre would have leverage over P-Cell by using one of their men? Why would they need leverage?

"Is this a direct order?"

"Huh? No, I... No, in effect, I'll be sneaking you in."

"I don't want you to get in trouble. Rules were made to be followed."

"Jack, the rules will separate you and I forever if they find out I've been consorting with P-Cell. But I have to do this. You need to know the truth. It's not a spooky fun house of creatures, it's just a normal manor—well, okay, so not *normal*. Will you come inside with me?"

Crossing his arms, Jack scanned the stretch of roadside. Not so much as a cricket chirping. Made sense, when the forest was guarded by nasty stone gargoyles.

If she possessed an ulterior motive, he couldn't figure it.

"Brilliant." He reached inside the Range Rover and retrieved the keys. Turning, he again found himself in Mersey's arms. The smell of her—sweet and citrusy, eatable—did things to his staunch desire to remain impartial until he knew what she was up to.

"Kiss me again," she whispered and slid her hands over his chest.

Her lips brushed his, a cool petal against stone. A sigh tickled his mouth. Unwilling to resist, Jack lifted Mersey up to sit upon the hood. She wrapped her legs around his hips.

"What are you up to, Mersey? Tell me, because you're driving me crazy."

"I'm just kissing you."

"Kissing me or killing me? You want to lead me inside a place forbidden to outsiders? Do you have ulterior intentions? I've just been chased out of that damned forest by two gargoyles. Living stone things. One chomp and I'm pretty sure I would have been monster supper."

"The threshold guardians," she said between kisses. And caresses, and slipping her hands up under his shirt. Wanting and greedy, she wouldn't allow him to deny the touch. "No one ever gets past them, or Ophelia."

"Ophelia?"

"Sweet little old lady who lives in the cottage."

"Let me guess—she has sharp teeth?"

"Even sharper senses. But we can avoid them if we take the back route on the ever-changing trail. Jack, I know this forest like I know my heart."

"Is that so?" He slid his palm over her soft sweater and nestled it below her breast. A strong, proud heartbeat there. And softness that tangled with his need to remain hard, impermeable and staunch. "And what does your heart say to you?"

"You really want to know?" So much wonder in her tone.

He considered it for a long moment. Darkness kissed his cheek. No, that was Mersey. And there, she traced the curve of his scar so that he sucked in a breath. She wore the proverbial heart on her sleeve. She was open to wonder and enchanted him with an electric draw. He was everything she was not, yet he wanted only to stand in her splendor and wish it to seep into him.

"Yes," he finally said, "I want to know what your heart knows."

"He is the one."

Spoken so distinctly, and without pause, Jack felt it like a shove against his chest. He pulled away and stepped around in front of the car. For he struggled with shapes inside himself that were dark and unwilling to be changed.

The one? He was no one's *one.*

"What sort of faery-tale nightmare are you playing with me, Mersey?"

"It's not a game. I thought we both felt the same way about each other?"

"Yes, but…"

Her hand slipped into his. He hadn't heard her shift from the car hood, yet now she stood next to him, her arm tight to his side and her head pressed against his shoulder. "You're the hero, Jack. The one my heart has always pined for."

He glanced to the corner of the car where the hood had been crunched into a wedge following his adventure in the snowstorm. First, the one, and now a hero?

Too trusting, this woman. It hurt Jack's heart that he could not embrace her so easily as she desired.

"I'm going to disappoint you, Mersey."

"Never." Soft, slightly cool lips met his in a sensual explosion of heat, and he couldn't make himself not kiss her back.

How one person could have so much faith in him frightened more than a brimstone-stinking dread demon. He didn't want to disappoint Mersey. But he didn't know how to make her imagined dreams of chivalry and romance come true.

The world didn't work that way. Not anymore. It had become every man for himself. Women and children first, but only if they could run fast enough, or if they had an armed man before them leading the way. Jack wanted to lead the way, but he wasn't sure Mersey would follow. She was too strong to be led.

Her warmth slipped away, and she stepped over to the edge of the road. Would she slip so easily from his life? Could he be the hero she wanted?

"Come on, Jack! I want to slip in during the night."

"The night?" Jack looked to the forest, and indeed, it had darkened. Yet, here on the road it was day.

"The rainbow will guide us."

"The rainbow?" He followed as Mersey tugged him along.

"The rainbow is always brightest at night and it ends right over the manor."

Jack felt the ground slope and he knew they were taking the ditch. It had become that dark. He gripped Mersey's hand, figuring if she were a familiar— "Can you see like a cat?"

"I can."

"Right then. Is it day or night right now?" He took another step, but Mersey had stopped.

"Day. But the forest changes at whim. I'd never lead you in if it was true night, because mortals who enter at night can never leave. And because it's so strange, you must promise me one thing before we enter the forest, Jack."

"What's that?"

She clasped his hand and stood up on tiptoes, and her breath dusted his chin. He thought she wanted another kiss and so bent close. Instead she whispered, "Don't let go of my hand. Ever. If you do, you will become pisky led, and you'll never find your way home."

"Pisky led?" Though the forest was dark, the sensation that they were being watched was very strong. "I believe it."

"Do you trust me?"

The question of the moment. With all his heart he wanted to trust this woman. And to walk through the forest, literally blind for the lack of light, he had to trust she would lead him well.

"Jack?"

"I do trust you." And, he did.

"And do you believe?" came her hopeful whisper.

"I…" Believe in there being one man for Mersey? No, he didn't believe in just one. But… He thought of the glass ball sitting on the front seat of the Rover. A thousand charging horses couldn't have made him toss it out now that it had returned to his life. *Should have brought it along.* "I do believe." In some things.

"That's my hero."

A soft kiss landed on his chin, and then, like the feline she was, Mersey padded into the darkest depths of the mysterious forest that was capped by a midnight rainbow.

"You don't need your fancy copper rods to witch a line?"

Jack followed, one hand in Mersey's as she sought a ley line, the source of the path, as she had explained.

"Not here in the forest. The concentration of energies is so strong I'll feel it immediately. It's very close."

As they broached the inner sanctum of the forest, the lacking light segued to an eerie green that wasn't quite twilight, but far from the blackness of midnight.

Still and silent, the air here was much fresher than in London proper. Jack wondered when he'd last breathed such clean air, then decided not to get too used to it. All good things...

He suspected eyes stared at him from every cranny and moss-covered depth. The proverbial skitter of dread traveled up the back of his neck. But his scar didn't pulse, so at least he didn't have to worry about a demonic presence.

While Jack hoped his enemy was clever enough to follow, he also prayed it would not harm Mersey. He had Mersey's back. He'd not let anything—demonic, living stone or otherwise—harm her.

A thick carpet of verdant moss coated the ground. It shaped over rocks and tree roots and crawled up the trunks.

This forest was not right. He could feel it as the moss received his footsteps, and shifted subtly, almost as if to trip him up. And the glimmer of dancing lights flashing in the grasses and overhead in the tree canopy? Best not consider the source.

"So, you spend a lot of time in this forest?" he asked as they twisted around a nonpath that trailed beneath a shelter of tree cover.

"I like to jog the path that surrounds the manor whenever I get a chance. It's always a new trail, though it starts and ends at the same point."

"I see." Brilliant. Moving trails and shifting ground. Dark when it should be daylight. And he'd done with the stone gargoyles. What next? Faeries flittering by? "Tell me how you became a demon hunter?"

"I was born to it," Mersey said. "I prefer to capture them as opposed to allowing them to tap me."

"Don't like it, eh?"

"I've had a bad experience. A demon kept me in a silver cage once when I was tapped while in my other shape."

"Not good."

"Nope. Silver will hold a familiar fast. Freedom is a good thing."

She skipped over a mossy rock and Jack did the same.

"My parents were members of the Cadre," she said. "So I was raised here."

"They still live here?"

"They're gone. My mother died when I was ten and my father, well...let's say he's absent."

Just like him, then. One parent gone, and his mother, she lived in the States and they spoke infrequently.

Mum had taken her curious fortune, sold the family land and moved to a Las Vegas retirement community in hopes of meeting Barry Manilow, her favorite singer. Jack didn't mind; it made him feel good to know his mother was getting on well.

"So," he said, "the Cadre must be like a family to you?"

"They like to think so. But it's not as if any of the initiates dole out hugs or serve as a warm shoulder to cry out your troubles to. There's Lady Dawn..."

She nimbly avoided a twisted tree root.

"Oh, never mind her. And forget about girl chats and dating advice. Not to mention, my experience with the dating scene. I don't have family, Jack."

"Family is overrated," he tried. "And you do dates just fine, if you ask me."

"Thanks. But family, it's all that I want. I don't think the Cadre is the place for me, but I feel so lost in London."

Mersey stopped suddenly and pressed a finger to her lips. She pointed across a clearing, and then pulled him to settle onto a moss-covered rock. Still holding a tight clasp on her hand, Jack knelt and watched the spectacle in fascinated silence.

If his eyes saw correctly, there were dozens of faeries fluttering in and about a round clearing. They were no bigger than dragonflies, and glowed like firebugs. Grass that looked to be trimmed by a mower, yet dotted with colorful flowers, marked out a wide circle. The air smelled like rosemary and grass and a crisp autumn stream.

"A faery version of a crop circle?" he wondered quietly.

"The faery round," Mersey said, close to his ear. Her breath entered his pores and coaxed him to her side. "Isn't it magical?"

"Is that one of those things that if a man walks into it—"

"He'll be dancing for decades with no cares in the world. Let's not go further. Even I don't want to upset the sidhe."

Sidhe. Another word for faery. Jack had scanned P-Cell's information about the sort, leaving the intense study for the gray seekers. Until now, his stint in P-Cell had revolved around demons. This was a welcome respite. As far as otherworldly happenings went, he could get behind this one. It appeared nonthreatening enough.

Something pale caught his attention and he bent to pick it up. A plastic bracelet. Jack examined the design. "Some girl must have lost this. Bunch of plastic skulls on it." He showed it to Mersey.

"Oh, Jack, throw it. Quickly. Over there into that bush!"

"Why?"

"Those aren't made of plastic. They're pisky skulls."

"Bloody hell." He flicked the bracelet away. "What kind of creature does something like that? And if it's lying on the ground, does that mean it's lurking?"

"A troll, likely. We've one that lives under the bridge over the stream, nasty thing. Trolls eat piskies like candy bars."

Jack couldn't help but think he'd pass next time he had the urge for sweets. Oh, he believed and all, but he knew demons, and had thus far only stalked them in mortal cities.

Everything about this forest gave him the creeps, and put him on guard.

"Oh, look," Mersey whispered, "they're dancing. I think it's a wedding."

Indeed, a procession of miniature lights danced with cockle-bells and formed a tunnel down which two faeries then floated. Jack kept a keen eye peeled for lurking trolls.

At his peripheral vision, he sighted the small creatures dancing and it gave him wonder.

"So…" He spread his arm around Mersey's waist and pulled her up against him. "You mentioned that you had kissed a faery. Tell me how one goes about snogging with one so little."

"They're not always so small. Some are, but others can shift to the more usual size. Most humanlike."

"I see." He knew that. Maybe.

"But you want details, am I right?"

He planted a kiss to her shoulder and then waggled an eyebrow. "As salacious as possible."

"Could you ever be jealous of a faery, Jack?"

"Hell, no."

"Even a faery who might fancy me?"

"I…" He didn't like to consider that there were some things in this world he couldn't understand, and never would. But he did know one thing. "I would be. Any person—" or *creature* "—that could win your affection over my own attentions would certainly put up my hackles."

Pushing up her loose sleeve, he kissed his way along Mersey's forearm, landing on the soft inner skin of her elbow. He liked it there. Fragrant and silken. He traced his tongue over her warm flesh.

"Oh, Jack. How can a man who lives by the gun be so gentle?"

"My weapon is a small part of what I do. It's not me, Mersey. I'd never harm you. You know that, don't you?"

The glimmer of faery lights twinkled behind Mersey as she turned to press her forehead against Jack's. "I know you have a gun with you. Did you intend to bring it inside the Cadre?"

Caught, red-handed.

"It's all right by me," she quickly added. "I'm not worried. You won't get past the foyer with it."

"I'd like to see a bloke try take it away from me."

"You won't even know it's missing." She smiled and ducked in to kiss him. The cool skim of the rings on her fingers tickled his cheek.

Drawing back, she held her beringed hand before him, waggling her fingers in display.

"You have three left," Jack noted. "Did all the rest break?"

"Yes." Saddened, she said, "I don't know why, but they've been falling away from me since meeting you."

"You said they were for protection? Maybe it's that you don't require it anymore?"

"Because I have you? *Do* I have you, Jack?"

"Always."

"Then I need to give you something." She slid off one of the rings from her middle finger and then slid it onto Jack's littlest finger. It stopped below the first knuckle. "You once had one similar?"

Jack ran his thumb along the inside curve of the highly polished ring. That freaky night he didn't need another reminder of.

"I did. These are common, yes?"

"Oh, sure. You can get them in bulk. But the ones I wear are bespelled."

He'd spent so much time trying to protect everyone else—to offer safety—and now she was offering a simple protection to him. And yet, while he didn't believe this object could manifest the power to protect, Beryth had alluded the rings kept him back from Mersey.

And he felt it, like a hand caressing his heart. Much like the gazing ball, embedded with childhood wonder.

"But you only have two left."

She kissed him again and pulled back with a grin. "Do you still have the other one, Jack?"

"I...no. But I have this one now, eh?" Another kiss. She took it with a sigh. "Mmm, can't get enough of you, love."

With Mersey fitting herself onto his lap, Jack didn't care if the bloody faeries staged an attack. He'd fend them off—all without breaking the kiss with his girl.

Yeah, his girl. Hematite rings and aviator cap and miles and miles of legs in sexy black boots with flirty satin ribbons. She could be his girl. It was easy to go there, even given his last tragic mistake with the opposite sex. Mersey wasn't Monica. And he felt that even the things he couldn't tell her, she might already know.

His claim to her?

Too bad that ring didn't exist.

"Be careful not to let go of my hand—Jack?"

Everything about her screamed to be touched. The soft sweater hugging all her curves. And her nipples were hard against his chest, begging to be stroked.

"No, don't let go of my—"

The faery lights blinked out.

Jack sat alone under the dark canopy of leaves.

Chapter 23

"—My hand. No!"

They had been going at it, kissing and hugging and…that had involved more than the one hand. Mersey had felt the brief shock of contact as Jack's fingers had stroked her nipple. Melting, she had wanted to become a part of him.

Now, she sat alone on the mossy rock, her hands pressed to her breasts. His touch was gone. Jack was gone.

The faery reel danced on behind her, oblivious to her loss.

She shifted on the rock and searched the merriment. Gay music shimmied in iridescent waves. Diaphanous clothing fluttered above the clearing, the dancers suspended between heaven and earth. Everywhere laughter played syncopation to the night.

Had they stolen Jack into the affair? He might be invisible to Mersey once ensconced within the circle, but she should detect his footsteps in the grass.

Nothing.

Now she noticed the others standing along the outside. Sized as normal mortals, and regal. The White and Black courts were not recognized here in the St. Yve wood—it was a neutral forest, a borderland that sheltered those seeking sanctuary, and a virtual stew of *paras*—but Mersey knew there were a few renegades from both sidhe courts who took refuge here.

"What did you do with him?" She rushed for the first sidhe, a male, who stood with his back to her.

Elegant brocade fitted him from collar to knee in homage to the eighteenth-century French courts. Lace fashioned of spider's silk fluttered at his wrists and collar. His breeches were of blackest leather. Gorgeous gossamer wings splayed in rest down his back, the palest violet filamented tips dusting the moss carpet.

"Where is—" Mersey gripped him by the shoulder and twisted him about. "Oh. Crap."

Her heart dropped to her knees. Courage wilted and sticky humiliation rose at the back of her throat.

Of all the faeries she had to run into. It was the one faery she had kissed.

And he wasn't smiling.

Jack stumbled and caught himself against the trunk of a crippled oak. The musty odor of bark and, at his feet, toadstools, filled his nostrils. Normally a forest smelled verdant and fresh. It smelled wrong now. Dead and rotting. Sinister.

He'd only wanted to touch Mersey. To imprint her curves against his palm. To lose himself in her serenity and banish the dark demons of his memories. And now she was gone.

Or was it he who was gone? Where was he?

He wandered aimlessly in the darkness, calling Mersey's name. He could see the shapes of trees and roots and stones in shades of gray. Gone were the fantastical greens and faery lights. The world wasn't right.

Wait, that rock. Jack touched the boulder. He was sure this was the one he and Mersey had been sitting on. And there, in the clearing, a perfect circle of cut grass, now murky and silent.

"I hope this isn't one of those decades-long losts," he murmured. "Bloody faeries."

Had he somehow slipped from the rock and fallen into the faery circle?

P-Cell had not trained him for this. He knew the basics about faeries. Had read a brief discourse on the varieties and their culture, but he'd never expected to be dealing with their kind. If he'd been shifted to the dark realm...

Swiping away low-hanging foliage from before his face, he paused, fingers spread to clutch a branch, and eyed the ring Mersey had slipped onto his little finger.

"Protection, eh? Christ, Mersey, what have we done?"

Jack lowered his head and clenched his jaw. This ring was all he had to connect him to a woman...he loved.

He'd never been keen on gifts. Especially rings. No matter from a cat, or now, a woman who was also a cat. And to actually fall in love with her?

No matter. "I've got something better than a stone wrapped around my finger."

Drawing out the .45, he cocked the trigger and wandered onward, cautious as his steps wobbled on the undulating ground. Could salt lay out a faery? What did he remember from Mum's faery tales? Iron! That should put them out for a while. Where to get iron when he needed it most?

An insect buzzed near his ankles. Jack strode in wide steps to avoid whatever creepies lurked.

A wisp of fuzzy whiteness fluttered before him. Jack blew it away. He stepped carefully, not wanting to trip up on the roots and definitely not wanting to move into the clearing. It was the same clearing he and Mersey had been sitting near before.

He'd walked a circle?

"The never-ending circle," he muttered. "Is this like her ever-changing trail? I don't abide faery magic!" He shouted that last statement as a warning for any who might attempt it against him.

The tuft of white moseyed by again. Jack swiped at the bit. It dodged and flickered brightly. A faery. Following him?

"What can I offer you to get me out of these woods?" he tried.

"A thousand kings' ransoms and one lusty sea siren who has never kissed a drowned sailor," sounded right at his ear.

Jack swung around. The wood was dark. Not a leaf fluttered. Glimmer of fine particles settled through the air. Faery dust?

He clasped the pistol handle with both hands. "Show yourself!"

This time the voice came from across the clearing, loud and bellicose. "Fire a gun in these woods, Jack Harris, and the bullet will boomerang back between your ugly mortal eyes."

Briefly, Jack focused on the scar over his chest. Not a tingle, nor twinge of pain. It was not Bcryth.

"No demons in these woods. I would scare them off," came the boastful voice right behind Jack.

Jack swung around, and the tip of the pistol grazed the outstretched finger of a man who stood as tall as him. Long dark hair fell over his shoulders and halfway down his chest. Lean but muscled, he stood with hands to his hips. His trousers looked like leather rock-and-roll gear. Bare feet perched upon the mossy stone.

"What are you?" Jack demanded.

The man tapped the pistol barrel. "Is there iron in that idiot stick?"

"Of course!" It was titanium and steel, but if the fool didn't know…

"Nasty business." He made a gesture with his fingers of throwing something away.

Inexplicably, Jack felt the gun shift, as if he wanted to toss it. But he held firmly.

"At least put it away, then," the man decided. "We cannot talk with that idiot stick between the two of us."

"Name!"

"That is none of your concern, Jack Harris."

It was likely a bloody faery. He remembered something about the faeries keeping their names to themselves. A mortal knowing the name of a faery would give them power over the being.

He didn't appear to be carrying a weapon, but these creatures could probably zap something out the ends of their fingertips, for all Jack knew.

"Boomerang," the man repeated. "Go ahead. Try it. I will duck and then laugh when your mortal brains splatter the sky."

Trickery or not, Jack wasn't willing to risk finding out. He tucked the gun in the waistband at the small of his back. "You know my name—"

"And you do not require mine."

The faery twisted gracefully and did a balance-beam walk across a thick root emerging from the ground. Reaching the end of the root, he tilted a look over his shoulder at Jack. Deep sapphire eyes held the fathomless sparkle of a jewel.

Jack avoided his gaze. Not so dangerous as a demon gaze, but he disliked the mocking insinuation he saw there.

From the faery's back, wings burst out much like a dragonfly's wings. Four lustrous appendages, two on each side, fluttered. A sheen of sapphire colored them like stained glass run through with reticulated veins.

Noting Jack's awe, the faery chuckled gleefully. "Rather spectacular, eh?" He darted to stand before Jack. "Do you have any tricks, mortal? A soft-shoe across the roots? Calisthenics through the air?"

"I have none."

"Of course not!" He drew up his arms to cross boldly over his chest. "Though my ears tell me you are a bold yet cowardly demon killer. Is that your talent? Cowardice?"

"I'm no such thing!"

"It is a coward who shoots without first assessing danger. Jack, you will never get to your mortal heaven that way."

"Not worried about that."

"Good and well! Perhaps it is leading demons you excel in."

"Beryth is not here."

"But he is near. What right do you have? Did you ask the demon why he wanted into the Cadre?"

How could this creature know—? He would not ask; it would show his weakness. "What do I care?"

"Oh, Jack. Daft, Jack. Time to have a conversation with your master."

"I answer to no master."

The faery reached out and touched Jack's shirt, right over his scar. "I guess differently."

"I'm not controlled by the demon, and have no worries for his destruction."

"Then I will not, either. So!" He bent forward, the schoolmaster admonishing a tardy student. "You, Jack, are wandering willy-nilly through a forbidden forest. Did she give you the slip?"

"You know where Mersey is?" Well, if he knew everything else, it was worth a try. "I dropped her hand."

"Ah. Mersey Bane. Should have known. Tough bit of luck then, old chap," the faery mocked.

Deciding he'd had enough of this joker, Jack started to walk the opposite way, but the flutter of white fuzz reappeared. He slapped at it, and it dodged expertly.

Zooming before him, the bit of white flashed again and there stood his tormentor in the path.

Those wings. Recognizing his wonder, Jack immediately pushed it back. These faeries, he had to remain alert to their dark enchantments.

"I need to get out of this forest," he insisted. "Mersey needs me. Can you show me the way?"

The faery lifted an arm and pointed over Jack's shoulder.

Turning, Jack saw the faery round glowed with a gorgeous green light. Someone stood in the center. A man, older, but still in his prime. Gnarled fingers clued Jack to his trade of working the fields.

Catching his breath, Jack clutched his gut. The ache of seeing him, standing there in simple white robes, lifted a moan to his throat.

The uneven ground did not stop his strides to the edge of the faery round. A soft, weird chatter filled the background. Tiny lights constellated above him. And there *he* stood, arms held out to him.

"Thought I'd never see you again, Jack," he said.

"Dad?"

"He's waiting for you." The dusting of a wing against Jack's spine momentarily stiffened him. The faery had followed, and Jack felt his luminous presence over his shoulder. "Go to him. Tell him all the things you never dared speak. He needs to hear what you have to say, Jack."

"Yes. There are things, Dad…" He took a step forward. The earth leveled as he left the tangled roots and neared the circle clearing. "I made a wish…"

"I know you did, Jack," his father answered.

Could he confess? Would it change things? *Could* it change things?

"It can change evv-rything," whispered in his ear.

Aware of his proximity to the circle, Jack knew one step would place him inside—next to his father.

"You wished for a curious fortune, and you got it, boy," his father snapped. "By stealing my life."

"No!"

Jack reached out. Pressure against the back of his right shoulder pushed him forward. He lifted a foot. He bowed his head. Decades of regret flooded his heart with acute ache. "It wasn't real. My wish couldn't possibly have killed him."

"Oh, but it did." The faery stretched out his thin arms and tilted back his head to announce "A child's heart is hale and powerful!"

Overhead the trees stirred with a flock of birds chirping and taking to flight upward toward the midnight rainbow.

The faery lowered his sapphire gaze back on Jack, bestilling

Jack with an unsettling sensation of being crawled over by insects. "Be careful what you wish for, Jack."

The faery leaned forward, craning his head to peer up into Jack's downcast face. "You, Jack Harris, are not worthy to be her hero. Go," it instructed. "Step forward."

And Jack took one more step.

Chapter 24

Raskin Rubythorn wore handsome as vain glory. His sapphire eyes lit upon Mersey, but she felt the disgust lingering behind his marvel. Not a touch of grace in the faery's cold soul.

"Mersey Bane," he said flatly. Raskin nodded to the companion he'd been speaking to, and with a gesture, directed Mersey to walk toward a chestnut tree. The massive bole had been hollowed out to form a gazebo. "Shall we?"

"I want to know what you did with him," she insisted. A squeeze of her fist and she felt a pinch. Another ring had broken. Only one left.

Raskin glided on, without mind for her anxiety. Briefly folding down his wings, he bowed to step inside the gazebo.

The bole had been carved in delicate cutouts resembling an Eastern Indian motif. Inside, plush chaises covered over with green velvet—though Mersey knew it to be moss so soft and fine that velvet would be bargain-rack next to it—were placed in the center. All of it fit for a prince, no matter he'd been ostracized from his court, the sidhe Black court that normally wintered well and mischievously, then crept into the shadows for the summer during the White court's reign.

"Your Jack Harris?" Raskin asked as he seated himself, crossing his legs and leaning back into the chaise. His wings flexed and propped high against the back, the filaments tufting the carved wall behind him. The fireflies at his toes remained in place as living jewels.

Mersey did not question how he had the man's name. Or that he labeled him hers. The sidhe knew things. She accepted that.

Striding to the center of the room, she fit her hands to her hips. *Maintain calm,* she coached inwardly. *Do not reveal your discomfort, or he will use it.*

"Jack's lost. I must find him."

A tilt of Raskin's fingers changed the pale light inside the gazebo to violet. The moss took on a gray cast and Raskin appeared like a cool jewel before her. A smirking jewel whom she had once coveted in her aching, crushing heart.

Deep sapphire eyes seeped into her psyche, prying open the loose ropes she'd wrapped round her soul following her last miserable encounter with the faery.

Her body softened and her breathing increased. Her shoulders fell back, lifting her breasts.

"You led an unapproved mortal into the forest," he spoke slowly, making every word an event. Not once did his eyes stray from hers. "That, my merciless Mersey Bane, is not allowed."

Swallowing, Mersey attacked the unwarranted desire with affront. "Oh, get over yourself, Rubythorn. So I made a mistake."

"Make it once, kitten, you shall never again make the same one."

Shoving her fists into her trousers pockets to keep from lashing out at the imperious bit of faery fluff, Mersey plopped herself onto the stool opposite his chaise.

Don't look into his eyes. There is where you always stumble.

The kiss from Raskin had been her first. Just eighteen, and comfortable with the forest and its inhabitants, gushing with longing for boys and men, Mersey had been beyond the world to know this gorgeous creature had wanted to press his lips to hers.

It had been summer solstice, a night that had glowed with joy and merriment. Mersey had become drunk on elderberry wine. But ever cautious never to enter the faery reel, for even a familiar could become trapped for eternity.

Raskin had paid particular attention to her that night. She'd known him from a previous exercise with Cadre initiates, as they'd learned the ins and outs of the forest and the ways of its inhabitants. Whispers from female initiates had labeled him the Enchanter. Raskin had been her guide, and taught her all she needed to know of the sidhe ways.

That he'd been ostracized from the Black court for seducing the White princess had only increased his attraction in Mersey's eyes. A bad-boy faery with a taste for trendy mortal fashion—eighteenth-century trends, however.

That night they'd kissed beneath a constellation of dancing faery couples. Mersey had closed her eyes and fallen into bliss. Skin flushing, her entire body had pressed up to the tall sidhe. Kissing was beyond all she had imagined.

Too quickly, Raskin had pulled away, pleading he'd forgotten a precious engagement.

Crestfallen, and yet brimming with the elation of one's first kiss, Mersey had watched as Raskin met up with a fellow sidhe behind the hornbeam wall at the edge of the festivities.

She had strained her heightened feline senses to hear their conversation. Raskin's friend had asked, "How was it?"

"Not so favorable."

Mersey had bravely swallowed back a cry. Pierced through the heart, she'd clutched the ache and fled the merriment. Later, the tears had come and she'd pressed her face into the pillow and wished for her long-passed mother's hug.

"Do you hate me, Mersey?"

She looked up to find Raskin had slid forward, elbows to knees. The sidhe moved like ghosts. Spider's lace spilled about his wrists and hands. The essence of rare night flowers perfumed his aura. The sapphires teased her to match his gaze—but she dared not. *So easy to fall again.*

"W-why do you ask that?"

"It is my curiosity. And very likely, my vanity. You never approach me during fetes. We were once quite companionable."

Once. And only for a moment. A moment that had embroidered humiliation upon Mersey's soul. The sidhe tended to twist every encounter to serve them best.

"You don't remember our kiss?"

He appeared to peruse memory, and then tapped the air between them. "Quick. Dry. Er… Well! It was not so memorable. Ah, so that is why you avoid me? Our fleeting forest snog remains quite the memory to you, my feline familiar?"

Bowing her head, Mersey could not force herself to meet his glittering eyes. The displeasure in his tone humiliated her further. He brushed off her first intimate experience as if sweeping crumbs under a table.

"It is simply we sidhe do not mix so well with familiars." The touch of his finger beneath her chin irritated. Mersey jerked away. "We prefer your kind as pets, really."

The idea of purring about Raskin's ankles made Mersey want to toss her cookies. She had no doubt if the faery could pull it off, he'd enslave her in cat form and do just that.

Why had she followed Raskin into the gazebo? Nothing good could ever come of conversation with the sidhe.

"I should leave." She stood, yet the mossy floor suddenly undulated, toppling her to again sit gracelessly on the stool.

"You will leave when it pleases me."

Raskin stretched languorously upon the chaise, the move bending his wings down and behind him. He reached back for one and curled it forward to toy with the tip. Looking up through his lashes, he captured the hidden tendril of desire Mersey still carried for the arrogant faery.

"Tell me you do not enjoy my presence, Mersey."

"I…" *Do.* He even smelled good. Like a fresh lilac panicle after a sun-drenched spring rain. "*Enjoy* is not the right word."

"Desire?"

"Yes. No!"

Focus, Mersey! *This faery holds no sway over you now.* She had moved beyond the humiliation. *Think of your new lover.* Yes, the man her mother had chosen for her.

"I don't have time to speak to you, Raskin. Please," she pleaded. "Jack is…"

"Is what? Your mortal lover?"

To give that information would serve Raskin too well, something he would eventually wield as a weapon. But Mersey knew the longer Jack remained lost, the deeper and more desperately he'd become fixed by enchantment. He might never be found. The forest would consume him forever.

And she could not conceive of never again seeing the man.

"Yes," she answered, straightening and dusting back her hair from her cheek. "He is my lover."

"Do tell."

"Tell what?"

"Sensational details. Sordid excerpts. Illicit moments. I insist!"

Mersey stood briskly. "I'm leaving."

"Does the hunter, who trails demons in his wake like a pied piper, care about you? Or does his mission serve a means to treachery? To further death? He does not love you, Mersey. Jack Harris is using you to gain access to the Cadre."

"I know that." And that Raskin knew infuriated her. "But I know that I can open Jack's eyes to a different viewpoint of the *paras* if only he could meet some of them."

"Like *moi?*"

"Er…" It was never a good idea to introduce the current boyfriend to the old one, especially when the old one would tell tales.

"I hate that term. *Paras.*" Raskin said it as if a bit of broccoli were stuck to his tooth.

She'd been wise earlier to realize this conversation would get her nowhere.

"The hunter has a nasty demon attached to him." Raskin ran the tip of a wing filament over his lips and gave a theatrical shiver. "I can feel the creature's presence even as we speak. It has followed its mortal slave into the forest."

"Ba'al Beryth?"

Raskin lifted a brow. "You would lure the mortal in, knowing so much? Mersey, Mersey." He tsk-tsked. "I am almost inclined to respect you for that. But I cannot allow you to show the demon into the Cadre."

"Since when have you been so devoted to the Cadre? Last I heard, you were admonished for preaching a rebellion against the forest guides, and anyone who would ally themselves with the Cadre."

"Alas, a futile uprising. Today it pleases me to ally myself to your little group. Tomorrow may be another day. Now, you should run along. Leave the mortal lost, as it is. Food is being brought to the round. I can smell the sweetmeats and wine." He slanted a rich gaze upon her. "You are not invited to the festivities, kitten. And I should not wish to endure your tears when you see the lovelies I have plans to kiss tonight."

Perhaps he was right. Jealously would rear up should she witness the harem Raskin could gather with a mere snap of his fingers.

If Jack snapped, she would go to his side. Jack. Her hero. The one man she had finally found.

"Raskin, is there nothing you can do?"

"Ah, you strike me with your misery. I can do many things. I can groom a whale. I can battle trolls. I can open a maiden's heart—"

"Raskin!"

"I—" he leaned closer and danced his fingers between them "—can reverse the foreverness of the lost."

"You can?"

Irritation made his eyes beam. "I just said I could."

"Yes, of course you can," she rushed in before she angered him further.

Mersey grabbed Raskin's hand. Without a thought, she begged her heart. "Please. I'll do anything if you will put Jack's hand back in mine."

The faery's thin dark brow lifted. "*Anything* covers quite a lot."

Yes, it did. Her heart lurched. Toggling the last remaining ring on her finger, she swallowed.

She had known Jack only a week. And yet she had known him forever. Since she had been a babe in her mother's belly. Jack Harris was the man for her. Jack Harris held her heart.

Mersey nodded. "I will require an additional favor, but…yes. In exchange, you may have…anything."

"Then it is done." Raskin clapped his palms together once.

And Mersey stood—

Chapter 25

—In the dark forest, her hand clasped within a warm, sweaty grip.

"Mersey?"

"Jack!" She tugged, as it seemed he was about to step forward into a faery round. "Don't go in there!"

"Never." He clung to her, wrapping his arms around her shoulders. Every part of her that touched him renewed his spirit, lifted him up from the dark.

"How did you find me?"

"I would do anything to find you, Jack."

"I'm not worthy," he murmured.

"Jack, your worth is immeasurable to me. Now, don't drop my hand again," she said.

He kissed her and spread away the hair from her face. Gorgeous green eyes glittered with moisture. "I won't. Let's get out of this dreaded wood."

She turned and pointed high above the treetops. A rainbow

stretched through the midnight sky, glittering as if slathered with faery dust.

"This way."

Finally, he felt the draw. Pulled down from the sky and into the depths of the St. Yve wood. Beryth allowed it to occur, his arms spread and corporeal body tumbling. Jack Harris, his familiar, would lead him inside the sacred walls of the hermetic order that had treated him so cruelly.

Cruelty, he could accept. But stealing away love?

Never.

"You asked to find me, and the faery prince simply helped you?"

Mersey smirked at Jack's disbelief. She couldn't tell him she'd ransomed something valuable for his freedom.

But it was worth it. Jack would not be wandering the forest forever. And she had got something additional out of the deal. Something that would allow Jack to see her world—without recourse.

"Simple as that," she responded.

A stacked stone cairn signaled the end of the ever-changing trail and full sunlight beamed upon a stately manor. Mersey paused to look over the manicured lawn behind the grounds of the St. Yve manor.

The air vibrated with a preternatural energy. Damselflies constellated the long grasses that decorated the west end of the pond. Threshold guardians maintained stealth guard over the centuries-old manor. The family wings were guarded with as many house demons as the Cadre's section.

An initiate required permission to bring a guest into the manor. Mersey knew P-Cell would never be allowed inside. But she so wanted to show Jack her world. She'd take the back door, access allowed only to Cadre initiates, and those forest residents who had been approved—including Raskin.

"Should I still hold your hand?" Jack wondered.

"Yes, but first—"

She peered behind them and sighted the rapidly moving spurt of glimmer headed their way.

Jack turned, and before he could mutter more than "What the—" a faery crashed into his chest, spuming him with a cloud of dust. The force sent both Jack and the faery reeling in opposite directions, but Jack managed to catch himself against a poplar trunk.

Shaking his head sent dust everywhere.

Mersey waved to the retreating faery—Raskin, wobbling from the impact—and called thanks.

"Now, you can hold my hand," she said, pleased with the transaction.

He merely stared at her fingers.

"It's a glamour," she offered. "You've just been given a free pass into the Cadre."

He patted his chest and studied his arm. The gray sweater he wore shimmered beneath the sunlight. "What does that mean?"

"For twenty-four hours you'll appear as Raskin Rubythorn to others. He has access to the manor. The glamour will get you past the guardians. Shall we try?"

"You mean I look like a faery? How do you see me?"

"As Jack, my hero." And she did, for one who orders the glamour can always see beyond it. And how thankful was she for that? If Jack resembled Raskin, Mersey was in trouble. "Let's go on."

At the servant's door where Mersey often entered after a jog through the forest, she flashed a smile to the guardian demon, followed by Jack who offered a roguish smirk. He wore the disguise well enough.

They made it all the way to her room without interference. Which surprised Mersey. She hadn't expected an armed guard to come and wrestle Jack away from her. She supposed whoever was on security was probably getting a smile at her and the faery.

"Council meeting," she said, remembering today would see most of the facility in a meeting to discuss bringing a certain former Cadre initiate—Damien Hancock, a vampire—back into the fold. The equinox was coming up, and the nasty Asmos demon would be expected to return. Capturing that *para* would require a specialized adept.

Mersey wasn't keen on vampires and would likely stay as far from the Cadre as possible should Mr. Hancock be approved for return.

"Easier than I thought," she said as she wandered into her room and released Jack's hand.

She watched him for a long time. They had actually parted hands and he had not disappeared. She knew so long as she remained in his presence, Jack was safe. But should they stray from the other's sight, all bets were off.

"You have your own room?" he wondered.

"Already taking notes to report back?"

"Yes. No. I don't know." He sat on the edge of her bed and absently traced the emerald square set in the quilt. "Mersey, you know I have orders."

"Yes, and I have no worries."

"Memory loss?" he guessed.

"What made you guess that?"

"P-Cell rumors. A few agents have attempted to get inside, with similar results. But you don't know anything about that, right?"

"Exactly."

He leaned back, crossing his hands behind his head and studying the long white sheers that ballooned across the window tops. "So you grew up around all this weird stuff?"

"I was born into this stuff, Jack, and it's not weird." She slid onto the high bed and climbed on top of him, fitting her knees to either side of his hips and grinding her mons against his already hard cock. "Just wait until the building tunes in to your feelings."

"What does that mean—oh, yes. Riiiight there…"

"The manor is alive with demon energy. But benevolent demons—they won't harm us. Although they are rather lusty and tend to feed off any sexy, erotic energy that is released here."

"Really? A regular peep show, eh?"

"I prefer to think of it as a sanctuary." Jack tugged her closer and she pulled the neckline of her sweater down to reveal the witch mark. "Taste me, Jack."

"You want to feed the demons with our lust?"

"Oh, yeah."

His hot tongue electrified her skin with a single touch. Dragging the back of her sweater up her ribs, he then pulled it over her head and tossed it aside. "But I thought you were going to take me around and introduce me to your friends?"

"Soon. They're all in meetings right now, so we've some time to waste."

"Right then. I just want you to know…"

Mersey tugged down her jeans and kicked them off. "Know what?"

"My opinion has already changed. I don't think I'll ever see otherworldly entities in the same way that I have been."

She bit her lower lip, holding back the urge to groan loudly. Though he chatted, after every other word, Jack lashed his tongue over the crescent mark, pushing her, goading her to surrender. "What—ohhh—made you change your mind?"

"You. And lately…everything. I…I saw my dad in the forest, just before you tugged me from the circle. It was an illusion. Some faery bloke made me see him. I think he wanted me to step into the circle."

Had it been Raskin? She had been suspicious that the sidhe had already seen Jack before speaking to her. Their kind could be everywhere and nowhere and then back again—it was called *bilocation.*

"Dad's my past now, Mersey. And just like you wearing the rings on one hand, because your past can never be changed, I can't change what happened. My world has done a complete one-eighty since meeting you. It's for the best. Because it brought me to you."

"Are you getting romantic on me, Jack?"

"Don't know how to do romance. I just know I like it when you're in my arms, and I don't like it when you're not."

He scouted her stomach with a lazy trail of tongue lashes. "Give me another purr. You know you purr like a pussycat when you're aroused? And you do that funny kneading thing against my shoulders."

"Funny?"

He kissed her quickly. "I like it. So does this glamour thing I've got on mean you're actually shagging a faery?"

"Oh, I...don't know. Well, it's you, Jack." She licked his demon mark. "Feels like you."

"What about the erotic energy? Are there...demons watch-ing us?"

Mersey glanced to the ceiling and then trailed her gaze down toward the window. Jack followed and saw a flit of faery lights. "So *we're* the show?"

"Oh, yes."

Digging her fingernails into his scar made Jack suck in his breath. She pressed her lips over it. He moaned aside her neck as her fingers wrapped around him and squeezed firmly. "Oh, sweetness..."

"Do you love me, Jack?"

Eyelids closing and jaw tense, Jack had fallen into the only moment he could manage while aroused—the cock ruled all. "What was that, love? Sure. What did you say?"

A firm tug on his cock wasn't going to make him pay closer attention; it redirected all blood flow to his torso and deprived the brain of clear thought. "Oh, love, please. I can't... That's so good. Don't make me think now, huh?" He parted her legs and dipped his tongue across her mark as his fingers traced the same motions inside her. Mersey's grip loosened. "We'll talk later, yes?"

"Yes," she purred. In a deft move, she wrapped her legs about his hips and drew him inside her warm and tight squeezing walls. "Talking...bad. This..."

"Good," Jack finished for her as he began to thrust to the rhythm of their heartbeats. Fast, steady. A new pace to him because this one involved setting his apprehensions aside and accepting what came to him.

"Kiss me," he murmured. Mersey slid her lips across his forehead and kissed him there. And there, at his temple. And there, at the crease of his eye. "Oh, yes, lover, kiss the demons from my dreams. Take them all away."

"All of them," intoned a dark, deep voice over their heads, "save me."

Jack pushed Mersey from him. The sudden loss of connection bit like a serpent. He groped the bedside for his gun. No weapon.

And overhead, the demon Beryth grinned at them.

Chapter 26

"This is how I prefer you, Jack." Beryth swept over the bed, its head and shoulders formed in thick red muscles and from hip down, a black mist. Sulfur wilted the air. "Charged up and ready to action. But looking a little strange. Those wings aren't yours, are they? And that you chose such a powerful familiar for your sex mate. Good boy, Jack."

Jack shifted beneath the sheet to cover Mersey. He felt something ping against his fingers and the shards of her final ring spilled onto his palm. Shit.

"Go back to hell," Jack shouted. "I didn't call you here."

"But you did, Jack." The demon formed into human shape, shaking out wavy black hair and landing on the floor with both feet.

What to use as a weapon? Jack's pistol had been removed from him upon entry. Put a simple shaker of table salt in hand and he could at least hold the thing off.

He pressed the ring shards into Mersey's palm.

Tilting a sad head shake at him, the demon then jumped onto

the end of the bed and crouched there like a primate. A wicked glimmer shot from its yellow eyes, which Jack did not look into. And he protectively lifted his hand to shield Mersey's eyes. "Don't look."

She slid a leg along his thigh beneath the sheet. "I know."

"I have always been a part of you, Jack. Belief is all that is required," Beryth cooed. Creeping forward, its hand pressed the counterpane over Jack's leg.

And the hand changed, growing thinner, more delicate. Blond hair shook out over the demon's shoulders. Monica's face smiled at Jack. "You've served your purpose, Jack. Now." She eyed Mersey. "I want her. She looks like her mother."

Mersey sat upright. "You killed my mother!"

"She was no longer mine when her death came. She'd given herself to that familiar."

"M-my father?"

"Wretched bastard."

"You continued to torment her after their marriage. She died to protect her family!"

"You invent stories to appease your broken heart. No wonder familiars are so easy to enslave. I was nowhere near Mirabelle when she breathed her final breath. Pity."

"You've no power within the walls of the Cadre," Mersey said to the demon. "Leave now and you remain free. But stay one moment beyond the time it takes me to fit that crystal into my hand—" all averted their eyes to the quartz pyramid on the bedside table "—and your arse is mine."

"Not if I can make your ass mine first," Beryth hissed in Monica's tone.

A long black tongue snaked toward Jack, attaching itself to the scar on his chest. Jack choked, felt a tugging deep within his heart. The tongue stirred at his insides. He couldn't bend his arms to grip the intrusion.

Would it eat his heart, as it had Monica's?

The demon chanted a few words.

To Jack's right, Mersey twisted and reached for the crystal. Beryth lashed out with a talon, knocking the pyramid to the floor. Mersey scrambled, naked, off the bed.

"So long, Jack boy, hello Miss Mersey Bane," the demon announced.

It retracted its tongue from Jack's body, an icy blade withdrawn with a bite. In its wake, flames burst upon Jack's chest. His brain told his hand to slap at the fire, but his arm wouldn't cooperate.

The motion of Beryth whisking off the bed extinguished the flame to a smoldering, stinging ache.

Great exhaustion melted Jack's muscles and limbs. He tried to reach for Mersey, but she wasn't on the bed. He could barely lift his head; his skull felt like a boulder rolling upon the pillow.

Released from the demon's control. That knowledge overwhelmed like fog creeping across his heart. For behind the fog formed acute clarity. And now Beryth was after something more powerful.

"Mersey," he managed to say. "Watch out!"

"I'm fine, Jack," he heard her shout.

But she wasn't. The ring had broken. She wore no protection. And if he couldn't move to help her—

The demon lifted Mersey above the bed. Out lashed its tongue.

A full-blood familiar, who wasn't tapped and who could get the demon into anything within the Cadre was the biggest prize.

Mersey did not hold the crystal. Jack pulled himself to the edge of the bed, the journey like a dying man dragging himself across the desert. The quartz pyramid sat on the floor.

Beryth growled. The creature changed to its natural state, horned, red and angry. One taloned claw held Mersey by the neck, dangling.

Jack spread his arms and lunged forward. He clasped Mersey's legs, but in that instant, she slipped from him. Completely vanished from the room.

And in the next moment, Jack found himself sitting in a thatch of stinging nettle. Outside. Full sun beamed upon his naked flesh. Two grinning stone gargoyles peered down upon him.

"I loved your mother."

"Demons cannot own that emotion," Mersey spat. Though she knew better. While a demon was focused to its directive—in Beryth's case, dread—the only other emotions it felt were lust and anger.

The cutting sting of Beryth's hand across Mersey's cheek sent her reeling. She groped for the leg of the stainless-steel lab table for support.

"We do know love. It's just so…random." It flicked a hand, gesturing dismissively. So human an action. "It strikes without warning. And it struck me hard."

"Love is not lust. You felt lust toward my mother. And when my father crystallized you, the Cadre should have kept you stored forever."

"The decade I spent in that icy prison was unwarranted. I would have never harmed Mirabelle."

"Then what did?"

"She called a war demon, quite by accident. Your mother wasn't prepared for the intensity of its rage."

"If you know that, then why didn't you stop it from murdering her?"

"I was in a damned crystal!" Beryth shivered and closed its red-lidded eyes. The demon clasped its black-taloned fingers near its chest. "And it was love. Mirabelle, she was…sublime."

"Don't speak of her. Please."

"No, of course not. She is *my* prize. The memory that got me through my hell. Now, you will help me to take revenge against the Cadre for imprisoning me in one of those officious crystals. Do you know what that experience is? You, who captures my kind as a profession! I deal dread, and yet, nothing can match imprisonment in an icy hell such as the one Caractacus consigned me to."

"You'll be back inside that hell soon enough. Jack will save me."

"Do you mean your hero? Perhaps he'll kill me, eh? Blast me to Kingdom Come? Do you think he'll consider the *fallout* before he pulls the trigger?"

Mersey wilted upon the stone floor. *Would* Jack think about the fallout? She was now tapped by Beryth. If Jack killed the demon, he would kill her, too.

Chapter 27

A dragonfly buzzed his nose—a dragonfly the size of a swan. Jack ducked and batted at the insect. Then he stood and looked around. The gated cottage sat before him. The gargoyle pair growled silently, though Jack felt their acute observance.

Somehow he'd been booted out of the manor.

"Because I'm not with her," he whispered, dread seeping into his pores. "I've done it again. Led the demon to another woman I love."

A surreptitious glance up and to the left spied one of the gargoyles. Cracked all over, but in one piece. That one had tasted his wrath; perhaps it would be leery.

"Mersey," he muttered, pleading for his lost lover. Even more than knowing Beryth had her was the horrid moment he'd felt her final protective ring fall away. "I've got to get back to her."

Leaping, he gripped the iron crossbar that topped the gate, and pulled himself up and over. Jack landed and turned to look into the soft cornflower eyes of a woman who could have been his mother's age.

"Out for a stroll in the woods, are you now?" she asked. There was no question the woman was *not* mortal. Her voice iced over him, raising the hairs on his arms. "Oh, but you'll take a nasty burn to your bits like that, you will."

Jack cupped his privates with both hands. "No time for small talk, Granny, I've been booted out of the Cadre's headquarters and I need to get back. You know what I'm talking about, I'm sure you do."

"Watch your tone with me, faery," she admonished sharply.

Right. The glamour. So he still looked like that Raskin bloke?

"Now," she resumed the sweet voice, "you look lost. I can point your way to the faery round, if you'll—"

"No!" Not caring if he was naked, Jack sideswiped her and made for the cottage, and the narrow oval door, surrounded by climbing red roses. "There is a woman inside the manor who needs my help. Her name is Mersey Bane, and she's been kidnapped by the demon Beryth. You understand me, lady?"

He reached for the lion's head doorknob, yet drew back with a yelp. Thorns as long as his fingers and brandishing a saber edge flashed in the sunlight.

"What the bloody—?"

He swung about to find the woman standing with a silver tea tray in hand. Behind her sat three white wicker chairs. A tablecloth laid over a small tea table fluttered in the afternoon breeze.

"Fancy a bit of tea?" she asked.

"Tea?"

On the verge of shaking the woman silly, out of the corner of his eye Jack sighted another figure. Toward the back of the cottage, exiting a garden, meandered a hunched old man, using a cane and wobbling at the speed of stop.

"I've no time for your brass, old lady," Jack said, controlling his anger. "I'm naked!"

"Tea tastes fine no matter one's clothing choice. But I'd caution you against spilling, I would."

He needed to remain calm. The wood was enchanted. Which meant this cottage was enchanted, and likely the old couple, as well. They must be some kind of threshold guardians, providing entrance to the castle—yes, he'd read about this while researching the Cadre. He had to play this right.

"Name's Jack Harris," he said. He didn't offer to shake her hand because he needed both of them to cover his privates.

"Pleased to meet you, Jack." She swept a slow gaze up his length. "All of you." The woman sat on a chair and patted the one next to her.

Jack sat. Behind him, the old man had got no farther than five feet from the garden.

"I've not heard of you, Jack Harris," she said. "New to the forest?"

"You could say that. Listen, I'm not what I seem."

She lifted a stern brow. "I sense that." Her eyes strayed to his crotch.

A cheery red-and-white checked tablecloth covered the tea table. Jack pulled a magician's move and succeeded in nabbing the cloth without upsetting the tea service. Laying it over his lap, he received an approving nod from his hostess.

"But I've been remiss with introductions. My name is Ophelia."

The very same Ophelia that Mersey had mentioned to have a keen bite?

"How's the tea? It's hawthorn."

He sipped the tea. It was… "Refreshing."

"It'll show the truth of you."

Jack tilted the cup to peer at his lap. Couldn't she already see enough of him?

"You know Mersey Bane?"

"I have had the pleasure of that name." Coy, she sipped again, her littlest finger pointing to the perfect white clouds overhead. Daylight here. Again. "She your girl?"

"Yes."

And yes! She was his girl, and Jack wasn't about to allow one more innocent's death because he couldn't be there to protect her. Though he knew Mersey was strong, she was no match to Beryth. And the rings! She had no protection now.

"She's in danger, Ophelia. Ophelia. That's a lovely name, by the way."

The woman lowered her eyes. Rosy blush filled her apple cheeks. "Have more tea, will you dear?"

"I'm not thirsty. Will you help me, Ophelia? I must get back inside the manor to rescue Mersey."

"Drink the tea."

Startled by the commanding tone, Jack lifted the cup and swallowed back the whole thing. He felt a strange sweat suddenly rise, gulped deeply, and then the air about him grew dense, as if his pores had expelled the dust.

"As I suspected," Ophelia said. "Wearing a glamour, were you?"

He patted his chest, seeing only himself, but suspecting the glamour had just been defeated. "Mersey got it for me. I wasn't trying to fool you."

"Bad form, Jack."

Now where had he heard that before? Could he not please any woman?

"From where do you hail, Jack Harris?"

"Hail? Me?" Truth, Jack. It was the only way. "London. I—I work for P-Cell."

"Makes sense." Soft blue eyes slashed over him with an admonishing cut. "You seem like a hunter."

"I protect innocent civilians. There *are* demons that only do harm—you must know that. Beryth is one of them."

"Miss Bane has been trained. She'll fare well enough."

"Well enough?" Jack crushed his hand into a fist. Porcelain cracked. He opened his fingers to let the shards of teacup spill to the ground. "I'm not sorry for that. In fact, your neck is next, old lady. Mersey is under Beryth's influence. The protection spell her mother gave her is completely gone. She cannot help herself."

"And you propose to do so?"

"Hell, yes!"

"It means sure death for one or the both of you."

"If you're talking me and Beryth, then bring it on. I don't care if I don't survive. All that matters is that Mersey is safe."

Jack huffed out an exhale. Yes, he meant it. He would sacrifice his life for Mersey's. Life was worth very little if it did not include Mersey Bane.

The woman stared at the teacup shards as if it were a child, broken in a fall.

"Ophelia!"

Jack jumped out of the chair, crouching to defend. Behind him the old man wavered, cane shaking, bushy white hair listing in the breeze.

"What in blue blazes are you doing with this naked man?" the geriatric demanded.

The woman nodded, attention still fixed to the teacup. "Not so much as I should dream to."

Jack pulled the tablecloth around his hips, sensing her leering scrutiny.

"Not right." The man wobbled forward. "Not right...*at all!*"

What was once old and frail transformed fluidly into a towering, muscle-wrapped white wraith. Jack could see through the figment to the apple trees dotted with red fruit in the backyard. But the hot breath flaming over his face made it very real.

"Apologize," the beast commanded.

"Right." Clutching the cloth like an apron, Jack stepped out of the chair, eyes to the creature. He didn't have a weapon. And how to punch through a figment? "S-sorry, Miss Ophelia. I-it's just... Mersey is..."

To give voice to an emotion that welled inside him and made

him warm and right? She lifted him out of the darkness and made him realize it was okay to mourn his past, but that he shouldn't dwell there.

Jack rubbed the hematite ring on his pinky finger along his hip. Mersey wanted to protect him. And she had—at the unexpected sacrifice of her freedom.

He didn't deserve her. But he did admire her. And Mersey must have the freedom she craved.

"I love her."

The wraith morphed back to an ailing geriatric. Cane abandoned on the ground, the old man put his attention to collecting it, one creaking bend of his spine at a time.

"You love her?"

Jack turned to find Ophelia stood next to him. Her eyes wandered downward, where her fingers toyed with the hem of the tablecloth that threatened to splay open his makeshift kilt. What was with these creepy sorts?

"I do love her. Honestly. I don't ever say things like that. But I mean it."

"Have you never said it before?" the woman interrogated sternly.

"What do you mean? Like, to another woman? No." He scratched his head.

"What about your Monica Price? You held love for her in your heart."

"And I still do. A different kind of love," he defended quickly. "I realize that now. Monica was comfortable, like family, and yes, I did desire her. But Mersey, she's everything." The words came easily and felt like air on his tongue. Light, encompassing, and necessary. "I've never felt this way about another woman. I don't want to live without her."

Ophelia lifted his hand and inspected the hematite ring wrapping his little finger. "She gave you this."

"Yes."

"Not her mother?"

"What? I…no. Mersey put this on my finger hours ago." And if he was gaining headway with this couple, then please hurry it up! But he had to restrain himself from pushing. "For protection," he said. "I was given one very similar to this as a child."

"By a black cat?" Ophelia asked.

"Yes. You…know the cat?" It wasn't a ridiculous question. Not after all Jack had learned in the past few days. "Mersey's mother?"

Ophelia exchanged gazes with the old man.

"Please, Miss Ophelia. I love her. I'm just one man. I can't protect everyone. But I believe Mersey's mother chose me. And if that is so, then I accept the challenge. I'd give my all for Mersey."

"You will!" The old man rallied, thrusting his cane to the sky.

Ophelia smiled and bowed her head. She gestured toward the front door of the cottage. Entrance granted.

But Jack couldn't go in yet. He thought of the Range Rover parked on the road, and the thing he'd brought along, not knowing why, but that there would be a reason.

A reason crystal clear to him now.

"I must get to my car first. There's something inside it I need."

"A weapon?"

"Yes!"

The woman's lips tightened, but in the next instant, Jack found himself standing next to his car. He would not bother to question the weird goings-on. Instead, he leaned inside and fit his palm about the glass ball.

Direct sunlight beamed into the clear globe, casting a rainbow across Jack's wrist. It felt lighter than usual, and yet heavy with possibility.

"Right then," Jack said, and when next he looked, he was back before the cottage.

When Jack made to walk toward it—tablecloth wrapped round his hips—Ophelia thrust out her hand, catching him across the chest.

"What's that?"

He tilted the hunk of glass. "Truth? It's a ball of guilt. I'm going to kill it all today. And if there's a demon in my path, then mores the better."

She nodded approvingly. "That weapon is well and fine. A true warrior you are, my son. But what will you offer for entry, Jack Harris, Demon Frightener?"

Jack thought for a few seconds. The tangible would not be considered. Not as if he had anything on him to offer anyway.

Offering the glass ball was out of the question.

Whatever he put forth, it had to be something true and worthy of Mersey's rescue. There was but one thing Jack owned that he could offer. "I'd give my life to look into Mersey's eyes one more time."

"So you offer your life?"

"Yes," he said, never more sure of anything. "Take it. Only get me in there now. Er…with clothes, if you can manage that."

Ophelia smiled and nodded. "Enter freely."

And this time, the thorns did not bite.

He wore clothes. Or rather, armor. Mesh chainmail that linked to below his hips and topped off suede trousers. Sturdy suede boots laced to below his knees. In a leather sack tied at his waist, the glass ball hung ominously. And he carried a broadsword so heavy he had to use both hands to lift it.

"You've got to be bloody kidding me," Jack muttered, but he didn't think on his anachronistic clothing overlong. He was inside the Cadre. He had to find Mersey.

Jack focused his thoughts toward Mersey. The essence of her lived in the ring on his smallest finger. That part of her that had embedded itself inside of him. He should be able to sense her….

"My heart will find you," he muttered.

The mail was heavy and loud. Jack plodded forward, down the

hallway that he recognized leading to Mersey's bedroom. The door was open.

A man stood inside.

Chapter 28

Jack rushed the room, sword held at the ready in both fists. He'd never used a broadsword before, yet he'd trained with an épée in the army. He figured the gist of the motions quickly. Swing, thrust and jab.

Someone stood by the window, curtain pulled aside. Jack thrust the blade toward the intruder.

"I surrender!" the man shrieked, backing his shoulders to the wall and putting up his hands.

"Name, rank and ID number, pronto."

"Uh, Squire Callahan, storage manager, and—sodding hell, I can't remember my ID number."

"You work here?"

The blond man nodded effusively. He didn't appear threatening, more frightened than anything.

Jack looked down the blade of the sword. "What are you doing in Mersey's room?"

"I was l-looking for her."

"You always come in her room when she's not around?"

Squire shrugged. "Wh-who are you? You're not an initiate. I...think I need to call for—"

The sword was heavy, and ridiculous. Jack tossed it to the bed, and with one step, fitted himself before Squire, lifting him by the front of his shirt. "You're not going anywhere. Mersey's in trouble. The demon Beryth has her."

"And you are?"

"Jack Harris," he said.

"P-Cell?" he gasped. "How did you—?"

"Doesn't matter. I need to know where in this place a demon might take a hostage."

"Has it tapped her?"

"Not sure."

"Blimey." Squire released a miserable exhale. "Mersey doesn't take to being tapped. Why didn't you protect her?"

"I..." Tried. It was a cop-out admittance. So he wouldn't put it to words. "The demon was using influence. Listen, I don't have time for chitchat. Do you know this place?"

"I live here. You won't get far though. As soon as I recite the code spell, security will pick you out and then there'll be hell to pay."

"I don't look like a faery to you?"

"Should you?"

So the glamour had depleted when Ophelia had put him here. Not that he needed it now.

"I'm surprised the alarms aren't sounding and the cavalry isn't here already. Where is everyone? How can one of their own be literally kidnapped and no alarms, no one rushes to save her?"

"Big meeting still going on. Talk about vampires and such. The ladies Maybank aren't due out until later this evening. I'm pretty much the only one about. There was no breach. I don't know how the demon got in."

Jack swiped a palm down his face. "It was me. I didn't think of the demon when Mersey gave me the glamour."

"*You* brought Beryth in?"

Jack slammed his palm against the man's shoulder, pinning him to the wall and fixing him with a stare. "Squire, right?"

The man nodded.

"I love Mersey, and I have to find her. You willing to lead me about this place?"

"You love her?" Squire gasped. "But, she…"

Apparently this man had feelings for Mersey as well. "We'll do the gauntlet over who wins the girl's favor later. Think, Squire. Where would a pissed-off demon go in this place?"

"The lab," Squire decided resolutely. "It's where we store his brethren."

"Let's go."

Squire scampered down the hallway, and Jack marched along behind him. The halls grew narrower, and a chill, musty odor rose as they took a twisting stairway down to what Squire explained was the dungeon, or rather, the laboratory.

"You don't have a weapon that will destroy the demon," Squire noted in huffing breaths as they bottomed the stairs. "How will you kill Beryth?"

"Can't kill it," Jack said. Which is why he'd left the broadsword behind in Mersey's bedroom. "It may have tapped Mersey."

"Bloody hell." The man sank against the rough stone wall, his face going paler than his hair. "Then we're out of luck."

"What about those fancy crystals Mersey uses?"

"Crystallization?"

"Can you do it?"

Squire nodded. "But I'm only an apprentice. We need someone with the skill to capture the thing. I mean, I know the spell, but I don't have that *quintessence,* you know? Like a certain innate power."

"The connection." As Jack had witnessed Mersey do that first night in the warehouse. She'd thrust the crystal high, whispered a chant and had drawn the demon to her. "Like Mersey does with the ley lines and such?"

"Exactly."

Jack reached into the leather pouch and produced the glass ball. "Think this'll work?"

Squire studied the ball, tapping it. "It's crystal, it should."

"Crystal? It's just glass."

"Glass doesn't striate like this. But you don't understand—"

"You said you know the spell?"

"Yes, but—"

"But nothing, Callahan. I remember the invocation words Mersey used that first night we met." Vividly. How could he forget a moment imprinted into his psyche by that magical surprise kiss in the warehouse? "If you can speak the spell, I can take out the demon."

"It'll never work," Squire insisted as Jack approached the door to the dungeon. "You're not an adept!"

Jack closed his eyes tightly. All his life he'd tried to run away from silly childhood belief. That he'd been responsible for losing his father. That he could be responsible for luring the demon to Monica. All that running had twisted him into a circle that had brought him right back into the thick of things.

But the thing was, he did believe. Had he ever truly stopped believing? If not in any of the crazy things he'd witnessed over the past few months, he did believe in one thing—Mersey.

Jack spun round and shoved the ball against Squire's chest. "It will work, because I *believe* it will."

Chapter 29

Wearied and naked, Mersey tried to lift her head from the cobbled stone dungeon floor. Unsuccessful. Cold and must tainted the air along with a mixture of herbs used for healing and spellcraft. She shivered, her bare flesh riddled with goose bumps. She needed something to cover herself.

And—she needed a hero.

Where was Jack? He could save her. He was the one her mother had chosen. And she didn't need a ring to know that. Jack Harris had fit himself into her heart the moment she'd met him.

But he could be struggling himself. She had no doubt the instant Beryth separated her from Jack that he had been ousted from the Cadre. Glamour or not, the uninitiated were not able to remain on Cadre grounds without a guide. The supernatural barriers would have deported him.

Which meant that Jack was outside the perimeter with no means to get inside. She hoped his glamour held. Disguised as a sidhe, he should have little trouble in the forest—or else, a whole lot of problems.

Dash it all. What an afternoon. As far as dates went, this one chalked a mark in the swimmingly disastrous column.

A tilt of her head spied a white lab coat fallen from a stool. She reached it and pulled it up an arm. Every part of her ached, yet the demon had done little more than transport her to the dungeon and throw her to the floor.

Was Beryth influencing the pain to keep her subdued and unable to flee?

The clack of crystals alerted her to the demon above her sorting through Squire's library of stored demons. Ba'al Beryth. Minister of Devilish Pacts and Rituals. The very demon that had once tried to kill her mother—and Mersey; Mirabelle had been pregnant at the time.

A war demon had killed her mother? Could she believe Beryth? She couldn't see the demon, but the brimstone was pungent.

If it wanted revenge against her mother and father, why go through the crystals? It would never get the stored demons out of the crystals without the proper spell. Only adepts mastered that skill. Even if it could find a way to release the stored demons, the dread demon had no power within this building. It was a literal prisoner.

She touched her witch mark; it felt hot. Tapped. This was not good.

Where was everyone? Weren't the alarms on? Squire usually activated them as soon as he entered the lab. He was no fool.

A cat could easily scamper out and seek help. Concentration determined that the energy required to shift was depleted. She couldn't do it.

"Oh, Jack." Mersey eased a hand up her arm. Her skin was tender and bruised where Beryth had grabbed her.

"How can I determine which demons are inside which crystals?" the demon hissed, impatience heightening its voice. "Bane?"

She gave a withering nod and closed her eyes. Mersey passed out.

The familiar served him little value, beyond anchoring him to this realm and providing another anchor to the Cadre. So Beryth would not release their bond. But her unconscious state left him to fend for himself, which he could muster. Though he didn't want to release any of his kind that would not serve him well.

The crystals were numbered, so there must be a storage log somewhere with corresponding information on the contents. He need only release a war demon or two, and his revenge against the Cadre could begin. They'd tear this castle down and devour the inhabitants.

'Course, Beryth would keep a few as slaves to release the remaining demons upon the world. Wouldn't that be delicious joy?

And perhaps, within the information and data, he'd find the location of that infernal Caractacus Bane, his jailer, his rival.

Jack pushed open the huge iron-banded door to the dungeon.

"Stay out here," he whispered to Squire, "until I need you to chant the spell."

From behind cover of the door, he observed. Inside the dungeon a high-tech lab had been trashed. Glass vials broken. Books shoved everywhere. Dozens of the storage crystals lay scattered across the stone floor. Each one pulsed with a dark shadow. Something was inside. Could Beryth release them?

Jack didn't spy Mersey, though he sensed her presence.

And there, sorting through the shelves of crystals stood Beryth, wearing the costume of a dark-haired human and black fitted suit. His back to Jack, the demon worked frantically through the crystals. Lifting them, peering into them, shaking them near his ear and then tossing them over his shoulder.

"Now or never."

Jack leaped inside the dungeon and stepped right into the lashing tongue that whipped toward him. He gripped the slimy appendage, struggling to hold it back, to keep the forked tip from touching any part of him. It was like holding a noodle.

The thing narrowed and slid from his fingers.

Ball of wonder clasped firmly, Jack raised it above himself and stood defiantly before the demon.

Beryth reeled in his tongue with a spit-flying lash. He tilted his head with an insectile jerk and regarded what Jack displayed above his head. "I know I taunted you about it earlier, Jack boy, but you don't believe that kiddie toy has any power over me?"

"It sent you running before."

Beryth brushed nonexistent lint from his shoulder. "A lucky shot."

"Twice?" Jack made to toss the thing.

"Wait!" Beryth stepped back and spread out his hands. Drawing in a breath, his chest puffed up unnaturally and it grew twice its size, taking on the red musculature that Jack preferred. Much easier to kill something that looked like a creature. "You need me, Jack."

Behind him he sensed Squire remained hidden. Good.

"Where's Mersey!" he demanded.

A groan from behind the steel table answered Jack's question. Beryth shifted to stand before the table as Jack stepped forward.

"Think about it, Jack. Without me," Beryth tried, "you cannot know your silly mortal love, because there would be no opposite in your heart."

"I've known sadness. And grief and pain. They are all opposite. Face it, Beryth, *you* need me. Without humans, demons have no purpose."

"You humans," Beryth bellowed. "You are crueler to each other than we demons can be to you. We inhabit you. We coerce, we tempt, we plant lust and fear." The demon gestured beyond Jack. It had seen Squire. "But you, you have free will. You can choose your actions. And what do you choose to do? Kill!"

"Only those deserving," Jack muttered.

"Oh? Ah. Well then. And so I am deserving?"

"You're a murderer, Beryth, and you will not leave this realm unpunished."

"Punishment is something you've no expertise in, Jack boy. But these Cadre sorts?" The demon grasped a darkened crystal from the table. "An icy hell, Jack. I did nothing. I harmed none."

"I saw you! You would have killed Mersey's mother!"

"I would have never harmed Mirabelle. I loved her! But the Cadre believed her when she claimed much the same, that I would have murdered her had some idiot boy not frightened me off. And those Cadre bastards saw fit to put me in one of these."

"Cry me another one, Beryth. Your arse is mine."

"Serve me your best." The demon bristled, drawing up to its full height, which was a good two feet higher than Jack. "Say, what if I could give her back to you, Jack? Your precious, unrequited Monica?"

Sucking in a breath, Jack hardened his grip on the ball. He'd had enough. Glancing back to Squire, he gave the signal wink.

Squire began to chant.

"Jack!" groaned out from behind the table. A hand slapped the floor and he saw a tuft of black hair. Not a single protective ring on those fingers.

Beryth drew his forked tongue across his lips and smacked them. A lift of brow and a bounce on his toes signaled his wicked delight.

"She'll never be yours," Jack warned.

"She already is. Just as her mother once was."

"So what—you once had a thing for Mirabelle Bane?"

The demon bristled.

"Get over it. Mersey is not her mother."

"She is that bastard Caractacus's progeny. It was he who kept me from—"

"Enslaving an innocent? I got your number, dread. You were in love, she chose another. Happens all the time. It's called heartbreak. You don't get to harm others because infatuation slapped you in the face. Now you may not have harmed Mirabelle, but you did murder an innocent human. Monica Price," Jack announced. "Time to pay for that crime."

"I need more time!" Squire yelled, then fell back into the chant.

Deep, bellicose laughter filled the room. The remaining glass vials on the table shattered. Beryth slashed out an arm, the length growing. Talons checked Jack's coat of mail.

"So you want a fight?" Jack asked. "Bring it."

Jack dropped the ball to the floor and came upright, charging for the demon. He head-butted the thing against the wall of crystals, which clattered down around them.

The demon could not control Jack's reflexes now he was not tapped.

"You ready, Squire?"

"Almost!"

"Face it, Jack the Demon Frightener. You've lost another to your own dread." The demon made a gesture with its arm.

Behind him, Squire soared through the air and landed against the wall with a bone-crunching thud. He sputtered and muttered a few Latin words, determined but obviously injured.

How to hold back the demon until the chant was complete?

There was one way to enchant a demon, and that was to give it something to feed off—a mortal's soul. Jack had been trained never to look a demon in the eye, for madness was guaranteed.

But he would not rest until Mersey was free. He locked onto the demon's yellow gaze with his own eyes.

Beryth grinned and chuckled grandly. "Oh, the cleverness of you, Jack! Will you dare it? Enchant me into your eyes."

Jack planted his feet. The demon's wide round yellow eyes opened into a vast and treacherous tunnel. Dry, itchy pain sizzled over Jack's eyes. This was nothing. He could do this gaze.

"Look deeper," Beryth cooed. Its talons clacked against the chain mail.

Squire's confused chanting segued to a fuzzy fugue at the back of Jack's brain. He thought Mersey screamed, but the buzzing of a thousand insects intensified in his ears.

No longer were Beryth's eyes yellow. Filled with red, crimson and scarlet. Very similar, the colors, but acutely different. The swirl of death, each shade representing a different life, a vile scream of lost breath. A stolen soul shattered in a sea of dread.

With a toss of its head, the demon transformed. Blond ringlets bounced upon its shoulders. Red, pursed lips drew into a sexy smile. Monica winked at him, then she bellowed as her heart was ripped from her body.

Biting down on his lip, Jack winced. The demon hadn't changed. He saw it all in Beryth's eyes. He thought to look away.

Do not!

He must hold the demon, keep it distracted from Mersey and Squire.

Rationally, he knew the images were not real. And yet the ache of death held his limbs in a catatonic freeze. Buzzing entwined his veins. It stung, a thousand bees bombarding his soul. He could not shake it off.

Mersey's smile brightened inside the demon's eyes. She kissed him. A field of lemons caught his plunging, falling heart. Jack felt the fluttering warmth of her smile upon his mouth. Something else soaked his hands and chest. Mersey's blood, crawling with bees, and there, amid a pool of glittering crimson, her head rolled at his feet.

"No," he moaned.

He could not look at his mistakes. But he must.

His father's pale dead face replaced Mersey's. His mother's wails as she beat upon her husband's deathbed. So many staring eyes as he'd walked the aftermath of bombs, raids and terrorist attacks.

"Ready, Jack!" Squire mumbled.

Fisting the air did not erase the horrors in the demon's eyes. Heartbeats racing erratically, Jack wasn't sure if they'd ever stop. He gulped for air.

Ready? Right then. Time to do this. He leaned down to pick up the ball.

Every tear he had never shed over his father's death he grasped and shoved out through his being. *"Te vincio!"*

He had not been to blame for wishing. He believed that.

He could not change the past. Only, he would learn from it.

Pray God, he could now save his future.

Jack's arm swung backward, as if he'd caught something in a mitt.

Leaning forward, he caught his free hand on a knee and groaned against the ache that was his body. He shook the globe and it stirred with dark swirling mist. Beryth no longer stood in the room.

Mersey crawled around the corner of the table. She shoved the hair from her eyes. Jack displayed the crystal ball before him, twisting it and proudly showing her what he had done.

"I'm free." Mersey sighed and smiled. "Good one, hotshot."

The buzz of a thousand bees overwhelmed Jack and dropped him to his knees.

He scratched at the invisible torments. They dribbled from Mersey's face like blood. Each red droplet sprouted pixie wings and buzzed back at his eyes, piercing the iris with a stinger.

"Jack, I'm here."

He felt something touch his cheek. He slapped it away.

"It's the gaze," she said. "Blimey, the demon gaze is dangerous. He's gone mad."

No, not mad. He couldn't be mad when he was aware of Mersey so close—dead at his feet.

"Jack, please, don't let this happen."

Softer, bringing forth tears bloody and buzzing. Can the dead talk?

Warmth pressed upon his mouth. A kiss? *Not right. Too tender.* He made to slap it away, but she caught his wrist. Something sat upon him. Buzzing, so much buzzing. He jerked his head to the left and the right.

"Open your eyes, Jack. Look at me!"

"No," he gasped. No more staring down things that weren't his own species.

"Kiss me, Jack. Please. You are the one."

Those two words echoed in his tormented brain. The one? What did that mean? He wasn't anyone's—

Yes, you are. You want to be. You can be!

Allow it to happen. Believe.

Mersey's mother. The cat in the field. Fright made its way

through Jack's system at the memory of watching the cat drop the hematite ring on his windowsill.

Warmth against his mouth again. Salvation. The buzzing segued to background cacophony.

"I love you, Jack."

Touch her. Feel her. Know love. There is no other. You are the one!

Yes, he knew it. She wasn't dead. The demon did not get her.

"Mersey?"

"Kiss me…."

But before Jack could embrace Mersey, a winged man materialized above them, arms crossed jauntily, and crooked grin just as haughty.

"Ah, ah," the faery chastised with a finger cutting the air. "Not so fast, my demented Jack Harris. This one is mine. It was part of the bargain."

"Bargain?" Jack looked to Mersey. He swiped at a bee.

"A pity, really. He held potential as a warrior." The faery hugged Mersey to his side, his wing curling forward to wrap possessively around the bits the white lab coat did not cover. "For your release from the forest, Jack—and that glamour you used to sneak into the Cadre—kitten here offered up her own freedom."

"No, she wouldn't. Mersey? But all you have is your freedom."

"I—" Her head lolled to the faery's chest. "Love you, Jack."

"Touching, but futile. Unless you have a claim to her, mortal, she is mine." The faery glanced about the room and toed the inert body of Squire. Dismissing it all with a shake of his head, he then clutched up Mersey. "Shall we, my pet?"

And the two of them disappeared.

Chapter 30

Jack remained inside the walls of the Cadre, deep in the dank air of the dungeon. The buzzing had given over but he continued to shake his head. The residual effects of the demon gaze clung heavily to his soul.

He'd seen Mersey dead. An image he could never erase from his mind.

He shouted, calling all the darkest shadows to the surface.

Jack shuddered, his body clenching. He fell forward, pressing his hands to the stone floor. His cry matched that of his mother's wailing in his head.

"Not real," Jack managed to say through his tight jaw. "Not…"

Her kiss. He had not opportunity for a final kiss from the woman he loved.

You are the one.

And she was the one for him.

And now, he did not have her.

"Agent Harris."

Chainmail *clishing,* Jack looked up to a woman with long auburn hair, hands on her hips. Green eyes not so vivid as Mersey's fixed him. She was flanked by a man to the left, and to the right by a woman sporting stern black-rimmed spectacles. The hum of insects faded into the background.

"You're on private property," she announced.

Back to the real world. Come on, Jack. Snap out of it!

Right then. Mersey is gone. Taken by that…faery.

Jack sniffed away the tears and punched the floor once. With a snap of his neck, he pushed up to stand. "And you are?" he asked.

"Lady Aurora Maybank." She crossed her arms. An air of refined grace surrounded her, yet beneath, he sensed her interior was hard as steel. "Your new worst enemy."

As if he had room on his slate for another?

"I see. Sorry, I'm a bit put out, or I'd fill in your name on the list, but at the moment I believe I have enough enemies."

"How did you get inside our facility, Agent Harris?"

Where the hell had the faery taken Mersey? To that bloody forest. He had to pursue.

"Agent—"

"I don't recall," he snapped.

"It doesn't matter. I know you had to be led inside, yet you didn't show on the monitors. Whatever charm Mersey used, it was a good one to get you past the threshold guardians. But I can see you now."

He gave a mock bow. "Charmed, I'm sure."

"At the moment I must overlook the fact that P-Cell has infiltrated our private headquarters. Most pressing is where is Mersey Bane?"

"Gone." The word fell from Jack's heart and splattered upon the floor before his feet. "With…the faery."

"Raskin Rubythorn?"

"I don't know what the hell his name was. The faery said Mersey had traded him the boon of her enslavement to rescue me from that sodding forest. Me? Can you imagine?"

"No, I cannot." Though, the tiniest smile appeared on the woman's delicate-featured face. Or was that a shadow of the bees Jack still heard buzzing in his brain?

"I'm in charge here, and you will respect our rules. The Cadre does not allow P-Cell into headquarters, so you will be expelled."

"For such a private establishment, you're sure handing me the information, Miss Maybank."

"You will not leave with it, so it is irrelevant. Now, I know Mersey had been investigating a leak in London. But that doesn't explain you. You and Mersey are—?"

Jack shrugged. Sighed. "I love her."

The woman's brow rose.

"I do. I love Mersey Bane. And I know I'm not supposed to be here. And Mersey broke every rule in the book by bringing me in. And I did lead Beryth here, to the detriment of no one but Mersey. I take full responsibility for that." He gestured to the glass ball at his feet. "Although, you do now have the dread demon crystallized."

"Crystallized?" She bent forward to study the ball, but didn't touch it. "Are we using a new form of containment, Squire?"

"Nuhuh," mumbled up from the floor where Jack spied a tuft of blond hair. Poor guy, he'd taken a good whack to the head.

"It's in there," Jack offered. He tried to get her to take it by nudging it toward her feet, but she wouldn't. "I don't want it, that's for sure."

"We appreciate you helping us to capture the demon, Mr. Harris. Beryth has been tops on our most-wanted list for a long time. Squire will ensure the demon is stored properly. Won't you, Squire?"

"I'm fine!" called out from the floor behind the lab table. "Just a little groggy. Thank you, Lady Aurora, for your ever-lacking concern."

She ignored the sarcasm. "Now, Harris, if you'll shuck off that ridiculous armor, I'll arrange for you to be transported back to your home, minus the memory of your escapades behind Cadre walls."

Without memory of the Cadre? Well, bring it on. Nothing but ill luck had come of this adventure.

But no way was Jack moving until all the ends were neatly tied up.

He planted his feet and stared at the woman. "I go nowhere without Mersey."

"Please, Agent Harris, don't make this more than it is. You did what you could, and we thank you."

Lady Aurora had a certain air about her that spoke command. But *he* was in love. And, he believed. That trumped all superior stare downs.

"I don't think you heard me, Lady Aurora. I know I just met Mersey a week ago. But if her mother hadn't picked me, I still would have found her, I'm sure of it. I love Mersey Bane. And I'm not leaving until I know she is safe."

"We'll see to her comfort."

"She's been taken captive by a sodding faery!"

Lady Aurora noticeably stiffened at his shout. Jack could hardly care for offending the gentry.

"Assign someone to lead me into the forest and ensure exit. I have a score to settle with the Rubythroat guy."

"It's Rubythorn, and he's a former prince of the Black court. Malicious mischief is his stock and trade. You'll get nothing settled with him if he's taken claim to Mersey. And if Mersey made a bargain—"

"So you're going to let the sprite keep one of your own captive because he *can?*"

"It's not wise to sever a bargain made with the sidhe."

"Bullocks." It slipped and Jack didn't care. "She's mine."

"Is she?" She smirked.

He pounded a fist against his chest. The chainmail clinked. "She is."

"Do you have proof that Mersey is yours? That you've a claim to her."

"I didn't mean it that way. I just—in my heart. She's mine. Here." Outrage mellowing, he fisted his chest again. "I love her with all my heart, as tainted as that may be. Can't you at least provide me with a guide? I'll deal with the faery in my own manner."

"I'm well aware of P-Cell's *manner*, Harris. Weapons are not allowed in the unaligned borderlands surrounding the St. Yve estate. Besides, the alliance between the Cadre and Rubythorn is very tenuous. I couldn't send a guide along with you if I wanted to. Politics."

"I see." Jack nodded. "She was right."

"Who?"

"Mersey said your lot considered yourself her family, but it's all a show. You don't really care about her. You all are so big on studying the OEs, you don't know how to relate on a real emotional level. With humans and with familiars—who are as human as they come, let me tell you."

"And you do know how to relate, Harris?"

Jack clasped his hands before him. The ring Mersey had given him clinked against the chainmail. "I'm learning."

The ring.

It is your claim to me, Jack.

Mersey's mother had known they would someday find each other. *You are the one, Jack.*

Kiss me. She'd kissed the demons from his dreams. Could he ever give her the freedom she desired?

He had to try.

"What if I can find proof? A claim to Mersey."

"Then you've the key to getting her back."

Jack pushed the ring toward the end of his finger. It looked exactly like the other one he'd been given as a child. Could he use this one and save time? There was a rat's chance in heaven the original even existed.

"What is your proof?" Lady Aurora prompted.

"You'll see." Jack unhooked the chain mail shirt and tossed it to the floor. It landed in a clatter upon half a dozen toppled crystals. Bare chest heaved as he took in a breath of bravery. He'd keep the leather trousers.

"I'll need a guide."

The woman nodded sharply. "Impossible."

"I'll go," came a weak voice from the floor.

"Squire, you—"

"If he has a means to get her back," Squire said as he pulled himself up along the table, "I'm there. You may not care about Mersey, but I love her like a sister."

Jack turned to Lady Aurora. Not a blink. Not a smile. She gave a single nod, then turned, and with her entourage, walked out.

"So." Squire shrugged long fingers through his hair. "This is my first excursion outside the hallowed halls of the Cadre. Can't—" he wobbled and sank to his knees "—wait."

Chapter 31

"Where is it?"

"I have no idea, Callahan." Jack searched the roadway for sign of his home—the place of his birth. "I buried it when I was eight."

The man in the passenger seat sighed. Jack figured him for about twenty-five, and good-natured. Though his nose still bled. The demon had clocked him a good one. Whether or not the man was human, Jack didn't want to know. He'd volunteered to help Mersey; that was all that mattered.

"Well," Squire said, "you know the basic area?"

"Sure. And it was before an oak tree."

"That should make things easier. Just look for a big old…"

Jack pulled up to the edge of an oak forest. Centuries-old oaks lined the border, surrounded by many younger oaks that had been growing for decades. Fall-browned leaves formed a canopy and shook down in plummeting sheets as squirrels scrambled at the arrival of a vehicle.

"Oh, this is bad," Squire said. "Easy as working formulas blind-folded and hanging upside down! All it is is oaks!"

Squire sneezed. "Did I mention I'm allergic to pollen?"

"I noticed. You were the one so wise to get out of the dungeon. Welcome to the real world, Callahan."

"Speaking of the real world." Squire turned on the seat to face Jack. "Here we are, back in the real world. *Away* from Cadre grounds. So why don't you just leave, Harris?"

"I don't understand."

"You've your freedom *and* your memory. If you leave now, you can have back your life. You don't think Lady Aurora will actually allow Rubythorn to keep Mersey."

"I have no clue."

"Well, she won't. It wouldn't reflect well on her supervisory skills. So you go on. Mersey will be fine."

"Can't."

"You want to return to ultimately get your memory wiped of Mersey? Dude, leave and you'll still have her. Here." Squire tapped his skull. "Any other scenario, and you'll walk right past her and not even give her a second glance."

The idea of physically losing Mersey was unthinkable. But losing her in his memory? To leave now would mean walking away from his promise to Mersey. To always protect her.

"Can't do it, Squire. Love her."

"Then you'll lose her."

"Yes." Would he think of her when he smelled lemon in a supermarket? Just how encompassing could a memory wipe be? Would he lose this insufferable buzzing that hummed at the periphery of his sanity? "But I'll know she's safe."

"No, you won't. Memory wipe, dude!"

"Come on. We don't have time for this. Every moment Mersey spends with that faery is another moment her spirit fades."

"Man, she must really love you, Harris. To trade her freedom for you?"

Ignoring Squire's remark, Jack stepped out onto the roadside. He plunged down the ditch and started across the overgrown field that sat before the forest.

Did she really love him?

What was love? It wasn't about being the one. Or someone's Mr. Right. He would always be Mr. Wrong, no matter what.

Was it the need to make everything in the world around him right? The desire to erase his guilt? Or the compulsion to never stop until he again saw Mersey.

None of the above, Jack suspected. He knew better now.

Love lived in him and filled his every fiber. It felt like Mersey's sighs. It tickled like her laughter. It was a feeling, not a memory, and he wagered no vicious memory wipe could ever erase that.

He hoped not.

He'd never felt this way with Monica. And Jack knew now that he never said anything to Monica because it wouldn't have been the truth. Only a need.

Mersey wasn't a need; she was his soul.

"Why didn't you just keep the ring?" Squire set up post on a rotting oak trunk frilled with mushrooms, and itched furiously at his ankles. The noon sun coaxed rivulets of sweat down his forehead.

"It scared me."

Jack inspected tree number seven. There weren't a lot of oaks he earmarked for twenty years growth that edged the clearing. But there were enough.

"And if you look beyond the nasty demon I saw that night, there was the other weirdness. The ring was given to me by a cat. Mersey's mother. I can't understand how her mother expected that the little boy she gave the ring to would actually hold on to it over the years and not lose it."

Squire shrugged, but it was more a frantic splay of limbs as he wildly scratched.

"Someone should have told me the rules." Jack pressed his forehead to the tree and closed his eyes.

If he had known then the ring would lead him to an incredibly amazing, smart, sexy woman, he would have had it locked away in a security box until he was older.

"Too bad Mersey wasn't here," Squire commented. "She could have witched her way to the right tree. Even I can feel the energy here."

Energy? Jack closed his eyes and tried to tap into it. What did it feel like? What did Mersey feel when she located a ley line?

"Jack."

"I'd do anything for her, Squire. Mersey is like me. We both strive to survive in a world we don't quite belong in. She's a part of the world I don't understand, and I'm a part of the one she wants to belong to. I know I'll probably never see her again after I've found her and returned her to the Cadre—bloody hell, I made a bargain, too—but I just want her to know how much I love her before that chance is taken away."

"Then open your eyes, Jack."

He did. And the sun glinted an inch before his nose—

—on the curved black arc of a hematite ring.

Pulling away a chunk of bark, with ring intact, Jack presented it like a triumphant flame to the sky. But his celebration lasted all of two seconds.

There would be time later for celebrating—with the woman he loved. The bark crumbled away easily. Fitting the ring onto his finger above the one Mersey had given him, he marveled as the rings magnetically clicked to one another. As if destined to be together.

"Let's go." He grabbed Squire by the shirt and pulled him onward.

Wild lavender spotted the overgrown field. Jack stepped high to breach the grasses. They plunged down the ditch and up onto the gravel road.

They didn't get far. Crouched upon the crunched metal roof of the Range Rover, a stone gargoyle glowered. The passenger door had popped open as a result of the weight bending the frame sharply inward.

And standing before the car? Ophelia, wearing a floaty white dress decorated all over with red roses and holding her hands in a clasp before her. Wispy gray hair curled at her ears. Jack had not noticed before how blue her eyes were, like gemstones lit from behind. Was she a faery?

"Hello, Mr. Harris. You look much different with your trousers on."

Squire flashed Jack a wonky look.

"Out for a bit of sun today?" she asked.

"What do you want, Ophelia?" With a raised hand, Jack cautioned Squire to remain behind him. "And would you call off the hound? Look what it did to my car."

"Doesn't matter. You don't need it, after all."

"And why is that?"

"The bargain, Jack. Oh, don't give me that I-don't-understand frown. You bargained your life for entrance into the Cadre. You were granted that entrance. Now, it's time to pay the price. Step forward, if you will. I don't wish the residual energy of the spell to zap your friend to death."

Squire took an immense step backward. "Nice knowing you, mate. You want I should take care of that ring for you?"

"I'm not going anywhere, Squire. And who are you? Soon as you think I'm gone, you move in on my girl?"

Squire offered a sheepish shrug.

"Boys, there's no time for dillydally. I've tea brewing on the stove, and must return to the cottage." Ophelia harrumphed.

"Can't do it," Jack said. He planted his feet and squared his hips.

"A man never goes back on his word. That makes you unworthy, Jack Harris."

"Yeah? So take a number and stand in line." He waggled his finger, displaying his find. "Got a pressing matter. Yes, I promised my life for Mersey's. And I won't renege on the deal. But she's not free yet. And until she is, I'm still on the clock."

"That wasn't the bargain. It was merely to get inside—" Ophelia's words choked abruptly as Jack grabbed her by the neck.

The gargoyle gave a silent, stony yowl and flapped its wings.

"Call off that sodding hunk of gravel," Jack warned, "or I'll snap your neck."

Ophelia made a gesture with her hand that quieted the gargoyle. Jack felt the heat of its stony-eyed stare, but he did not relent.

"I'm going back into the St. Yve wood," he said. "Some Ruby-throat faery has my girl."

"Rubythorn," Ophelia rasped. "He's a bugger."

"You're telling me." Jack released the woman, and she smoothed a hand down her throat. "Let me rescue Mersey, then you can collect on your bargain. Deal?"

"You're fortunate I like you, Jack."

"I don't see how wanting to take a bloke's life shows much in way of liking him, but if that's your style…"

"You have entrance into the forest?" Ophelia asked now, all sweetness and tea.

"Squire here will lead me."

The woman looked over Jack's companion, her disapproval obvious. "If he's the best you can summon, then I send my blessings with you, Jack. You'll need them. And to ensure you make it out in one piece—"

"So you can claim that piece?"

"Oh, Jack, you tease." Ophelia harrumphed again. "I offer you this."

Two black ribbons fluttered out from nowhere before Jack and landed at his feet. They snaked about as if alive and the ends joined, forming into a branch.

"Use this when entering the faery camp," Ophelia said. "It's elder, a most sacred tree to the sidhe. We shall meet again. And next time there'll be no delaying the inevitable."

"Look forward to it."

The gargoyle leaped to the gravel road with a crunch and, spreading down one wing, allowed Ophelia to climb on.

Squire whistled appreciatively as he watched the creature take to flight, its passenger sitting sidesaddle upon its back. "Never saw those things do that before," Squire said. "Wicked."

Jack grabbed Squire by the shoulder and shoved him inside the car. "You drive. I'll sit and hold the door shut. Take me as close to the faery round as you can. From there, we'll walk."

Chapter 32

Was it worth it? Sitting now in a cage, a thing to be teased, while the bargain had won Jack's freedom from a never-ending consignment to the forest?

Yes.

A man like Jack Harris could go mad forever trapped in the St. Yve woods, walking endlessly after. And certainly Mersey would have had no way to find or contact him.

She was at peace with her decision. Jack would live to return to London. She hoped he'd be more thoughtful before blasting away at demons, and knew, in her small pounding feline heart, he would be. He had captured the demon Beryth with a crystal—a feat that had amazed her. It was Jack's belief, she knew, that had allowed him to perform the difficult task.

The man could do anything he set his heart to. Including stealing hers.

Crossing her forepaws one over the other, Mersey laid her skull upon her paws and closed her eyes. She did not want to peer out the silver cage bars. She must be content now with memories of her one true love.

Jack carried the elder branch before him on a palm, while he held Squire's hand in his other. Black ribbons fluttered across his knees as he took the mossy path in sure strides. Much as he wanted to charge forth, he knew the dangers of an unescorted venture into this wicked forest.

The air fell heavily upon his shoulders, the sky a warning pre-storm green. Any moment the heavens would crack open and gush down.

Before him, the faery round appeared amid centuries-old oaks and rowans and rocks that may have been washed up from the sea millennia ago. But the air was dead still...silent.

The ominous quiet crowded the back of his throat. He just wanted this to be done, to again see Mersey.

A pouf of dandelion seedling meandered before Jack, entering the circle with careless abandon. He squinted at it, wondering if it was the same faery he'd earlier encountered. The seedling floated away.

"Is this the right way?" he whispered to Squire.

"Who knows?"

Jack shot a look over his shoulder at the man.

"I don't know the forest. Dungeon master, remember? Don't get out much. I'm here to ensure your passage in and out."

"Right then. I'll just...follow my heart."

Squire returned a wink.

Drawing in a breath, Jack worked his shoulders, releasing the tension that had sprung up unawares. A bee buzzed his ear, but he didn't flinch. *Not real. Don't forget that.* He thought briefly it would have been great to have a weapon, but as quickly knew it wasn't wise, if simply unnecessary.

"Where are you, Mersey?" he said softly. Closing his eyes, he listened and sniffed and felt the wind touch his bare chest. Was that a hint of lemon he scented?

Jack opened his eyes.

Twilight grew around him so swiftly, he felt the light recede and pull from his flesh like winter growing over summer. Everywhere twinkling lights appeared, beeswax candles apported upon roots winding across the ground and nestled in knotholes pocking elm and oak trunks and twisting branches.

The sidhe had known of his presence before he'd even entered the forest. Now to wait for an invitation.

"Mersey, I will not leave without you," he murmured, feeling determination spread through his every fiber. "I promise you that."

Taking in the periphery, Jack began to notice the eyes peeking at him from within the grasses, or there, behind the cover of a ground leaf as wide as an elephant's ear. Toadstools harbored congregations of whispering sprites, faeries and small bug-like creatures.

Anxiety rose, stiffening his neck and straightening his shoulders. Jack coached himself to remain at ease; after all, he came in peace. A new costume for him to wear, but one that did not feel as confining as he'd expected.

Determined to show him a new vision of the strange creatures that inhabited his own world, Mersey had done him well merely by entering his life. Jack wasn't sure what he would do when he returned to London and to P-Cell. Blasting indiscriminately at anything that said boo now made little sense. The collateral damage was not acceptable.

His superiors wouldn't approve.

Wouldn't matter anyway, if he did not return with Mersey's hand in his.

Lifting the elder branch over his head, he called out, "I enter your domain in peace, and bearing proof of my claim to Mersey Bane."

A scurry of movement appeared like a sped-up movie, colors blending and figures darting, while Jack remained a dizzied spectator.

And from somewhere low, perhaps beneath the earth, the mournful cry of a bagpipe sweetened the candlelit night.

"This way," hissed close near his ear.

Jack spun. A thin faery with pointed ears and braided black hair gestured with fingers too long for gloves. It turned and strode over a twist of mossy roots. Jack took two steps for each one the faery made.

And then he realized he no longer held Squire's hand. "Callahan?"

"Just follow, Jack." Sounded like the dungeon master's voice, but Jack didn't take the time to wonder.

He turned and saw the elaborately carved chestnut trunk. It formed a huge room, much like an outdoor canopy for parties. Jasmine scented the air and the bell-like giggles of miniature yet unseen observers rang in his ears. He entered, and the carpet crushed beneath his steps.

His unease, present since setting foot in the forest, increased. Heartbeats muffled in his ears and his palms grew clammy.

Here be faeries. And not the sort that decorated greeting cards or sat as silent statuary in gardens. These faeries were mischievous and malicious, if not deadly.

"That way," his guide said and pointed to the door at the opposite side of the trunk.

A door no higher than a cat's shoulders and no wider.

Jack turned to question the guide, but found he stood alone in the small room. Outside, the candles blinked out, yet the trunk he stood in remained illuminated by flittering firebugs.

He bent to inspect the door. A small crystal doorknob and knocker were set into the chestnut door. "Mersey could get in there—if she were a cat. Hmm…"

Never one to turn away from a door that led to opportunity, Jack plucked the doorknob between thumb and forefinger. It opened. He poked a hand inside. The force that suctioned him into the void tore his limbs to a vicious stretch and muffled a scream from his lungs.

But it was nothing compared to a demon gaze. And recovery was instant.

He stood in the same forest, but it was a room of sorts. Smooth green moss designed a floor, the walls fashioned of close-spaced trees, their limbs curving overhead to form a ceiling. Upon closer inspection, the furniture seemed alive, glittering like sun upon the sea. A silver cage hung suspended over a grand emerald velvet chaise. Inside lay a black cat, its head hung over the cage edge, looking bored.

"Mersey!"

Jack rushed toward the cage. A crushing force squeezed his lungs and his breath expelled. Pressed backward, he landed on the ground. Before him stood a male faery, his hand extended, palm flat. The very same who had tried to coax Jack into the faery circle earlier.

The cat in the cage mewled. She could easily walk between the bars—why did she not?

"Mersey tells me you are her mortal lover," the faery announced. "Stand up. Be bold, Jack Harris." The sidhe's sapphire eyes glinted and briefly widened in acknowledgment. "You may have my name now, it matters little once Ophelia calls on your debt. I am Raskin Rubythorn. Master of your lover."

The branch in Jack's hand cracked in half. He tossed it to the floor before the chaise. That Mersey remained in the cage hurt Jack's heart. Did she feel obligated to do so?

"Mister, er—" Lady Aurora had told him this one was ostracized royalty. "My lord Rubythorn," he tried, giving it the protocol he suspected the faery felt he deserved. "I come in peace."

"I have heard that one before." The faery seated himself on the chaise. Silken fabric splayed across the back slinked down in puddles at his feet.

"You, mortal, you disturb my eyes. Come! Anyone!" Raskin snapped his long fingers crisply. "Bring me some henbane ointment to put this mortal out from my eyes."

"I have a claim to Mersey Bane that no sidhe must deny."

Jack avoided looking at the cat. He couldn't bear seeing Mersey trapped. Her greatest fear.

"Impossible," Raskin declared. With a nod, he directed Mersey toward his lap.

It cut to Jack's soul to watch Mersey glide between the silver bars and pounce onto the chaise. Head down and black ears flat, she settled on the faery's lap. The bastard stroked her back.

"I hear no mention of thanks," Raskin prompted.

"For imprisoning the woman I love? I'll save that gratitude."

"You used my glamour to enter the Cadre. Ungrateful death merchant."

He was not here to argue, or start a row. But it took all Jack's resolve to swallow a retort and keep his fists from forming.

For Mersey. Sacrifice your pride.

"Thank you," Jack said. "And now, I have this."

Slipping both rings from his littlest finger, Jack presented them upon his palm.

"What is that?" Raskin asked. "Trinkets? I have a thousand rings in the finest metals and crystals. Your dark little stone does not intrigue me, demon frightener. Can you do better?"

Jack peered into the sapphire eyes that simultaneously smirked and sneered. Much as he wanted to take the bastard down, he knew the outer appearance was deceptive, and that faeries were hale and powerful. Besides, if Mersey had bargained, he must win her back properly.

"Mersey's mother gave me this ring," he said. "She approved me as mate for her daughter while she carried Mersey in her belly."

"Is this man telling the truth?"

The cat meowed.

"Liar!"

"She does not lie!" Jack tamped down his anger. It was so difficult not to grab the fey thing by the neck and squeeze. "Please, if you will not accept this symbol of our destiny, then you must grant me one favor. Allow Mersey to change shapes. I must see her one last time."

"You can see her quite plainly—"

"In human form!"

"Do not raise your voice to me, mortal."

"I will stand here and shout to the skies until you give me that one request."

"I've given you enough already."

"Very well, then I'll begin." And Jack shouted anything he could conjure, which just so happened to be a ribald pub ditty.

Raskin pressed his palms over his ears. "Very well! Show yourself, kitten."

And the cat nuzzled her nose beneath the swathes of violet and mauve silk—and changed. The brilliant glow of her transformation was so bright Jack blinked. Within four seconds, his lover sat upon the chaise, shawls about her shoulders, tears in her eyes.

"Oh, Mersey, my love, don't cry."

"For Hern's sake!" Raskin huffed. "Get on with it, demon hunter. Say your farewell."

Jack held out the smaller ring that he knew was Mersey's and slid it onto her finger. "This one is yours." He displayed the other ring on his littlest finger. "And this one is mine."

"You found it," she gasped.

"You found me." He stroked her hair from her cheek, regretting that he could not steal her away from the world, and yet feeling he must not leave without her. He would not. He would kill the faery if he had to. "We were meant to find one another, Mersey."

"Jack," Mersey murmured.

Pressing their palms up, they held but four inches apart, wanting to touch, but both unsure of the faery who witnessed this farewell. Suddenly, their palms snapped to one another. The rings clicked, two long-lost mates reunited.

"I love you, Mersey."

"I love you, Jack."

"Oh, bloody elves!" Raskin stomped over to the two of them, Jack kneeling before Mersey, and inspected their joined hands. He made to touch the rings, but flinched away. "I can feel it. There *is* something there."

"Yes," Jack agreed. "True and deep and destined."

"Dash me to the dark realm! You do have a claim to her!" Raskin shouted in a storm of noise that shook the leaves on the branches. "Just…take her and be gone. But know you have incurred my wrath, Jack Harris!"

"Take a number!" Jack grabbed Mersey and thrust a hand through the doorway.

Jack woke. It was dark, yet a glimmer of sunlight toyed on the horizon outside the window. He lay in his bed.

"What kind of dream…?" He rubbed his forehead and studied his hand. The thin black band he'd worn—for how long?—tightened below his knuckle. "Faeries?"

"Bloody dreams." He lay back and closed his eyes. "Bloody P-Cell. This job is going to be the death of me," he murmured and drifted back to sleep.

Mersey sat on the marble steps outside the St. Yve manor, a plaid blanket wrapped about her shoulders. Beneath, the silk faery raiments sifted across her naked flesh. The lab coat had been lost when she'd shifted to cat shape.

Squire sat to her right, itching insect bites that spotted his neck as if he'd been a victim at a vampire orgy.

"Jack," she said. "He's gone."

Squire had told her about Jack's bargain with the threshold guardians. He'd sacrificed his life to save hers.

Gone. As in dead. Never again would she see him.

Mersey tucked her head into the folds of blanket. Tears slipped over her cheeks. Didn't Jack realize that to remove himself from this world would devastate her even more than imprisonment in a faery's silver cage?

She twisted the ring about her finger. Never would she forget the moment the two rings had connected. They belonged to one another.

"He was doing what he felt he had to save you," Squire offered between scratches. "He didn't care about his own demise. Hero stuff, that bloke. He could have killed Beryth, but he knew the risk to your safety. All he wanted was your freedom."

"I wanted a hero." Mersey sighed. And she had got one.

"You should come inside, Mersey. Cook has some hot chocolate with that wonderful ginger sugar in it," Squire said, trying on a hopeful tone.

"No, thank you," she said, head still tucked down. Most especially? She wanted to get herself as far from the Cadre as possible. "Leave me alone, Squire."

"If you wish. But believe me, I know about Ophelia," Squire offered. "Her bark is much worse than her bite."

"What does that mean?"

"Oh, I don't know. Maybe that she had a thing for your hero. I saw her looking him over when she could have ordered her gargoyle to stomp him. She didn't. The Cadre doesn't, as a rule, exterminate people, you know that. We're a peaceable crew, if not a bit pretentious at times."

"Then what?"

"Memory wipe, of course."

Suddenly hope renewed. Jack wasn't dead? How could she have believed the Cadre would even allow such a thing!

Mersey looked to Squire. "You think he's still alive?"

The dungeon master shrugged. "It's likely. But I wouldn't expect the man's brain to be in order. Most assuredly he's lost all memory of the past week. Including you."

"You think so? Squire, you wouldn't be saying this to get my hopes up?"

"Mersey, don't tell me you'd actually go looking for the man.

You can't! The Cadre and P-Cell— And if you look beyond that, he doesn't know who you are now."

"Doesn't matter." She leaped up and tugged the blanket around herself to cover her naked body.

"It will matter if you want to stay at the Cadre."

"He's the one, Squire! The only one."

"He may be the one," a woman said from the doorway. "But he isn't right for a Cadre initiate."

Mersey turned to Lady Aurora.

"Full moon," Aurora said with a nod of her head toward the full white moon in the velvet sky. "We should head to London to close the tear."

"Yes." In fact, Mersey could think of no other place she'd rather be.

"The drive will give us a chance to talk."

"Oh?"

"There's the matter of your sneaking P-Cell into the Cadre."

"But Jack's forgotten all that now."

"He may have, but I have not."

Chapter 33

Two weeks later...

He stood alone looking over the land. The London Eye capsule had reached an apex and he floated at the top of the world.

Not sure why, Jack had simply followed a compulsion to ride the Eye. He had never liked the thing. Today though, he pressed his palms to the clear Plexiglas wall and looked as far as he could. Beyond the city. West. There, where his attention fell upon a forest, gorgeous and enchanted.

Weird that he even cared about the landscape. Or used such words to describe it. Since a few weeks ago, Jack had been taking things slower. Appreciating things.

He felt as though he'd come back into this world after being, well...disemworlded. An odd word, but it appropriately described the feeling.

And last night, when he'd been on stakeout, instead of blasting straight away, he'd paused and asked the demon what its business was in this realm. Turned out the thing had been called by a familiar and wasn't sure what it was doing in the mortal realm itself.

Jack had directed it to Lawrence Prentice. He'd looked up the man in the phone book—of all places—and now kept his number handy. The freelance familiar offered wayward demons a return to the dark realm. It was his job to redirect the confused.

The idea that he'd not blasted away had sat well with Jack.

But it did not sit with P-Cell. He'd been asked to leave for reasons that remained a blur to him. Belladonna told him he'd had his memory tampered with, and it was best for all. He'd received a severance, and hadn't heard from P-Cell since.

But he couldn't stop hunting. It was in his blood. The world needed protection from the big bads, and Jack was the man for the job.

The capsule neared the landing, though Jack thought to go another round. He could ride this thing all day. He closed his eyes and bowed his head. He heard one person board, but kept his head tucked down.

Whoever it was sat in his row, two seats down. A woman, he guessed, since the chairs shifted little with her weight. She smelled nice, like fruit. Made him smile and he tapped his ring finger against the white plastic seat.

He'd once loved a gorgeous woman who smelled like this. Hadn't he? Hadn't been Monica Price. A tragedy, but he had moved on. Monica wouldn't have wanted him to carry guilt or remorse around with him. He'd been told she'd died during a shootout. He couldn't recall that evening. Weird. But—knowing his memory wasn't up to par—he accepted it. Sometimes bad things happened to good people. It was the way of the world.

So who had he loved? Had he lost someone recently? Someone tangled in the stolen bits of his memory? He felt the sense of loss so strongly, but he could not begin to touch a single clue.

Jack stretched his arms across the backs of the plastic chairs and accidentally touched the woman's hair. "Sorry."

"No problem." He heard her twist on the seat and guessed she must be looking over at him. "That's an interesting ring. Where did you get it?"

Jack toggled the hematite ring on his littlest finger. He wouldn't take it off. Never. But he wasn't sure why. "Truth? I got it from a cat."

That was one day he'd never forget. Thank God he still retained the wonders of his childhood.

"I believe you."

Jack turned on the seat. A gorgeous set of green eyes smiled at him. She wore an aviator cap, which hid most of her hair, and her face was delicate, yet strong, as if she was ready to take on the world and woe to any man who thought to stand in her way.

Instant affection emerged. A bit kooky, what with the goggles and cap, but very appealing. He could feel her in his heart, like a pulse beat.

And he knew.

Tapping the ring against the back of the chair, he said, "I thought I'd lost it years ago. Now here it is. Isn't it strange how things find their way back to where they really belong?"

She leaned closer and her perfume surrounded Jack's senses. "It's called destiny."

"Maybe. Sort of like you."

"What do you mean?"

"You seem…familiar."

"I do?"

Jack laid his hand before hers, slipping his fingertips in between hers so they just touched. "Are you…this will sound odd, but…" He instinctually knew. "Do you like cats?"

"You…know me?"

"We know each other, right?"

She nodded.

He blew out a breath. "Good, didn't want to freak you out. I recognize you, but I don't know you. Does that make sense? I've lost some bits of memory, but I'd never forget lemons."

"My perfume."

"And your kiss?"

"Yes? We've kissed," she encouraged.

"It tasted like…wintergreen, I think."

"Oh, Jack."

"You know me?"

"I love you, Jack." She came around and stood before him.

Jack rose and tentatively touched her, wanting to embrace and anticipating that it would be like holding a piece of his heart. He held out a palm, flat and parallel to her chest. She put up her palm. Their rings clicked together, as if magnetically attracted.

"What's your name?"

"Mersey Bane. Sounds like the disposition—"

"Spelled like the river," he finished, tickled that he knew such a thing. But again, he simply *knew.* "Mersey, can I… Can I kiss you?"

"Allow me." She kissed him.

There, in the gorgeous whirl of wintergreen and lemons, Jack fell into the wondrous moment of knowing. He still didn't know exactly what it was he should know about Mersey Bane, but he felt, without doubt, that he did know her.

And he also knew that she had changed his world.

"So, er, how did we meet?"

"Demon hunting," she said.

"You know what I am?"

"P-Cell," she offered.

"I was ousted from P-Cell. I'm not keen on the details but I think I might have failed a mission for them. It's better this way. I'm freelancing now." He dug into his pocket and handed her a card. It read Jack Harris, Pest Control.

"I knew that," she said and tucked the card away. Hooking her thumbs in her trousers pockets, she swayed side to side. A bashful tint colored her cheeks and she peered up at him through hopeful eyes. "Need a partner? I can help you determine the good demons from the bad ones."

"Brilliant." He kissed her, sliding his hands down her long coat, and from her pocket, he pulled out a crystal pyramid. "Why do I know that this thing will hold a demon in it?"

She shrugged. "There's a lot of things you know, Jack."

"I know you," he said, initially just saying it because it felt right, but then as the words were spoken, he *knew* it. "I love you?"

"Let's take it slow, hotshot. I hear there's been an incident in Knightsbridge involving a vengeance demon."

"Right then. Let's find us some demons."

* * * * *

Welcome to cowboy country...

Turn the page for a sneak preview of
TEXAS BABY
by
Kathleen O'Brien
An exciting new title from Harlequin Superromance
for everyone
who loves stories about the West.

Harlequin Superromance—
Where life and love weave together in emotional
and unforgettable ways.

CHAPTER ONE

CHASE TRANSFERRED his gaze to the road and identified a foreign spot on the horizon. A car. Almost half a mile away, where the straight, tree-lined drive met the public road. He could tell it was coming too fast, but judging the speed of a vehicle moving straight toward you was tricky.

It wasn't until it was about two hundred yards away that he realized the driver must be drunk…or crazy. Or both.

The guy was going maybe sixty. On a private drive, out here in ranch country, where kids or horses or tractors or stupid chickens might come darting out any minute, that was criminal. Chase straightened from his comfortable slouch and waved his hands.

"Slow down, you fool," he called out. He took the porch steps quickly and began walking fast down the driveway.

The car veered oddly, from one lane to another, then up onto the slight rise of the thick green spring grass. It just barely missed the fence.

"Slow down, damn it!"

He couldn't see the driver, and he didn't recognize this automobile. It was small and old, and couldn't have cost much even when it was new. It was probably white, but now it needed either a wash or a new paint job or both.

"Damn it, what's wrong with you?"

At the last minute, he had to jump away, because the idiot behind the wheel clearly wasn't going to turn to avoid a collision. He couldn't believe it. The car kept coming, finally slowing a little, but it was too late.

Still going about thirty miles an hour, it slammed into the large, white-brick pillar that marked the front boundaries of the house. The pillar wasn't going to give an inch, so the car had to. The front end folded up like a paper fan.

It seemed to take forever for the car to settle, as if the trauma happened in slow motion, reverberating from the front to the back of the car in ripples of destruction. The front windshield suddenly seemed to ice over with lethal bits of glassy frost. Then the side windows exploded.

The front driver's door wrenched open, as if the car wanted to expel its contents. Metal buckled hideously. Small pieces, like hubcaps and mirrors, skipped and ricocheted insanely across the oyster-shell driveway.

Finally, everything was still. Into the silence, a plume of steam shot up like a geyser, smelling of rust and heat. Its snakelike hiss almost smothered the low, agonized moan of the driver.

Chase's anger had disappeared. He didn't feel anything but a dull sense of disbelief. Things like this didn't happen in real life. Not in his life. Maybe the sun had actually put him to sleep....

But he was already kneeling beside the car. The driver was a woman. The frosty glass-ice of the windshield was dotted with small flecks of blood. She must have hit it with her head, because just below her hairline a red liquid was seeping out. He touched it. He tried to wipe it away before it reached her eyebrow, though, of course that made no sense at all. Her eyes were shut.

Was she conscious? Did he dare move her? Her dress was covered in glass, and the metal of the car was sticking out lethally in all the wrong places.

Then he remembered, with an intense relief, that every good medical man in the county was here, just behind the house, drinking his champagne. He found his phone and paged Trent.

The woman moaned again.

Alive, then. Thank God for that.

He saw Trent coming toward him, starting out at a lope, but quickly switching to a full run.

"Get Dr. Marchant," Chase called. "Don't bother with 911."

Trent didn't take long to assess the situation. A fraction of a second, and he began pulling out his cell phone and running toward the house.

The yelling seemed to have roused the woman. She opened her eyes. They were blue and clouded with pain and confusion.

"Chase," she said.

His breath stalled. His head pulled back. "What?"

Her only answer was another moan, and he wondered if he had imagined the word. He reached around her and put his arm behind her shoulders. She was tiny. Probably petite by nature, but surely way too thin. He could feel her shoulder blades pushing against her skin, as fragile as the wishbone in a turkey.

She seemed to have passed out, so he put his other arm under her knees and lifted her out. He tried to avoid the jagged metal, but her skirt caught on a piece and the tearing sound seemed to wake her again.

"No," she said. "Please."

"I'm just trying to help," he said. "It's going to be all right."

She seemed profoundly distressed. She wriggled in his arms, and she was so weak, like a broken bird. It made him feel too big and brutish. And intrusive. As if touching her this way, his bare hands against the warm skin behind her knees, were somehow a transgression.

He wished he could be more delicate. But he smelled gasoline, and he knew it wasn't safe to leave her here.

Finally he heard the sound of voices, as guests began to run around the side of the house, alerted by Trent. Dr. Marchant was at the front, racing toward them as if he were forty instead of seventy. Susannah was right behind him, her green dress floating around her trim legs.

"Please," the woman in his arms murmured again. She looked at him, the expression in her blue eyes lost and bewildered. He wondered if she might be on drugs. Hitting her head on the windshield might account for this unfocused, glazed look, but it couldn't explain the crazy driving.

"Please, put me down. Susannah… The wedding…"

Chase's arms tightened instinctively, and he froze in his tracks. She whimpered, and he realized he might be hurting her. "Say that again?"

"The wedding. I have to stop it."

* * * * *

Be sure to look for TEXAS BABY,
available September 11, 2007,
as well as other fantastic Superromance titles
available in September.

Welcome to Cowboy Country...

TEXAS BABY

by Kathleen O'Brien

#1441

Chase Clayton doesn't know what to think.
A beautiful stranger has just crashed his
engagement party, demanding that he not
marry because she's pregnant with his baby.
But the kicker is—he's never seen her before.

Look for TEXAS BABY and other fantastic
Superromance titles on sale September 2007.

Available wherever books are sold.

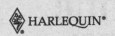
HARLEQUIN®

EVERLASTING LOVE™
Every great love has a story to tell™

Third time's a charm.

Texas summers. Charlie Morrison.
Jasmine Boudreaux has always connected
the two. Her relationship with Charlie
begins and ends in high school. Twenty
years later it begins again—and ends again.
Now fate has stepped in one more time—
will Jazzy and Charlie finally give in to
the love they've shared all this time?

Look for

Summer After Summer
by
Ann DeFee

**Available September
wherever books are sold.**

www.eHarlequin.com   HESAS0907

REQUEST YOUR FREE BOOKS!

2 FREE NOVELS PLUS 2 FREE GIFTS!

Silhouette®

nocturne™

Dramatic and Sensual Tales of Paranormal Romance.

YES! Please send me 2 FREE Silhouette® Nocturne™ novels and my 2 FREE gifts. After receiving them, if I don't wish to receive any more books, I can return the shipping statement marked "cancel." If I don't cancel, I will receive 4 brand-new novels every other month and be billed just $4.47 per book in the U.S. or $4.99 per book in Canada, plus 25¢ shipping and handling per book plus applicable taxes, if any*. That's a savings of about 15% off the cover price! I understand that accepting the 2 free books and gifts places me under no obligation to buy anything. I can always return a shipment and cancel at any time. Even if I never buy another book from Silhouette, the two free books and gifts are mine to keep forever.

238 SDN ELS4   338 SDN ELXG

Name	(PLEASE PRINT)	
Address		Apt. #
City	State/Prov.	Zip/Postal Code

Signature (if under 18, a parent or guardian must sign)

Mail to the **Silhouette Reader Service™:**
IN U.S.A.: P.O. Box 1867, Buffalo, NY 14240-1867
IN CANADA: P.O. Box 609, Fort Erie, Ontario L2A 5X3

Not valid to current Silhouette Nocturne subscribers.

Want to try two free books from another line?
Call 1-800-873-8635 or visit www.morefreebooks.com.

* Terms and prices subject to change without notice. NY residents add applicable sales tax. Canadian residents will be charged applicable provincial taxes and GST. This offer is limited to one order per household. All orders subject to approval. Credit or debit balances in a customer's account(s) may be offset by any other outstanding balance owed by or to the customer. Please allow 4 to 6 weeks for delivery.

Your Privacy: Silhouette is committed to protecting your privacy. Our Privacy Policy is available online at www.eHarlequin.com or upon request from the Reader Service. From time to time we make our lists of customers available to reputable firms who may have a product or service of interest to you. If you would prefer we not share your name and address, please check here. ☐

SN07

Don't miss the first book in the
BILLIONAIRE HEIRS trilogy

THE KYRIAKOS VIRGIN BRIDE
#1822

BY TESSA RADLEY

Zac Kyriakos was in search of a woman pure both
in body and heart to marry, and he believed that Pandora
Armstrong was the answer to his prayers. When Pandora
discovered that Zac's true reason for marrying her was
because she was a virgin, she wanted an annulment. Little
did she know that Zac was beginning to fall in love with
her and would do anything not to let her go....

On sale September 2007 from Silhouette Desire.

BILLIONAIRE HEIRS:
They are worth a fortune...but can they be tamed?

Also look for
THE APOLLONIDIES MISTRESS SCANDAL
on sale October 2007
THE DESERT BRIDE OF AL SAYED
on sale November 2007

Available wherever books are sold.

nocturne™

KISS ME DEADLY

by

MICHELE HAUF

When vampire Nikolaus Drake swears
vengeance on the witch who almost killed
him, a misdirected love spell causes him
instead to fall in love with his enemy—
Ravin Crosse. Now as the spell courses
through him, Nikolaus must choose
between loyalty to his tribe and the
forbidden desires of his heart....

*Available September
wherever books are sold.*

SN61771

nocturne™

COMING NEXT MONTH

#23 RISING DARKNESS • Cynthia Cooke
Dark Enchantments (Book 2 of 4)

Determined to protect Emma McGovern from a curse that will rob her of her soul, demon hunter and vampire Damien Hancock finds himself losing his heart to her. And as the evil demon Asmos arrives in the guise of his wolves, Damien must question if his feelings are real… or a result of the wolf's curse.

#24 KISS ME DEADLY • Michele Hauf

When vampire Nikolaus Drake swears vengeance on the witch who almost killed him, a misdirected love spell causes him instead to fall in love with his enemy Ravin Crosse. Now, as the spell courses through him, Nikolaus must choose between loyalty to his tribe, and the forbidden desires of his heart.…

A face—round and blurry—appeared right above her. Wide-set blue eyes shone with compassion and the same brilliance as her white smile. "I'm Tammy, your ICU nurse." Cool fingers secured the cannula back into place and brushed across her forehead.

What was she doing in the ICU? On a hospital bed in the ICU? And why had the nurse been calling her Julie?

That wasn't her name.

"I know someone who's been looking forward to talking with you. If you're ready, I'm going to let Detective Jones know that he can come in and see you. He's been waiting to talk with you for three days."

She tried to shake her head. A detective? As in a police officer? Why were the police coming to see her? What had she done?

Can Julie remember her past to save her future?
Pick up STOLEN MEMORIES wherever
Love Inspired Suspense books are sold to find out.

LISEXP0214

SPECIAL EXCERPT FROM

Love Inspired

*An attack stole her memory. Can she get it back in time
to save a missing child? Read on for a preview of
STOLEN MEMORIES by Liz Johnson,
the next exciting book in the*
WITNESS PROTECTION *series
from Love Inspired Suspense.*

Everything before that moment was blank.

It took considerable effort, but she pried her right eye open far enough to cringe at the glaring light wedged between white ceiling tiles. Pain sliced like a knife at her temple. She tried to lift her hand to press it to her skull. Maybe that would keep it from shattering. But her arm had tripled in size and weighed more than a beached whale. She could only lift it an inch from where it lay at her side.

Fire shot from her elbow to the tip of her middle finger, a sob escaping from somewhere deep in her chest and leaving a scar inside her throat as it escaped.

"Julie?"

Julie? She turned to look in the direction of the voice to see who else was in the room, but something plastic tugged against her nose. An oxygen mask. She didn't even try to lift her hand to adjust it, instead rolling her eyes as far as she could.

A gentle hand with cold fingers pressed against her forearm, but the face was just out of reach. "Julie? How are you feeling?"

Who was Julie? There wasn't anyone else in her limited line of sight, but that didn't mean the other girl wasn't close by.